JONAH'S GOURD VINE

JONAH'S GOURD VINE

A NOVEL

ZORA NEALE HURSTON

WITH A FOREWORD BY RITA DOVE
AND AN AFTERWORD BY HENRY LOUIS GATES, JR.

AMISTAD

An Imprint of HarperCollins*Publishers*

AMISTAD

First Perennial Library edition published 1990.
First Harper Perennial Modern Classics edition published 2008.

Designed by Cassandra J. Pappas

Library of Congress Cataloging-in-Publication Data is available upon request.

ISBN: 978-0-06-135019-1 (pbk.)

21 LSC 11

To
Bob Wunsch
Who is one of the long-wingded angels
Right round the throne
Go gator and muddy the water

FOREWORD

✦

"You laks dat ole train Ah see," the Negro said to John, watching him as he all but fell down into the railroad cut, trying to keep sight of the tail of the train.

"Yeah, man Ah lakted dat. It say something but Ah ain't heered it 'nough tuh tell whut it say yit. You know whut it say?"

"It don't say nothin'. It jes' make uh powerful racket, dass all."

"Naw, it say some words too. Ahm comin' heah pleny mo' times and den Ah tell yuh whut it say."

When the publishing house of J. B. Lippincott inquired if the author of the short story "The Gilded Six Bits" was working on a novel, Zora Neale Hurston took paper and pencil and headed for home. She rented a room in Sanford, Florida, next door to the all-black town where she had grown up, and began to write *Jonah's Gourd Vine*. In October 1933, a scant four months later, the manuscript was accepted for publication.

Jonah's Gourd Vine takes the classic form of the *Bildungsroman:* John, an unlettered but determined young man, ventures forth to make his fortune. What he learns of the world and his own nature form the trajectory of his life and the novel.

Like those of many black Americans, John's origins are

murky. His mother Amy bears him while working on Alf Pearson's farm; she marries Ned Crittenden and moves to the other side of Big Creek. Ned, who was raised a slave, despises John for what he represents—for there is every indication that John is the illegitimate son of the white judge.

Even as a young man, John is aware of the power of utterance. His fear of the first locomotive he sees is quickly replaced by the desire to understand it. And though he never learns to speak to his own soul, he is fascinated by the infinite variety of nature's music:

> . . . John sat on the foot-log and made some words to go with the drums of the Creek. Things walked in the birch woods, creep, creep, creep. The hound dog's lyric crescendo lifted over and above the tree tops. He was on the foot-log, half way across the Big Creek where maybe people laughed and maybe people had lots of daughters. The moon came up. The hunted coon panted down to the Creek . . . [t]he tenor-singing hound dog went home. Night passed. No more Ned, no hurry. No telling how many girls might be living on the new and shiny side of the Big Creek. John almost trumpeted exultantly at the new sun. He breathed lustily. He stripped and carried his clothes across, then recrossed and plunged into the swift water and breasted strongly over.

This passage contains all the elements of John's spirit—his exuberant masculine energy, his gift for language, and his intense relationship between his interior self and the natural world, both his headstrong lustiness and his ability for provident forethought. (He carries his clothes across the river, then recrosses before swimming over.)

This scene, however, occurs right after his mother's repeated warning not to swim the Songahatchee and John's parting promise to her to stop "runnin' and uh rippin' and clambin' trees and rocks and jumpin'." The seeds of his inner conflict are evident.

In an ironic twist recalling the incestuous relationships in the South, John leaves home to find work under Alf Pearson, who remarks, "Your face looks sort of familiar but I can't place you" before giving him the cast-off clothes of his legitimate son. But when the judge's wife objects to John driving their coach, he is put to work in the barns.

John, who adopts Pearson as his surname, is an immediate success among the black workers, especially the women: they seduce him right and left. He focuses his attention on the fiery little Lucy Potts, the smartest black girl in the area. Her excellence inspires John to "eat up dat school," and he joins the church when he is told that Lucy sings in the choir. After a determined courtship, Lucy and John become man and wife.

Although John left home at the suggestion of his mother, he soon learns the temptation of flight. Whenever things get sticky, he runs away. And, just as he is able to break a promise to his mother minutes afterward without a second thought, John sees no discrepancy in enjoying a stream of women while swearing to love Lucy body and soul. Even before marriage, John must leave the Pearson place and find work at a logging camp to escape a jealous husband; and though he swears to Lucy that "Ah loves you and you alone," after marriage he still cannot stay away from other women. There is Mehaley and Big 'Oman and then Delphine, who comforts John while Lucy lies in labor with their fourth child. When Lucy's brother takes their marriage bed in partial payment of a debt, John beats him up and is consequently summoned to court. Alf Pearson gives him money along with some "fatherly" advice: "John, distance is the only cure for certain diseases."

John moves to the all-black settlement of Eatonville, Florida (Hurston's home town) and sends for Lucy. He grows in confidence and takes his place in the community as a man, while Lucy's energy is taken up by children; all her fierce intelligence is channeled into advising her husband. Together they forge John's reputation as minister of Zion Hope Church and eventually mayor in the neighboring town of Sanford.

Actually, John's "disease" is that he is too smooth a talker. He is carried away by his own words, just as he is carried away by his body. His stirring prayers convince him and everyone else at Zion Hope that he has been called to preach, although his wife warns him against confusing talent with commitment:

> "Lucy, look lak Ah jus' found out whut Ah kin do. De words dat sets de church on fire comes tuh me jus' so. Ah reckon de angels must tell 'em tuh me."
> "God don't call no man, John, and turn 'im loose uh fool."

Perhaps his most despicable flight occurs when his younger daughter Isis lies desperately ill; terrified that she will die, he runs into the arms of another woman until she recovers. (Ironically, later it is the nine-year-old Isis who stands by her dying mother.) John returns, shamefaced, with gifts for Lucy—a new dress and a pineapple—that seem as blasphemous as they are ludicrous.

The procession of women continues until John meets Hattie Tyson, who enjoins the aid of a conjure woman to keep him at her side. Lucy's sound advice grows wearisome to him, and her cautious inquiries into his infidelities finally enrage him. Remembering John's poor track record with promises, it is with foreboding that we hear him swear to Lucy: "Li'l Bit, Ah ain't never laid de weight uh mah hand on you in malice." When Lucy falls ill, John continues to see other women, and Lucy makes a decisive pronouncement on John's sin-now-atone-later attitude: "You can't clean yo'self wid yo' tongue lak uh cat." Stung by the truth, John slaps her. She turns her face to the wall, withdrawing her support from him, and dies.

This act of malice, which hastens Lucy's death, is the worm that cuts down the great vine:

> And the Lord God appointed a plant, and made it come up over Jonah, that it might be a shade over his head, to save him from this discomfort. So Jonah was exceedingly glad because of the plant. But when dawn came up the next day,

God appointed a worm which attacked the plant, so that it
withered.

Jonah 4: 6–7

Indeed, John Pearson is a rapidly growing vine, and every-
thing he touches blossoms under his hand: he is a favorite with
the women, he is popular with the men, he is a good worker
and a gifted storyteller, and finally, as minister and mayor, he
becomes both a spiritual and a community leader. His philan-
dering ways do not seem to slow him down until he commits
the ghastly sin of striking his wife on her deathbed.

The worm, however, could also be Hattie, who is willing
to use magic more compelling than feminine wiles to topple
the preacher. John marries Hattie, and beats her after discov-
ering that he's been "conjured." When Hattie slyly pleads her
case before Deacon Harris (who is jealous of John's successes
with women), Harris assures her, "Ah'd cut down dat Jonah's
gourd vine in a uh minute, if Ah had all de say-so." When she
files for divorce, John does not confute her testimony.

The worm of malice burrows through the church commu-
nity. Long uneasy about the preacher's philanderings, the con-
gregation of Zion Hope plans to dethrone him. On the day
of reckoning, John preaches the sermon of his life.

John's final sermon is taken nearly verbatim from Hurston's
field notes on a country preacher. It is a meditation on martyr-
dom and heroism, reflecting John's position before the
church; after a brief rhapsodic digression on the creation of
earth, he zeroes in on Jesus, come on his "train of mercy" to
save mankind. In John's depiction of the Resurrection, the
train of mercy turns into the "damnation train," which in a
bizarre but effective conclusion is derailed when the cow-
catcher rams into Jesus's side. Final Judgment is pictured as a
convention where "de two trains of Time shall meet on de
trestle."

Surrounded by enemies who had once been friends, bitten
through at the root, John steps down from the pulpit and walks
out of the church. He decides to earn a living as a carpenter,

but his honest efforts fail in the face of the community's delight in persecuting a fallen idol.

Are we to sympathize with John as a victim of malicious ill-wishers, or condemn him for his despicable conduct toward his wife? Since Hattie has a spell put on him, is he to blame for his actions at all?

If we look at the Biblical story of Jonah and the vine, John's "case" becomes clearer: the prophet has predicted the fall of the great city of Nineveh, upon which its inhabitants repent by fasting and covering themselves in sackcloth and ashes. Moved to pity, the Lord revokes his sentence, and Jonah takes to the hills to sulk. After God has caused the vine to wither, he orders the sun to beat down until Jonah bemoans the loss of shade and exclaims that he is "angry enough to die." The Lord replies:

> "You pity the plant, for which you did not labor, nor did you make it grown, which came into being in a night, and perished in a night. And should not I pity Nineveh, that great city, in which there are more than a hundred and twenty thousand persons who do not know their right hand from their left, and also much cattle?"
>
> Jonah 4:10–11

Sudden growth—fame achieved without thought or labor—must maintain a precarious balance. Perhaps John's fatal flaw is his inability to listen to himself and consequently his reluctance to put any effort into changing his ways. Unable to accept responsibility for his actions, he either runs away or "licks himself clean" with fast talking. Even the heaped-on tribulations that follow Lucy's death fail to lead him to an understanding of his selfishness: all he can see is the hypocrisy of others. And when Lucy finally returns to him in a dream, he is oblivious to the warning:

> He killed the snake and carried Lucy across in his arms to where Alf Pearson stood at the cross roads and pointed

down a white shell road with his walking cane and said, "Distance is the only cure for certain diseases," and he and Lucy went racing down the dusty white road together. Somehow Lucy got lost from him, but there he was on the road—happy because the dead snake was behind him, but crying in his loneliness for Lucy.

Instead of seeing the dream as a condemning portrait of the pattern of his life, John believes he is meant to leave town—to run away again, and to seek his fortune elsewhere. The proper and rich widow Sally Lovelace takes him in, and John's luck begin to turn: they marry, his carpentry business picks up, and Zion Hope asks him back. His triumphant homecoming, resplendent in the new car Sally has bought him, brings with it the admiration of his former enemies as well as the irresistible blandishments of a sweet young thing named Ora. In no time at all, John succumbs to lust again; appalled at his weakness, he flees Sanford and heads back to his wife. So sunk in self-recrimination is he that he fails to see an oncoming train. He is killed instantly. A man who does not learn from his mistakes is doomed to repeat them. In many ways, John has cut himself down.

They called for the instrument that they had brought to America in their skins—the drum—and they played upon it. . . . The drum with the man skin that is dressed with human blood, that is beaten with a human shin-bone and speaks to gods as a man and to men as a God.

Does *Jonah's Gourd Vine* hold up today, apart from its unquestionable value as a portrait of Southern black life in the first decades of the twentieth century—or does a sympathetic portrait of a philandering preacher seem antiquated as a work of literature, politically retrograde? As his first name attests, John is Everyman, and Pearson is a surname with multitudinous echoes. In a bitter reference to the lost ancestry of black slaves, he is someone's (but whose?) son; like that archetypal Son of God, he is "pierced" by those he has trusted; conversely, he is a man, pierced by Adam's rib, and his human frailty eventually causes his downfall.

Lucy, on the other hand, is almost a parody of the faithful, betrayed wife: she subordinates her dreams to his ambitions, she is rebuked and dies, the husband remarries, the children get farmed out. And yet no one can take Lucy's place. She haunts the novel, and her absence is at least as compelling as John's suffering.

For its time, Zora Neale Hurston's first novel, produced in four months when the author was forty-two, is a remarkable achievement. Written in the vicinity of her birthplace, *Jonah's Gourd Vine,* unsurprisingly, does not stray far from the autobiographical—John and Lucy are based on Hurston's father and mother, and Lucy's deathbed scene can be found in its original (with Zora as the nine-year-old daughter) in Hurston's autobiography, *Dust Tracks on a Road.* What is striking, however, is that this young woman did not make one of the major mistakes of first novelists—sticking too faithfully to the "true story"—but knew how to fashion of her parents' lives a tale of compelling pathos and majesty.

As a work of fiction, *Jonah's Gourd Vine* certainly has its flaws: transitions that jog, a little too much "local color." And though Hurston can hardly be blamed for wanting to infuse the text with the fieldwork she had done as an anthropologist, all too often her eloquent commentary stands full-blown and self-contained, interrupting the narrative flow. John's final sermon is a case in point, for even its masterful train imagery seems too heavy-handed a foreshadowing when the locomotive comes barreling out of the blue, a modern-day *deus ex machina,* to seal John's fate.

But Hurston's language is superb, rich with wordplay and proverbs—not only compelling when it comes to rendering the dialect of the Southern rural black but also as an omniscient narrator who neither indulges nor condemns the actions of her characters but offers the complexity of life in a story that leaves judgment up to the reader. John Pearson is presented as a human being in all his individual paradoxes—troubled and gifted, dignified and lascivious, pure and selfish—and as the exemplification of the country preacher, he is both poet and philosopher. If language is the chief visible sign of human beings' pre-eminence over beasts, then poetry is the purest expression of man's spiritual quest. *Jonah's Gourd Vine* is a glorious paean to the power of the word, an attestation to the promise made in Langston Hughes's famous 1926 essay, "The Negro Artist and the Racial Mountain":

> We younger Negro artists who create now intend to express our individual dark-skinned selves without fear or shame. If white people are pleased we are glad. If they are not, it doesn't matter. We know we are beautiful. And ugly too. The tom-tom cries and the tom-tom laughs. If colored people are pleased we are glad. If they are not, their displeasure doesn't matter either. We build our temples for tomorrow, strong as we know how, and we stand on top of the mountain, free within ourselves.

RITA DOVE

JONAH'S GOURD VINE

CHAPTER 1

✦

God was grumbling his thunder and playing the zig-zag lightning thru his fingers.

Amy Crittenden came to the door of her cabin to spit out a wad of snuff. She looked up at the clouds.

"Ole Massa gwinter scrub floors tuhday," she observed to her husband who sat just outside the door, reared back in a chair. "Better call dem chaps in outa de cotton patch."

" 'Tain't gwine rain," he snorted, "you always talkin' more'n yuh know."

Just then a few heavy drops spattered the hard clay yard. He arose slowly. He was an older middle-age than his years gave him a right to be.

"And eben if hit do rain," Ned Crittenden concluded grudgingly, "ef dey ain't got sense 'nough tuh come in let 'em git wet."

"Yeah, but when us lef' de field, you told 'em not to come till you call 'em. Go 'head and call 'em 'fo' de rain ketch 'em."

Ned ignored Amy and shuffled thru the door with the chair, and somehow trod on Amy's bare foot. " 'Oman, why don't you git outa de doorway? Jes contrary tuh dat. You needs uh good head stompin', dass whut. You sho is one aggervatin' 'oman."

Amy flashed an angry look, then turned her face again to

1

the sea of wind-whipped cotton, turned hurriedly and took the cow-horn that hung on the wall and placed it to her lips.

"You John Buddy! You Zeke! You Zachariah! Come in!"

From way down in the cotton patch, "Yassum! Us comin'!"

Ned shuffled from one end of the cabin to the other, slamming to the wooden shutter of the window, growling between his gums and his throat the while.

The children came leaping in, racing and tumbling in tense, laughing competition—the three smaller ones getting under the feet of the three larger ones. The oldest boy led the rest, but once inside he stopped short and looked over the heads of the others, back over the way they had come.

"Shet dat door, John!" Ned bellowed, "you ain't got the sense you wuz borned wid."

Amy looked where her big son was looking. "Who dat comin' heah, John?" she asked.

"Some white folks passin' by, mama. Ahm jes' lookin' tuh see whar dey gwine."

"Come out dat do'way and shet it tight, fool! Stand dere gazin' dem white folks right in de face!" Ned gritted at him. "Yo' brazen ways wid dese white folks is gwinter git you lynched one uh dese days."

"Aw 'tain't," Amy differed impatiently, "who can't look at ole Beasley? He ain't no quality no-how."

"Shet dat door, John!" screamed Ned.

"Ah wuzn't de last one inside," John said sullenly.

"Don't you gimme no word for word," Ned screamed at him. "You jes' do lak Ah say do and keep yo' mouf shet or Ah'll take uh trace chain tuh yuh. Yo' mammy mought think youse uh lump uh gold 'cause you got uh li'l' white folks color in yo' face, but Ah'll stomp yo' guts out and dat quick! Shet dat door!"

He seized a lidard knot from beside the fireplace and limped threateningly towards John.

Amy rose from beside the cook pots like a black lioness.

"Ned Crittenden, you raise dat wood at mah boy, and you gointer make uh bad nigger outa me."

2

"Dat's right," Ned sneered, "Ah feeds 'im and clothes 'im but Ah ain't tuh tuh do nothin' tuh dat li'l' yaller god cep'n wash 'im up."

"Dat's uh big ole resurrection lie, Ned. Uh slew-foot, drag-leg lie at dat, and Ah dare yuh tuh hit me too. You know Ahm uh fightin' dawg and mah hide is worth money. Hit me if you dare! Ah'll wash *yo'* tub uh 'gator guts and dat quick."

"See dat? Ah ain't fuh no fuss, but you tryin' tuh start uh great big ole ruction 'cause Ah tried tuh chesstize dat young-un."

"Naw, you ain't tried tuh chesstize 'im nothin' uh de kind. Youse tryin' tuh fight 'im on de sly. He is jes' ez obedient tuh you and jes' ez humble under yuh, ez he kin be. Yet and still you always washin' his face wid his color and tellin' 'im he's uh bastard. He works harder'n anybody on dis place. You ain't givin' 'im nothin'. He more'n makes whut he gits. Ah don't mind when he needs chesstizin' and you give it tuh 'im, but anytime you tries tuh knock any dese chillun 'bout dey head wid sticks and rocks, Ah'll be right dere tuh back dey fallin'. Ahm dey mama."

"And Ahm de pappy uh all but dat one."

"You knowed Ah had 'm 'fo' yuh married me, and if you didn't want 'im round, whut yuh marry me fuh? Dat ain't whut you said. You washed 'im up jes' lak he wuz gold den. You jes' took tuh buckin' 'im since you been hangin' round sich ez Beasley and Mimms."

Ned sat down by the crude fireplace where the skillets and spiders (long-legged bread pans with iron cover) sprawled in the ashes.

"Strack uh light, dere, some uh y'all chaps. Hit's dark in heah."

John obediently thrust a piece of lightwood into the embers and the fire blazed up. He retreated as quickly as possible to the farther end of the cabin.

Ned smoked his strong home-grown tobacco twist for a few minutes. Then he thrust out his feet.

"Pour me some water in dat wash-basin, you chaps, and

3

some uh y'all git de washrag."

There was a scurry and bustle to do his bidding, but the drinking-gourd dropped hollowly in the water bucket. Ned heard it.

" 'Tain't no water in dat air water-bucket, Ah'll bound yuh!" He accused the room and glowered all about him, "House full uh younguns fuh me to feed and close, and heah 'tis dust dark and rainin' and not uh drop uh water in de house! Amy, whut kinda 'oman is you nohow?"

Amy said nothing. She sat on the other side of the fireplace and heaped fresh, red coals upon the lid of the spider in which the bread was cooking.

"John!" Ned thundered, "git yo' yaller behind up offa dat floor and go git me some water tuh wash mah foots."

"You been tuh de house longer'n he is," Amy said quietly. "You coulda done been got dat water."

"You think Ah'm gwine take uh 'nother man's youngun and feed 'im and close 'im fuh twelve years and den he too good tuh fetch me uh bucket uh water?" Ned bellowed.

"Iss rainin' out dere, an' rainin' hard," Amy said in the same level tones.

"Dass right," Ned sneered, "John is de house-nigger. Ole Marsa always kep' de yaller niggers in de house and give 'em uh job totin' silver dishes and goblets tuh de table. Us black niggers is de ones s'posed tuh ketch de wind and de weather."

"Ah don't want *none* uh mah chilluns pullin' tuh no spring in uh hard rain. Yo' foots kin wait. Come hawg-killin' time Ah been married tuh you twelve years and Ah done seen yuh let 'em wait uh powerful long spell some time. Ah don't want mah chilluns all stove-up wid uh bad cold from proagin' 'round in de rain."

"Ole Marse didn't ast *me* of hit wuz rainin' uh snowin' uh hot uh col'. When he spoke Ah had tuh move and move quick too, uh git a hick'ry tuh mah back. Dese younguns ain't uh bit better'n me. Let 'em come lak Ah did."

"Naw, Ned, Ah don't want mine tuh come lak yuh come nor neither lak me, and Ahm uh whole heap younger'n you.

4

You growed up in slavery time. When Old Massa wuz drivin' you in de rain and in de col'—he wasn't don' it tuh he'p you 'long. He wuz lookin' out for hisself. Course Ah wuz twelve years old when Lee made de big surrender, and dey didn't work me hard, but—but dese heah chillun is diffunt from us."

"How come dey's diffunt? Wese all niggers tuhgether, ain't us? White man don't keer no mo' 'bout one dan he do de other."

"Course dey don't, but we ain't got tuh let de white folks love our chillun fuh us, is us? Dass jest de pint. We black folks don't love our chillun. We couldn't do it when we wuz in slavery. We borned 'em but dat didn't make 'em ourn. Dey b'longed tuh old Massa. 'Twan't no use in treasurin' other folkses property. It wuz liable tuh be took uhway any day. But we's free folks now. De big bell done rung! Us chillun is ourn. Ah doan know, mebbe hit'll take some of us generations, but us got tuh 'gin tuh practise on treasurin' our younguns. Ah loves dese heah already uh whole heap. Ah don't want 'em knocked and 'buked."

Ned raked his stubbly fingers thru his grisly beard in silent hostility. He spat in the fire and tamped his pipe.

"Dey say spare de rod and spile de child, and Gawd knows Ah ain't gwine tuh spile nair one uh dese. Niggers wuz made tuh work and all of 'em gwine work right long wid me. Is dat air supper ready yit?"

"Naw hit ain't. How you speck me tuh work in de field right long side uh you and den have supper ready jes' ez soon ez Ah git tuh de house? Ah helt uh big-eye hoe in mah hand jes' ez long ez you did, Ned."

"Don't you change so many words wid me, 'oman! Ah'll knock yuh dead ez Hector. Shet yo' mouf!"

"Ah change jes' ez many words ez Ah durn please! Ahm three times seben and uh button. Ah knows whut's de matter wid *you*. Youse mad cause Beaseley done took dem two bales uh cotton us made las' yeah."

"Youse uh lie!"

"Youse uh nother one, Ned Crittenden! Don't you lak it,

don't you take it, heah mah collar come and you shake it! Us wouldn't be in dis fix ef you had uh lissened tuh me. Ah tole you when dey hauled de cotton tuh de gin dat soon ez everything wuz counted up and Beasley give us share for yuh tuh take and haul it straight tuh dis barn. But naw, yuh couldn't lissen tuh me. Beasley told yuh tuh leave hit in *his* barn and being he's uh white man you done whut he told yuh. Now he say he ain't got no cotton uh ourn. Me and you and all de chillun done worked uh whole year. Us done made sixteen bales uh cotton and ain't even got uh cotton seed to show.''

''Us et hit up, Major Beasley say. Come to think of it 'tis uh heap uh moufs in one meal barrel.''

''No sich uh thing, Ned Crittenden. Fust place us ain't had nothing but meal and sow-belly tuh eat. You mealy-moufin' round cause you skeered tuh talk back tuh Rush Beasley. What us needs tuh do is git offa dis place. Us been heah too long. Ah b'longs on de other side de Big Creek anyhow. Never did lak it over heah. When us gather de crops dis yeah less move.''

''Aw, Ah reckon we kin make it heah all right, when us don't have so many moufs in de meal barrel we kin come out ahead. 'Tain't goin' be dat many dis time when Ah goes to de gin house.''

''How come?''

''Cause Ah done bound John over tuh Cap'n Mimms. Dat's uh great big ole boy, Amy, sixteen years old and look lak he twenty. He eats uh heap and den you won't let me git de worth uh mah rations out of 'im in work. He could be de finest plowhand in Alabama, but you won't lemme do nothin' wid 'im.''

''He don't do nothin'? He's uh better hand wid uh wide sweep plow right now dan you is, and he kin chop mo' cotton dan you, and pick mo' dan Ah kin and you knows Ah kin beat you anytime.'' Then, as if she had just fully heard Ned, ''Whut dat you say 'bout boundin' John Buddy over tuh Cap'n Mimms? You ain't uh gonna do no sich uh thing.''

''Ah done done it.''

In the frenzied silence, Amy noticed that the rain had

ceased; that the iron kettle was boiling; that a coon dog struck a trail way down the Creek, and was coming nearer, singing his threat and challenge.

"Ned Crittenden, you know jes' ez good ez Ah do dat Cap'n Mimms ain't nothin' but po' white trash, and he useter be de overseer on de plantation dat everybody knowed wuz de wust one in southern Alabama. He done whipped niggers nigh tuh death."

"You call him po' when he got uh thousand acres under de plow and more'n dat in wood lot? Fifty mules."

"Don't keer if he is. How did he git it? When Massa Pinckney got kilt in de war and ole Miss Pinckney didn't had nobody tuh look atter de place she took and married 'im. He wan't nothin' but uh overseer, lived offa clay and black m'lasses. His folks is so po' right now dey can't sit in dey house. Every time you pass dere dey settin' in de yard jes' ez barefooted ez uh yard dawg. You ain't gwine put no chile uh mine under no Mimms."

"Ah done done it, and you can't he'p yo'seff. He gwine come git 'im tuhmorrer. He's gwine sleep 'im and feed 'im and effen John Buddy's any account, he say he'll give uh suit uh close come Christmas time."

"Dis heah bindin' over ain't nothin' but uh 'nother way uh puttin' us folks back intuh slavery."

"Amy, you better quit talkin' 'bout de buckra. Some of 'em be outside and hear you and turn over you tuh de patter roller, and dey'll take you outa heah and put uh hun'ed lashes uh raw hide on yo' back. Ah done tole yuh but you won't hear."

The clash and frenzy in the air was almost visible. Something had to happen. Ned stood up and shuffled towards the door.

"Reckon Ahm gwine swill dat sow and feed de mules. Mah vittles better be ready when Ah git back."

He limped on out of the door and left it open.

"John Buddy," Amy said, "you and Zeke go fetch uh bucket full uh water and hurry back tuh yo' supper. De rest uh y'all git yo' plates and come git some uh dese cow-peas and

7

pone bread. Lawd, Lawd, Lawd. Je-sus!''

There was a lively clatter of tin plates and spoons. The largest two boys went after water, Zeke clinging in the darkness to his giant of a brother. Way down in the cotton Zeke gave way to his tears.

"John Buddy, Ah don't want you way from me. John Buddy,—" he grew incoherent. So John Buddy carried him under his arm like a shock of corn and made him laugh. Finally John said, "Sometime Ah jes' ez soon be under Mimms ez pappy. One 'bout ez bad as tother. 'Nother thing. Dis ain't slavery time and Ah got two good footses hung onto me." He began to sing lightly.

They returned with the water and were eating supper when Ned got back from the barn. His face was sullen and he carried the raw hide whip in his hand.

Amy stooped over the pot, giving second-helpings to the smaller children. Ned looked about and seeing no plate fixed for him uncoiled the whip and standing tiptoe to give himself more force, brought the whip down across Amy's back.

The pain and anger killed the cry within her. She wheeled to fight. The raw hide again. This time across her head. She charged in with a stick of wood and the fight was on. This had happened many times before. Amy's strength was almost as great as Ned's and she had youth and agility with her. Forced back to the wall by her tigress onslaught, Ned saw that victory for him was possible only by choking Amy. He thrust his knee into her abdomen and exerted a merciless pressure on her throat.

The children screamed in terror and sympathy.

"Help mama, John Buddy," Zeke screamed. John's fist shot out and Ned slid slowly down the wall as if both his legs and his insides were crumbling away.

Ned looked scarcely human on the floor. Almost like an alligator in jeans. His drooling blue lips and snaggled teeth were yellowed by tobacco.

"Lawd, Ah speck you done kilt yo' pappy, John. You didn't mean tuh, and he didn't had no business hittin' me wid dat raw

8

hide and neither chokin' me neither. Jesus, Jesus, Jesus, Jeesus!"

"He ain't dead, mama. Ah see 'im breathin'." Zachariah said, "John Buddy sho is strong! Ah bet he kin whip ev'ry body in Notasulga."

Ned got up limpingly. He looked around and sat upon the bed.

"Amy, Ahm tellin' yuh, git dat punkin-colored bastard outa dis house. He don't b'long heah wid us nohow."

"He ain't de onliest yaller chile in de world. Wese uh mingled people."

Ned limped to the fireplace and Amy piled his plate with corn bread and peas.

"Git dat half-white youngun uh yourn outa heah, Amy. Heah Ah done took 'im since he wus three years old and done for 'im when he couldn't do for hisseff, and he done raised his hand tuh me. Dis house can't hol' bofe uh us. Yaller niggers ain't no good nohow."

"Oh yes dey is," Amy defended hotly, "yes dey is—jes' ez good ez anybody else. You jes' started tuh talk dat foolishness since you been hangin' 'round old Mimms. Monkey see, monkey do."

"Well, iss de truth. Dese white folks orta know and dey say dese half-white niggers got de worst part uh bofe de white and de black folks."

"Dey ain't got no call tuh say dat. Is mo' yaller folks on de chain-gang dan black? Naw! Is dey harder tuh learn? Naw! Do dey work and have things lak other folks? Yas. Naw dese po' white folks says dat 'cause dey's jealous uh de yaller ones. How come? Ole Marse got de yaller nigger totin' his silver cup and eatin' Berksher hawg ham outa his kitchin when po' white trash scrabblin' 'round in de piney woods huntin' up uh razor back. Yaller nigger settin' up drivin' de carriage and de po' white folks got tuh step out de road and leave 'im pass by. And den agin de po' white man got daughters dat don't never eben smell de kitchin at the big house and all dem yaller chillun got mammas, and no black gal ain't never been up

9

tuh de big house and dragged Marse Nobody out. Humph! Talkin' after po' white trash! If Ah wuz ez least ez dey is, Ah speck Ah'd fret mahself tuh death.''

"Aw naw," Ned sneered, "de brother in black don't fret tuh death. White man fret and worry and kill hisself. Colored folks fret uh li'l' while and gwan tuh sleep. 'Nother thing, Amy, Hagar's chillun don't faint neither when dey fall out, dey jes have uh hard old fit.''

"Dass awright, Ned. You always runnin' yo' race down. We ain't had de same chance dat white folks had. Look lak Ah can't sense you intuh dat.''

"Amy, niggers can't faint. Jes' ain't in 'em.''

"Dass awright. Niggers gwine faint too. May not come in yo' time and it may not come in mine, but way after while, us people is gwine faint jes' lak white folks. You watch and see.''

"Table dat talk. Dat John is gwine offa dis place effen Ah stay heah. He goes tuh Mimms uh he goes apin' on down de road way from heah. Ah done spoke.''

"Naw Ned," Amy began, but John cut her off.

"It's all right, mama, lemme go. Ah don't keer. One place is good ez 'nother one. Leave him do all de plowin' after dis!''

With his mouth full of peas and corn bread, Ned gloated, "De crops is laid by.''

"Yeah, but nex' year's crops ain't planted yit," John countered.

So John put on his brass-toed shoes and his clean shirt and was ready to leave. Amy dug out a crumpled and mouldy dollar and gave it to him.

"Where you goin', son?''

"Over de Big Creek, mama. Ah ever wanted tuh cross over.''

"Ah'll go piece de way wid yuh tuh de Creek, John. Gimme uh li'dud knot, dere, Zeke, so's Ah kin see de way back.''

"Good bye, pap," John called from the door. Ned grunted over a full mouth. The children bawled dolefully when John called to them.

Amy threw a rag over her bruised head and closed the door

after her. The night was black and starry.

"John, you wuz borned over de Creek."

"You wuz tellin' me dat one day, Ah 'member."

"Dey knows me well, over dere. Maybe Ah kin pint yuh whar some work is at."

"Yassum. Ah wants tuh make money, so's Ah kin come back and git yuh."

"Don't yuh take me tuh heart. Ah kin strain wid Ned. Ah jes' been worried 'bout you and him. Youse uh big boy now and you am gwine take and take offa 'im and swaller all his filth lak you been doin' here of late. Ah kin see dat in yo' face. Youse slow, but wid him keerin' on lak he do now, hit takes uh Gawd tuh tell whut gwine happen in dat house. He didn't useter 'buke yuh lak dat. But his old mammy and dat old cock-eyed sister uh his'n put 'im up tuh dat. He useter be crazy 'bout yuh. 'Member dat big gol' watch chain he bought fuh you tuh wear tuh big meetin'? Dey make lak he love you better'n he do de rest on 'count youse got color in your face. So he tryin' side wid dem and show 'em he don't. Ahm kinda glad fuh yuh tuh be 'way from 'round 'im. Massa Alf Pearson, he got uh big plantation and he's quality white folks. He know me too. Go in Notasulga and ast fuh 'im. Tell 'im whose boy you is and maybe he mought put yuh tuh work. And if he do, son, you scuffle hard so's he'll work yuh reg'lar. Ah hates tuh see yuh knucklin' under 'round heah all de time. G'wan, son, and be keerful uh dat foot-log 'cross de creek. De Songahatchee is strong water, and look out under foot so's yuh don't git snake bit."

"Ah done swum dat ole creek, mama—'thout yuh knowin'. Ah knowed you'd tell me not tuh swim it."

"Dat's how come Ah worries 'bout yuh. Youse always uh runnin' and uh rippin' and clambin' trees and rocks and jumpin', flingin' rocks in creeks and sich like. John, promise me yuh goin' quit dat."

"Yassum."

"Come tuh see me when yuh kin. G'bye."

Amy was gone back up the rocky path thru the blooming

11

cotton, across the barren hard clay yard. For a minute she had felt free and flighty down there as she stood in the open with her tall, bulky son. Now the welts on her face and body hurt her and the world was heavy.

John plunged on down to the Creek, singing a new song and stomping the beats. The Big Creek thundered among its rocks and whirled on down. So John sat on the foot-log and made some words to go with the drums of the Creek. Things walked in the birch woods, creep, creep, creep. The hound dog's lyric crescendo lifted over and above the tree tops. He was on the foot-log, half way across the Big Creek where maybe people laughed and maybe people had lots of daughters. The moon came up. The hunted coon panted down to the Creek, swam across and proceeded leisurely up the other side. The tenor-singing hound dog went home. Night passed. No more Ned, no hurry. No telling how many girls might be living on the new and shiny side of the Big Creek. John almost trumpeted exultantly at the new sun. He breathed lustily. He stripped and carried his clothes across, then recrossed and plunged into the swift water and breasted strongly over.

CHAPTER 2

❖

There was a strange noise that John had never heard. He was sauntering along a road with his shoes in his hand. He could see houses here and there among the fields—not miles apart like where he had come from. Suddenly thirty or forty children erupted from a log building near the roadside, shouting and laughing. He had been to big meeting but this was no preaching. Not all them li'l' chaps. A chunky stern-faced man stood in the door momentarily with a bunch of hickories in his hand. So! This must be the school house that he had heard about. Negro children going to learn how to read and write like white folks. See! All this going on over there and the younguns over the creek chopping cotton! It must be very nice, but maybe it wasn't for over-the-creek-niggers. These girls all had on starchy little aprons over Sunday-go-to-meeting dresses. He stopped and leaned upon the fence and stared.

One little girl with bright black eyes came and stood before him, arms akimbo. She must have been a leader, for several more came and stood back of her. She looked him over boldly from his tousled brown head to his bare white feet. Then she said, "Well, folks! Where you reckon dis big yaller bee-stung nigger come from?"

Everybody laughed. He felt ashamed of his bare feet for the

13

first time in his life. How was he to know that there were colored folks that went around with their feet cramped up like white folks. He looked down at the feet of the black-eyed girl. Tiny little black shoes. One girl behind her had breasts, must be around fourteen. He looked at her again. Some others were growing up too. In fact all were looking a little bit like women—all but the little black-eyed one. When he looked back into her face he felt ashamed. Seemed as if she had caught him doing something nasty. He shifted his feet in embarrassment.

"Ah think he musta come from over de Big Creek. 'Tain't nothin' lak dat on dis side," the little tormenter went on. Then she looked right into his eyes and laughed. All the others laughed. John laughed too.

"Dat's whar Ah come from sho 'nuff," he admitted.

"Whut you doin' over heah, then?"

"Come tuh see iffen Ah could git uh job uh work. Kin yuh tell me whar Marse Alf Pearson live at?"

The little girl snorted, "Marse Alf! Don't y'all folkses over de creek know slavery time is over? 'Tain't no mo' Marse Alf, no Marse Charlie, nor Marse Tom neither. Folks whut wuz borned in slavery time go 'round callin' dese white folks Marse but we been born since freedom. We calls 'em Mister. Dey don't own nobody no mo'."

"Sho don't," the budding girl behind the little talker chimed in. She threw herself akimbo also and came walking out hippily from behind the other, challenging John to another appraisal of her person.

"Ah calls 'em anything Ah please," said another girl and pulled her apron a little tight across the body as she advanced towards the fence.

"Aw, naw, yuh don't, Clary," the little black-eyed girl disputed, "youse talkin' at de big gate now. You jus' want somebody tuh notice yuh."

"Well, effen you calls 'em Mista, Ah kin call 'em Mista too," John talked at the little spitfire. "Whar at is Mista Alf Pearson's place?"

14

"Way on down dis road, 'bout uh mile uh mo'. When yuh git long dere by de cotton-gin, ast somebody and dey'll tell yuh mo' exact."

John shifted from one foot to another a time or two, then started off with the long stride known as boaging.

"Thankee, thankee," he threw back over his shoulder and strode on.

The teacher poked his head out of the door and all the other girls ran around behind the school house lest he call them to account for talking to a boy. But the littlest girl stood motionless, not knowing that the others had fled. She stood still akimbo watching John stride away. Then suddenly her hands dropped to her sides and she raced along the inside of the fence and overtook John.

"Hello agin," John greeted her, glad at her friendliness.

"Hello yuhself, want uh piece uh cawn bread look on de shelf."

John laughed boisterously and the girl smiled and went on in another tone, "Whyn't *you* come tuh school too?"

" 'Cause dey never sont me. Dey tole me tuh go find work, but Ah wisht dey had uh tole me school. Whut Ah seen of it, Ah lakted it."

From behind her the irate voice of a man called, "Lucy! Lucy!! Come heah tuh me. Ah'll teach yuh 'bout talkin' wid boys!"

"See yuh later, and tell yuh straighter," John said and walked off.

John strode on into Notasulga, whistling; his tousled hair every which away over his head. He saw a group of people clustered near a small building and he timidly approached.

"Dis heah mus' be de cotton-gin wid all dem folks and hawses and buggies tied tuh de hitchin' postes."

Suddenly he was conscious of a great rumbling at hand and the train schickalacked up to the station and stopped.

John stared at the panting monster for a terrified moment, then prepared to bolt. But as he wheeled about he saw everybody's eyes upon him and there was laughter on every face.

He stopped and faced about. Tried to look unconcerned, but that great eye beneath the cloud-breathing smoke-stack glared and threatened. The engine's very sides seemed to expand and contract like a fiery-lunged monster. The engineer leaning out of his window saw the fright in John's face and blew a sharp blast on his whistle and John started violently in spite of himself. The crowd roared.

"Hey, dere, big-un," a Negro about the station called to John, "you ain't never seed nothin' dangerous lookin' lak dat befo', is yuh?"

"Naw suh and hit sho look frightenin'," John answered. His candor took the ridicule out of the faces of the crowd. "But hits uh pretty thing too. Whar it gwine?"

"Oh eve'y which and whar," the other Negro answered, with the intent to convey the impression to John that he knew so much about trains, their habits and destinations that it would be too tiresome to try to tell it all.

The train kicked up its heels and rattled on off. John watched after it until it had lost itself down its shiny road and the noise of its going was dead.

"You laks dat ole train Ah see," the Negro said to John, watching him as he all but fell down into the railroad cut, trying to keep sight of the tail of the train.

"Yeah, man, Ah lakted dat. It say something but Ah ain't heered it 'nough tuh tell whut it say yit. You know whut it say?"

"It don't say nothin'. It jes' make uh powerful racket, dass all."

"Naw, it say some words too. Ahm comin' heah plenty mo' times and den Ah tell yuh whut it say." He straightened up and suddenly remembered.

"Whar de cotton-gin at?"

"Hit's right over dere, but dey ain't hirin' nobody yit."

"Ain't lookin' tuh git hiahed. Lookin' fuh Mist' Alf Pearson."

"Dere he right over dere on de flat-form at de deepo', whut yuh want wid 'im?"

16

"Wants tuh git uh job."

"Reckon you kin git on. He done turned off his coachman fuh stovin' up one uh his good buggy hawses."

John stalked over to the freight platform.

"Is you Mist' Alf?" he asked the tall broad-built man, who was stooping over some goods.

"Why yes, what're you want?"

"Ah wants uh job uh work, please suh."

The white man continued to examine invoices without so much as a glance at the boy who stood on the ground looking up at him. Not seeing what he wanted, he straightened up and looked about him and saw John at last. Instead of answering the boy directly he stared at him fixedly for a moment, whistled and exclaimed, "What a fine stud! Why boy, you would have brought five thousand dollars on the block in slavery time! Your face looks sort of familiar but I can't place you. What's your name?"

"Mama, she name me Two-Eye-John from a preachin' she heered, but dey call me John Buddy for short."

"How old are you, John?"

"Sixteen, goin' on sebenteen."

"Dog damn! Boy you're almost as big as I am. Where'd you come from?"

"Over de Big Creek. Mama she sont me over here and told me tuh ast you tuh gimme uh job uh work. Ah kin do mos' anything."

"Humph, I should think you could. Boy, you could go bear-hunting with your fist. I believe I can make a lead plow-hand out of you."

"Yassuh, thankee, Mista Alf, Ah knows how."

"Er, who is your mama?"

"Amy Crittenden. She didn't useter be uh Crittenden. She wuz jes' Amy and b'longed tuh you 'fo surrender. She say Ah borned on yo' place."

"Oh yes. I remember her. G'wan get in my rig. The bay horses with the cream colored buggy. Fetch it on over here and drive me home."

17

John went over by the courthouse to get the rig. It was some distance. As soon as he was out of earshot, one of Alf Pearson's friends asked him, "Say, Judge, where'd you get the new house-nigger from?"

"Oh a boy born on my place since surrender. Mama married some stray darky and moved over the Big Creek. She sent him over here to hunt work and he ran into me and I'm hiring him. Did you ever see such a splendid specimen? He'll be a mighty fine plow hand. Too tall to be a good cotton-picker. Sixteen years old."

"Humph! Plow-hand! Dat's uh house-nigger. His kind don't make good field niggers. It's been tried. In his case it's a pity, because he'd be equal to two hands ordinary."

"Oh well, maybe I can do something with him. He seems willing enough. And anyway I know how to work 'em."

When John brought the horses to a satisfactory halt before the white pillars of the Pearson mansion, his new boss got down and said, "Now John, take those horses on to the stable and let Nunkie put 'em away. He'll show you where the quarters are. G'wan to 'em and tell old Pheemy I said fix you some place to sleep."

"Yassuh, thankee suh."

"And John, I might need you around the house sometimes, so keep clean."

"Yassuh."

"Where's the rest of your clothes?"

"Dese is dem."

"Well, you'll have to change sometime or other. I'll look around the house, and perhaps I can scare you up a change or two. My son Alfred is about your size, but he's several years older. And er, er, I'll fetch 'em down to the quarters in case I find anything. Go 'long."

Ole Pheemy gave John a bed in her own cabin, "Take dis bed heah if hit's good 'nough fuh yuh," she said pointing to a high feather bed in one corner.

"Yassum, thankee ma'am. Ah laks it jes' fine, and dis sho is uh pritty house."

He was looking at the newspapers plastered all over the walls.

Pheemy softened.

"Oh you ain't one uh dese uppity yaller niggers then?"

"Oh no ma'am. Ahm po' folks jes' lak you. On'y we ain't got no fine houses over de Creek lak dis heah one."

"Whus yo' name?"

"John, but Zeke and Zack and dem calls me John Buddy, yassum."

"Who yo' folks is over de Big Creek?"

"Mama she name Amy Crittenden—she—"

"Hush yo' mouf, you yaller rascal, you! Ah knowed, Ah seed reckerlection in yo' face." Pheemy rushed upon John, beating him affectionately and shoving him around. "Well, Lawd a'mussy boy! Ahm yo' granny! Yo' nable string is buried under dat air chanyberry tree. 'Member so well de very day you cried." (First cry at birth.) "Eat dis heah tater pone."

The field hands came in around dusk dark, eyeing John suspiciously, but his utter friendliness prevented the erection of barriers on his birth place. Amy's son was welcome. After supper the young folks played "Hide the Switch" and John overtook and whipped most of the girls soundly. They whipped him too. Perhaps his legs were longer, but anyway when he was "it" he managed to catch every girl in the quarters. The other boys were less successful, but girls were screaming under John's lash behind the cowpen and under the sweet-gum trees around the spring until the moon rose. John never forgot that night. Even the strong odor of their sweaty bodies was lovely to remember. He went in to bed when all of the girls had been called in by their folks. He could have romped till morning.

In bed he turned and twisted.

"Skeeters botherin' yuh, John Buddy?" Pheemy asked.

"No'm Ahm jes' wishin' Mist' Alf would lak mah work and lemme stay heah all de time." Then the black eyes of the little girl in the school yard burned at him from out of the darkness and he added, "Wisht Ah could go tuh school too."

19

"G'wan tuh sleep, chile. Heah 'tis way in de midnight and you ain't had no night rest. You gotta sleep effen you wanta do any work. Whut Marse Alf tell yuh tuh do?"

"He ain't tole me nothin' yit."

"Well, you stay heah tuh de house. Ontell he send fuh yuh. He ain't gwine overwork yuh. He don't break nobody down. Befo' surrender he didn't had no whippin' boss on *dis* place. Nawsuh. Come tuh 'membrance, 'tain't nothin' much tuh do now. De crops is laid by, de ground peas ain't ready, neither de cawn. But Ah don't speck he gointer put you in de fiel' nohow. Maybe you hand him his drinks uh drive de carridge fuh him and Ole Miss."

"Yassum," drifted back from John as he slid down and down into sleep and slumber.

That night he dreamed new dreams.

"John."

"Yassuh."

"I see the clothes fit you."

"Yassuh, Ahm powerful glad dey do, 'cause Ah laks 'em."

"John, I don't reckon I'll have you to drive us again. I thought to make a coachman out of you, but the mistress thinks you're too, er, er—large sitting up there in front. Can't see around you."

"Yassuh," John's face fell. He wasn't going to be hired after all.

"But I've got another job for you. You feed the chickens and gather the eggs every morning before breakfast. Have the fresh eggs in the pantry at the big house before seven o'clock so Emma can use some for our breakfast."

"Yassuh."

"And John, see to it that Ceasar and Bully and Nunkie keep the stables, pig pens and the chicken houses clean. Don't say anything to 'em, but when you find 'em dirty you let me know."

"Yassuh."

"And another thing, I want you to watch all of my brood

sows. As soon as a litter is born, you let me know. And you must keep up with every pig on the place. Count 'em every morning, and when you find one missing you look around and find out what's become of it. I'm missing entirely too many shoats. I'm good to my darkies but I can't let 'em eat up all my hogs. Now, I'm going to see if I can trust you."

"Yassuh."

"Can you read and write, John?"

"Nawsuh."

"Never been to school?"

"Nawsuh, yassuh, Ah passed by dat one d'other day."

"Well, John, there's nothing much to do on the place now, so you might as well go on down to the school and learn how to read and write. I don't reckon it will hurt you. Don't waste your time, now. Learn. I don't think the school runs but three months and it's got to close for cotton-picking. Don't fool around. You're almost grown. Three or four children on this place go so you go along with them. Go neat. I didn't have slouchy folks on my place in slavery time. Mister Alfred, my son, is studying abroad and he's left several suits around that will do for you. Be neat. Let's see your feet. I don't believe you can wear his shoes but I'll buy you a pair and take it out of your wages. You mind me and I'll make something out of you."

"Yassuh, Mister Alf. Thankee. Youse real good tuh me. Mama said you wuz good."

"She was a well-built-up girl and a splendid hoe hand. I never could see why she married that darky and let him drag her around share-cropping. Those backwoods white folks over the creek make their living by swindling the niggers."

John didn't go to school the next day. He had truly been delighted at the prospect of attending school. It had kept him glowing all day. But that night the young people got up a game of "Hide and Seek." It started a little late, about the time that the old heads were going to bed.

Bow-legged, pigeon-toed Minnie Turl was counting, "Ten, ten, double ten, forty-five, fifteen. All hid? All hid?"

From different directions, as the "hiders" sought cover, "No!"

> "Three li'l' hawses in duh stable,
> One jumped out and skint his nable.
> All hid? All hid?"

"No!" from farther away.

John ran down hill towards the spring where the bushes were thick. He paused at a clump. It looked like a good place. There was a stealthy small sound behind it and he ran on. Some one ran down the path behind him. A girl's hand caught his. It was Phrony, the womanish fourteen-year-old who lived in the third cabin from Pheemy's.

"Ah'll show yuh uh good place tuh hide," she whispered, "nobody can't find yuh."

She dragged him off the path to the right and round and about to a clump of sumac overrun with wild grape vines.

"Right under heah," she panted from running, "nobody can't find yuh."

"Whar you goin' hide yuhself?" John asked as he crept into the arboreal cave.

"Iss plenty room," Phrony whispered. "Us bofe kin hide in heah."

She crept in also and leaned heavily upon John, giggling and giggling as the counting went on.

> "Ah got up 'bout half-past fo'
> Forty fo' robbers wuz 'round mah do'
> Ah got up and let 'em in
> Hit 'em ovah de head wid uh rollin' pin.
> All hid? All hid?"

"Yeah."

"All dem ten feet round mah base is caught. Ahm comin'!"

There were screams and shouts of laughter. "Dere's Gold-Dollar behind dat chanyberry tree. Ah got yuh."

22

"Whoo-ee! Ahm free, Minnie, Ah beat yuh in home."

"Less we run in whilst she gone de other way," John whispered.

"Naw, less we lay low 'til she git tired uh huntin' us and give us free base."

"Aw right, Phrony, but Ah loves tuh outrun 'em and beat 'em tuh de base. 'Tain't many folks kin run good ez me."

"Ah kin run good, too."

"Aw, 'tain't no girl chile kin run good ez me."

"Ah betcha 'tis. Lucy Potts kin outrun uh yearlin' and rope 'im."

"Humph! Where she at?"

"She live over in Pottstown. Her folks done bought de ole Cox place. She go to school. Dey's big niggers."

"She uh li'l' bitty gal wid black eyes and long hair plats?"

"Yeah, dat's her. She leben years ole, but she don't look it. Ahm fourteen. Ahm big. Maybe Ah'll git married nex' year."

"Ahm gwine race huh jes' soon ez Ah gits tuh school. Mista Alf gwine lemme go too."

"Dat's good. Ah done been dere las' yeah. Ah got good learnin'. Reckon Ah'll git uh husban' nex'."

Cry from up the hill, "John and Phrony, come on in. You get free base!"

They scrambled out. John first, then Phrony more slowly, and trudged up the hill. A boy was kneeling at the woods chopping-block base when they came into the crowd. The crowd began to disperse again. John started off in another direction. He looked back and saw Phrony coming behind him, but Mehaley cut in from behind a bush and reached him first.

"Come on wid me, John, lemme show yuh uh good place." He started to say that he didn't want to hide out and talk as he had done with Phrony. He wanted to pit his strength and speed against the boy who was counting. He wanted to practise running, but he felt a flavor come out from Mehaley. He could almost sense it in his mouth and nostrils. He was cross with Phrony for following them. He let Mehaley take his hand

and they fled away up the hill and hid in the hay.

"De hair on yo' head so soft lak," Mehaley breathed against his cheek. "Lemme smoothen it down."

When John and Mehaley came in, Minnie Turl was counting. Everybody was hid except Phrony who sat bunched up on the door step.

"Y'all better go hide agin," she said.

"Somebody else count and lemme hide," Minnie wailed. "Ah been countin' most all de time." She came and stood near John.

"G'wan hide, Minnie, Ah'll count some," John said.

"Heh! Heh!" Phrony laughed maliciously at Minnie. Minnie looked all about her and went inside the house and to bed.

"Haley, where mah hair comb you borried from me las' Sunday? Ah wuz nice enough tuh len' it tuh yuh, but you ain't got manners 'nough tuh fetch it back." Phrony advanced upon Mehaley and John.

"You kin git yo' ole stink hair comb any time. Ah'll be glad tuh git it outa mah house. Mama tole me not tuh comb wid it 'cause she skeered Ah'd git boogers in mah haid."

"Youse uh lie! Ah ain't got no boogers in mah haid, and if you' mamy say so she's uh liar right long wid you! She ain't so bad ez she make out. Ah'll stand on yo' toes and tell yuh so."

"Git back outa mah face, Phrony. Ah don't play de dozens!" Mehaley shoved. Phrony struck, and John and all the hiders, who came running in at the sound of battle, had trouble stopping the rough and tumble.

"Did y'all had words befo' yuh fell out?" Charlie asked.

"We ain't had no words," said Mehaley.

"Whut y'all fightin' 'bout, if yuh ain't mad?"

"Aw, ole fish-mouf Phrony mad 'cause John wouldn't hide wid her and he took and hid wid me."

"Youse uh liar, madam! He did so hide wid me."

"He wouldn't stay, and Ah'll betcha Alabama wid uh fence 'round it he won't never hide wid yuh no mo'."

Mehaley preened herself akimbo and rotated her hips insolently.

"Sh-sh—" Charlie cautioned, "de old heads liable tuh wake up, and dey'll haul off and take and frail everybody. Less all tip in tuh bed. Iss way after midnight anyhow."

So John overslept next morning and by the time that he had gathered the eggs and counted the hogs it was too late for school. He didn't want to see Lucy anyway. Not the way he felt that day, but late in the afternoon as he wandered over the place, he found a tiny clearing hidden by trees.

"Dis is uh prayin' ground," he said to himself.

"O Lawd, heah 'tis once mo' and again yo' weak and humble servant is knee-bent and body bowed—Mah heart beneath mah knees and mah knees in some lonesome valley cryin' fuh mercy whilst mercy kinst be found. O Lawd! you know mah heart, and all de ranges uh mah deceitful mind—and if you find any sin lurkin' in and about mah heart please pluck it out and cast it intuh de sea uh fuhgitfulness whar it'll never rise tuh condemn me in de judgment."

That night John, deaf to Mehaley's blandishments, sat in the doorway and told tales. And Brer Rabbit and Brer Fox and Raw-Head-and-Bloody-Bones walked the earth like natural men.

Next morning, bright and soon he stood at the school-house door. The teacher was a stodgy middle-aged man who prided himself on his frowns. Every few moments he lifted his head and glared about the room. He yearned to hold his switches in his hand. He had little ambition to impart knowledge. He reigned. Later John found out he was Lucy's uncle.

"Come heah, you," he pointed his ruler at John. "Don't you know no better'n to come in my school and sit yo'self down without sayin' a word to me?"

"Yassuh," he approached the deal table that went by the name of desk.

"If you know better, why did you do it? I ought to put forty lashes on yo' bare back. You come to school?"

"Yassuh."

"Don't say 'yassuh' to me. Say 'Yes suh.' "

The room tittered.

"What's yo' name?"

"John."

"John whut? You got some other name besides John."

"Mama, she name me Two-Eye John—"

They burst into loud laughter. John colored and he stole a glance at Lucy. She wasn't laughing. Her hands and lips were tense. She must be put out with him for being a fool. She wasn't laughing like the rest.

"But mama and all of 'em at home calls me John Buddy."

"Buddy is a nickname. What's yo' papa' name?"

John scratched his head and thought a minute.

" 'Deed Ah don't know, suh."

There was another short silence.

"Where do you live?"

"On Mista Alf Pearson's place."

"Was you born there?"

"Yes suh."

"Well, Ah'll jus' put you down as John Pearson and you answer by that, you hear?"

"Yes suh."

"Ever been to school before?"

"Naw suh."

"Well, you get over there in de A B C class and don't let me ketch you talkin' in school."

John was amazed at the number of things to be learned. He liked to watch Lucy's class recite. They put so many figures on the board and called it long division. He would certainly be well learnt when he could do that. They parsed sentences. They spelt long words.

He studied hard because he caught Lucy watching him every time he recited. He wrote on the ground in the quarters and in a week he knew his alphabet and could count to a hundred.

"Whut you learnin' in school, John—A, B, Ab's?" Charlie asked him.

26

"Ah already know dat, Charlie. Ah kin spell 'baker' too."

"Don't b'lieve it. Not dis quick, yuh can't."

"B-a-k-bak-e-r-er baker."

"Boy, you sho is eatin' up dat school!"

"Ain't ez smart ez some. Take Lucy Potts for instink. She's almost uh 'fessor now. Nobody can't spell her down. Dey say she kin spell eve'y word in Lippincott's Blue-back Speller."

"Shucks! You ain't tryin' tuh buck up tuh her in book learnin', is yuh? Dey tell me she kin spell 'compresstibility,' and when yuh git dat fur 'tain't much mo' fuhther fur yuh tuh go."

"She sho kin spell it, 'cause Ah heered 'er do it. Some say she kin spell 'Constan-ti-nople' too."

"Ah b'lieve it. All dem Potts is smart. Her brother leads de choir at Macedony Baptis' Church, and she trebles right 'long wid dem grown women and kin sing all de notes—de square ones, de round ones, de triangles."

"Ah'll be dere tuh heah her do it nex' big meetin'. Charlie, Ah loves tuh heah singin'."

"Whyn't yuh join de choir? You oughter be able tuh sing lak git out wid all dat ches' you got."

"B'lieve Ah will, Charlie. Ah laks big meetin'."

It was three weeks from the time that John started to school 'til cotton-picking time. Prodded on all sides, he had learned to read a little and write a few words crudely.

He was sorry when school closed for the cotton-picking but he kept on studying. When the school re-opened for its final month he wanted to get promoted again. He found himself spelling out words on barns and wagons, almanacs, horse-medicine-bottles, wrapping-paper.

He had been to church; he hadn't enough courage to join the choir, but every meeting he was there. Lucy tossed her head and sang her treble and never missed a note.

When the cotton-picking began on his place, Alf Pearson said to John, "You better go across the Creek and let your mama know how you're getting along. If you see any good cotton pickers—anybody that can pick more than two hundred a day—tell 'em I need some hands, and you be back by tomorrow night. I bought a brood sow over round Chehaw and I want you to go get her.''

There was great rejoicing in Amy's house when John climbed the hill from the Creek.

They didn't know him in his new clothes. They made great '' 'miration'' over everything. Amy cried.

"Jes' tuh think, mah boy gittin' book-learnt! Ned, de rest uh dese chillun got tuh go tuh school nex' yeah. Sho is.''

"Whut fur? So dey kin lay in de peni'ten'ry? Dat's all dese book-learnt niggers do—fill up de jails and chain-gangs. Dese boys is comin' 'long all right. All dey need tuh learn is how tuh swing uh hoe and turn a furrer. Ah ain't rubbed de hair offa mah haid 'gin no college walls and Ah got good sense. Day ain't goin' tuh no school effen Ah got anythin' tuh say 'bout it. Jes' be turnin' 'em fools!''

Stormy weather. John cut in.

"Mama, Mista Alf say if Ah could find some good cotton pickers tuh tell 'em he need hands. You know any? He payin' fifty cent uh hund'ed.''

"Dat's more'n dey payin' over heah,'' Ned cut in eagerly, "Amy, whyn't you take Zeke and Zack and y'all g'wan make dat li'l' change? Ah'll take keer de li'l' chillun and pick up whut li'l' Ah kin git over heah. Cotton open dat side de Creek fust anyhow. By time y'all finish over dere hit'll jis' be gittin' in full swing over heah.''

"Reckon us could make li'l' money. Tell 'im, 'Yeah,' John Buddy, we's comin'.''

"Zack!'' Ned called, "Take dis heah jug and run over tuh de Turk place and tell Ike tuh send me uh gallon. Pay 'im nex' week some time.''

When the cotton was all picked and the last load hauled to the gin, Alf Pearson gave the hands two hogs to barbecue.

That was a night. Hogs roasting over the open pit of oak coals. Negroes from three other plantations. Some brought "likker.'' Some crocus sacks of yellow yam potatoes, and bushels of peanuts to roast, and the biggest syrup-kettle at Pear-

28

son's canemill was full of chicken perleau. Twenty hens and six water-buckets full of rice. Old Purlee Kimball was stirring it with a shovel.

Plenty of music and plenty of people to enjoy it. Three sets had been danced when Bully took the center of the hard-packed clay court upon which they were dancing. He had the whole rib of a two-hundred-pound hog in his hands and gnawed it as he talked.

"Hey, everybody! Stop de music. Don't vip another vop 'til Ah says so. Hog head, hog bosom, hog hips and every kind of hog there ever wuz is ready! Come git yourn. De chickens is cacklin' in de rice and dey say 'Come git it whilst iss fitten 'cause t'morrer it may be frost-bitten!' De yaller yams is spilin' in de ashes. It's uh shame! Eat it all up, and den we's gointer dance, 'cause we'll have somethin' tuh dance offa."

The hogs, the chickens, the yams disappeared. The old folks played "Ole Horse" with the parched peanuts. The musicians drank and tuned up. Bully was calling figures.

"Hey you, dere, us ain't no white folks! Put down dat fiddle! Us don't want no fiddles, neither no guitars, neither no banjoes. Less clap!"

So they danced. They called for the instrument that they had brought to America in their skins—the drum—and they played upon it. With their hands they played upon the little dance drums of Africa. The drums of kid-skin. With their feet they stomped it, and the voice of Kata-Kumba, the great drum, lifted itself within them and they heard it. The great drum that is made by priests and sits in majesty in the juju house. The drum with the man skin that is dressed with human blood, that is beaten with a human shin-bone and speaks to gods as a man and to men as a God. Then they beat upon the drum and danced. It was said, "He will serve us better if we bring him from Africa naked and thing-less." So the buckra reasoned. They tore away his clothes that Cuffy might bring nothing away, but Cuffy seized his drum and hid it in his skin under the skull bones. The shin-bones he bore openly, for he thought, "Who shall rob me of shin-bones when they see no drum?" So he laughed with cunning and said, "I, who am borne away to become an orphan, carry my parents with me. For Rhythm is she not my mother and Drama is her man?" So he groaned aloud in the ships and hid his drum and laughed.

"Dis is jes' lak when Ah wuz uh girl," Amy told Pheemy and offered her body to the voice.

Furious music of the little drum whose body was still in Africa, but whose soul sung around a fire in Alabama. Flourish. Break.

> Ole cow died in Tennessee
> Send her jawbone back to me
> Jawbone walk, Jawbone talk
> Jawbone eat wid uh knife and fork.
> Ain't Ah right?
>
> CHORUS: Yeah!
> Ain't I right? Yeah!

Hollow-hand clapping for the bass notes. Heel and toe stomping for the little one. Ibo tune corrupted with Nango. Congo gods talking in Alabama.

> If you want to see me jabber
> Set me down to uh bowl uh clabber
> Ain't Ah right? Yeah!
> Now, ain't Ah right? Yeah!
>
> Ole Ant Dinah behind de pine
> One eye out and de other one blind
> Ain't Ah right? Yeah! Yeah!
> Now, ain't Ah right? Yeah!

"Looka dat boy uh yourn, Amy!" Zeke Turk urged. "Didn't thought he knowed how tuh dance. He's rushin' de frog tuh de frolic! And looka 'Big 'Oman,' dat gal dancin' wid 'im. Lawd, she shakin' yonder skirt."

Wisht Ah had uh needle
Fine ez Ah could sew
Ah'd sew mah baby to my side
And down de road Ah'd go.

Double clapping—

Down de road baby
Down de road baby
It's killing mama
Oh, it's killing mama.

Too hot for words. Fiery drum clapping.

"Less burn dat old moon down to a nub! Is dat you, Pheemy?"

"Yeah Lawd. Mah head is tilted to de grave, but Ah'll show y'all Ah ain't fuhgit how. Come on out heah, Dink, and help ole Pheemy do de Parse me lah."

"Heel and toe. Don't call no figgers."

"Aw yeah, less call figgers. Go 'head Bully, but don't call it lak you call for white folks and dey go praipsin 'cross the floor lake dey steppin on eggs. Us kin dance. Call 'em, Bully."

"Awright, choose yo' partners."

"Couples tuh yo' places lak hawse tuh de traces."

"Sixteen hands up!"

"Circle four."

"Y'all ain't clappin' right. Git dat time.

Raccoon up de 'simmon tree
Possum on de ground
Raccoon shake dem 'simmons down
Possum pass 'em round."

The fire died. The moon died. The shores of Africa receded. They went to sleep and woke up next day and looked

31

out on dead and dying cotton stalks and ripening possum persimmons.

As the final day of school closing drew near, John found life tremendously exciting. The drama of Pearson's plantation yielded to the tenseness around the school house. He had learned to spell his way thru several pages in his reader. He could add, subtract and divide and multiply. He proved his new power to communicate his thoughts by scratching Lucy's name in the clay wherever he found a convenient spot: with a sharp stick he had even scratched it on the back of Pheemy's chimney.

He saw Lucy at school every day. He saw her in church, and she was always in his consciousness, but he had never talked with her alone. When the opportunity presented itself he couldn't find words. Handling Big 'Oman, Lacey, Semmie, Bootsie and Mehaley merely called for action, but with Lucy he needed words and words that he did not have. One day during the practice for school closing he crowded near her and said, "Wisht Ah could speak pieces lak you do."

"You kin speak 'em better'n me," Lucy said evenly, "you got uh good voice for speakin'."

"But Ah can't learn no long ones lak you speaks. When do you learn 'em?"

"In de night time round home after Ah git thru wid mah lessons."

"You ain't got many mo' days tuh be studyin' of nights. Den whut you gwine do wid yo'self?"

"Mama always kin find plenty fuh folks tuh do."

"But Ah mean in de night time, Lucy. When youse thru wid yo' work. Don't you do nothin' but warm uh chair bottom?"

Lucy drew away quickly, "Oooh, John Buddy! You talkin' nasty."

John in turn was in confusion. "Whuss nasty?"

"You didn't hafta say 'bottom.'"

John shriveled up inside. He had intended to recite the rhymes to Lucy that the girls on the plantation thought so witty, but he realized that—

would drive Lucy from him in disgust. He could never tell her that. He felt hopeless about her. Soon she was recalled to the platform to recite and John's chance was gone. He kept on thinking, however, and he kept on making imaginary speeches to her. Speeches full of big words that would make her gasp and do him "reverence." He was glad when he was selected as the soldier to sing opposite Lucy in the duet, "Oh Soldier, Will You Marry Me?" It meant something more than singing with gestures beside a girl. Maybe she would realize that he could learn things too, even if she could read the better. He meant to change all that as quickly as possible. One day he shyly overtook her on her way home.

"Dey tell me you kin run fast," he began awkwardly.

"Dey told you right," Lucy answered saucily, "whoever tole you. Ah kin outrun most anybody 'round heah."

"Less we race tuh dat sweet-gum tree and see who kin beat," John challenged.

They were off. Lucy's thin little legs pumping up and down. The starchy strings of her blue sunbonnet fluttering under her chin, and her bonnet lying back of her neck.

"Ah beat yuh!" John gloated over the foot or two that he had gained with difficulty.

"Yeah, you beat me, but look how much mo' legs you got to run wid," Lucy retorted. "Bet if Ah had dem legs nobody couldn't never outrun me."

"Ah didn't mean tuh beat yuh. Gee, us done come uh good ways! How much further you live from heah, Lucy?"

"Oh uh little ways cross de branch."

"B'lieve Ah'll go see how yo' ole branch look. Maybe it got uh heap uh fish in it."

" 'Tain't got no fish in it worth talkin' 'bout. 'Tain't hardly knee deep, John, but iss uh great big ole snake down dere."

"Whut kinda snake?"

"Uh great big ole cotton-mouf moccasin. He skeers me,

John. Everytime Ah go 'cross dat foot-log Ah think maybe Ah might fall in and den he'll bite me, or he might reah hisself up and bite me anyhow."

"How come y'all don't take and kill 'im?"

"Who you reckon goin' down in de water tuh strain wid uh moccasin? He got uh hole back under the bank where you kin see 'im, but you can't git 'im 'thout you wuz down in de branch. He lay all 'round dere on de ground and even on de foot-log, but when he see somebody comin' he go in his hole, all ready for yuh and lay dere and dare yuh tuh bother 'im."

"You jes' show 'im tuh me. Ah can't stand tuh be aggravated by no ole snake and then agin Ah don't want 'im slurrin' *you.*"

"Sh-sh, watch out, John! He 'round heah somewhere. Can't you smell 'im? Dere he is goin' in his hole!"

John took a good look at the snake, then looked all about him for a weapon. Finding none he sat down and began to remove his shoes.

"You ain't goin' in dat branch!" Lucy gasped.

"Turn me go, Lucy. If you didn't want yo' ole snake kilt yuh oughta not showed 'im tuh me." He exulted, but pretended not to see her concern was for him.

He looked carefully to see that no other snakes were about, then stepped cautiously down into the water. The snake went on guard, slowly, insolently. Lucy was terrified. Suddenly, he snatched the foot-log from its place and, leaning far back to give it purchase, he rammed it home upon the big snake and held it there. The snake bit at the log again and again in its agony, but finally the biting and the thrashing ceased. John fished the snake out and stretched it upon the grass.

"Ooh, John, Ahm so glad you kilt dat ole devil. He been right dere skeerin' folks since befo' Ah wuz borned."

"He won't skeer nobody else, lessen dey skeered uh dead snakes," John answered in the tone that boys use to girls on such occasions.

"Reckon his mate ain't gonna follow us and try tuh bite us for killin' dis one?"

34

"Lucy, he can't foller bofe us, lessen us go de same way."

"Thass right, John. Ah done forgot, you live over on de Alf Pearson place."

"Yeah, dat's right."

"Where M'haley and Big 'Oman live."

"Unh hunh, Ah speck dey do live dere. Ah seen uh lot uh pullet-size girl chillun 'bout de place. Nearly uh hund'ed head uh folks on dat plantation."

A heavy silence fell. Lucy looked across the shallow stream and said,

"You ain't put de foot-log back, John."

"Dat's right. Sho nuff Ah done fuhgot. Lemme tote you 'cross den. Ah kin place it back for de other folks."

"Doncha lemme fall, John. Maybe 'nother ole snake down dere."

"How Ahm gonna let uh li'l' bit lak you fall? Ah kin tote uh sack uh feed-meal and dat's twice big ez you. Lemme tote yuh. Ah 'clare Ah won't drop yuh."

John bore Lucy across the tiny stream and set her down slowly.

"Oh you done left yo' book-sack, Lucy. Got tuh take yuh back tuh git it."

"Naw, you hand it tuh me, John."

"Aw, naw, you come git it."

He carried Lucy back and she recrossed the stream the third time. As he set her down on her home side he said, "Little ez *you* is nobody wouldn't keer how fur he hafta tote you. You ain't even uh handful."

Lucy put herself akimbo, "Ahm uh li'l' piece uh leather, but well put t'gether, Ah thankee, Mist' John."

"Mah comperments, Miss Lucy."

Lucy was gone up the hill in a blue whirlwind. John replaced the foot-log and cut across lots for home.

"She is full uh pepper," John laughed to himself, "but ah laks dat. Anything 'thout no seasonin' in it ain't no good."

At home, Lucy rushed out back of the corn crib and tiptoed

to see if her head yet touched the mark she had made three weeks before.

"Ah shucks!" She raged, "Ah ain't growed none hardly. Ah ain't never gointer get grown. Ole M'haley way head uh me!"

She hid and cried until Emmeline, her mama, called her to set the table for supper.

The night of school closing came. John in tight new shoes and with a standing collar was on hand early. Saw Lucy enter followed by the Potts clan. Frowning mama, placid papa, strapping big sister, and the six grown brothers. Boys with "rear-back" hair held down by a thick coating of soap. Boys hobbling in new shoes and tight breeches. Girls whose hair smelled of fresh hog-lard and sweet william, and white dresses with lace, with pink or blue sashes, with ruffles, with mothers searching their bosoms for pins to yank up hanging petticoats. Tearful girls who had forgotten their speeches. Little girls with be-ribboned frizzed-out hair who got spanked for wetting their starchy panties. Proud parents. Sulky parents and off-spring. Whispered envy.

"Dere's Lucy Potts over dere in uh fluted dress. Dey allus gives her de longest piece tuh speak."

"Dat's 'cause she kin learn more'n anybody else."

"Naw 'tain't, dey muches her up. Mah Semmie could learn jes' ez long uh piece ez anybody if de give it tuh her—in time. Ahm gwine take mah chillun outa school after dis and put 'em tuh work. Dey ain't learnin' 'em nothin' nohow. Dey makes cake outa some uh de chillun and cawn bread outa de rest."

Opening prayer. Song. Speech by white superintendent. Speeches rattled off like beans poured into a tin can.

"A speech by Miss Lucy Potts."

The shining big eyes in the tiny face. Lacy whiteness. Fierce hand-clapping. Lucy calm and self-assured.

"A chieftain to the highland bound, cried 'Boatman do not tarry' "—to the final "My daughter, oh my daughter." More applause. The idol had not failed her public.

"She kin speak de longest pieces and never miss uh word

36

and say 'em faster dan anybody Ah ever seed." It was agreed Lucy was perfect. Time and speeches flew fast.

> Little fishes in de brook
> Willie ketch 'em wid uh hook
> Mama fry 'em in de pan
> Papa eat 'em lak uh man.

"Duet—Miss Lucy Potts, bassed by Mr. John Pearson." They sang and their hearers applauded wildly. Nobody cared whether the treble was treble or the bass was bass. It was the gestures that counted and everybody agreed that John was perfect as the philandering soldier of the piece and that Lucy was just right as the over-eager maid. They had to sing it over twice. John began to have a place of his own in the minds of folks, more than he realized.

CHAPTER 3

❖

One morning in the early spring John found Amy sitting before the fire in Pheemy's house.

"Howdy, mam."

"Howdy, son."

She rubbed her teeth and gums with the tiny snuff-brush. She had something to say and John knew it.

"How's everybody makin' it over de Big Creek, maw?"

"Right middlin', John. Us could do better but yo' pappy always piddlin' from piller tuh post and dat keep de rest uh us in hot water."

"Yessum. What's de trouble now?"

"Yuh know Beasley took and beat us out uh our cotton and we ain't hardly had nothin' tuh eat, so day 'fo' yistiddy Ned took and kilt one uh Beasley's yearlings way down dere in de hammock and fetched it home dere and us cooked and et some of it and put some of it down in salt. We thinkin' nobody'd ever know de diffunce, but Beasley heard de cows bellerin' when dey smelt de blood where it wuz kilt and went down dere and found de hide. So us had tuh pack up our things in meal sacks and when it wuz black dark us went on over tuh de Shelby place, and us goin' work dere dis year."

"Dat's uh whole heap better'n Beasley's place, but 'tain't

39

nigh good ez heah. Wisht y'all would come work fuh Mist' Alf."

"Ned, he too hard-headed tuh do dat. Ah done tried and tried but his back don't bend. De only difference 'tween him and uh mule is, de mule got four good foots, and he ain't got nairn. De minute anybody mention crossin' dat creek, he's good tuh make disturbiment and tear up peace. He been over dat creek all his life jes' ez barefooted ez uh yard dawg and know he ain't even got uh rooster tuh crow fuh day, yet and still you can't git 'im 'way from dere."

"How come you don't quit 'im? Come on, and fetch de chillun wid you!"

"You can't know intuh dat yit, John. In times and seasons, us gwine talk dat, but Ah come tuh take you back wid me, John."

"Me, mama?" John asked in agonized surprise, "you know Ah don't want no parts of over dat Creek."

"Mama know, son, but Mist' Shelby asted where wuz you de fust thing and say he don't want us 'thout you."

"Mama, Ah don't wanta go 'way back over dere in dem woods. All you kin hear 'bout over dere is work, push-hard and pone-bread, ole cawn bread wid nothin' in it but salt and water! Ah laks it over here where dey talks about biscuit-bread some time."

"Yeah, John Buddy, mama know jes' how yuh feels and her heart is beatin' right wid yourn. Mama love flour bread too. But, you know, lots uh white folks ain't gwine be bothered wid Ned, and us got tuh find some place tuh lay our heads. Mist' Shelby ain't uh mean man, but he don't b'lieve us kin make de crop 'thout you. Reckon you better git yo' things and come 'long."

Amy got up wearily, the ruffles of her faded calico skirt sweeping the floor as she moved.

"Ahm goin' and see Marse Alf 'bout takin' yuh. Be ready 'ginst Ah git back, John Buddy."

John watched her out of the door, then slowly he went out himself and wandered about; but finally he was standing back

40

of Pheemy's cabin and gazing at the rude scratching on the adobe chimney. "Lucy," "Lucy Ann," "Lucy Potts," "Lucy and John," "Lucy is John's girl," "No 'nife can cut our love into," "Lucy Pearson."

"Oh," John sobbed, "she ain't gonna want no over-de-creek-nigger."

He stood there a long time before he went inside and began to collect his things. Then he came upon the song book that Lucy's terrifying brother had given him when he joined the choir. There was a crude drawing of a railroad train on it. No, he couldn't leave Notasulga where the train came puffing into the depot twice a day. No, no! He dropped everything and tore out across the fields and came out at last at the railroad cut just below the station. He sat down upon the embankment and waited. Soon in the distance he heard the whistle, "Wah-ooom! Wahup, wahup!" And around the bend came first the smoke stack, belching smoke and flames of fire. The drivers turning over chanting "Opelika-black-and-dirty! Opelika-black-and-dirty." Then as she pulled into the station, the powerful whisper of steam. Starting off again, "Wolf coming! Wolf coming! Wolf coming! Opelika-black-and-dirty, Opelika-black-and-dirty! Auh—wah-hoooon"—into the great away that gave John's feet such a yearning for distance.

The train had been gone a long time when Alf Pearson's buggy pulled up beside John.

"What are you doing down here, John, with Amy looking all over Macon County for you?"

"Jes' come down tuh hear whut de train say one mo' time, Mist' Alf."

"Get in and drive me down to get the mail, John. How's the hogs getting on?"

"Jes' fine, Mist' Alf. S'pectin' two mo' litters dis week. Dat make five litters since New Year's. Ain't lost one since Chris'-mas, neither."

"Splendid, John, splendid."

"Mist' Alf, Ah don't treasure 'cross dat creek. Lemme stay heah wid you, please suh."

41

"John, I'm not sending you over there. Your mother is taking you. If you're ever in need of a job, come on back here and behave yourself and I'll look after you. No matter where you are, don't steal and don't get too biggety and you'll get along. Touch the horses up a little. I'm in a hurry."

CHAPTER 4

✣

There was work a plenty on the Shelby place. John and Ned were plowing the rocky hillsides. As they turned the furrows John always strode several feet in advance of Ned. The older man limped behind his plow, stumbling now and then, slashing the mule and swearing incessantly.

"Gawd uhmighty! Git up heah, you hard-tailed bastard! Confound yuh, gee! John Buddy, whar you gwine?"

"Ahm goin' tuh git me uh sweat-rag tuh wipe mah face wid. Ahm tired uh sweat runnin' intuh mah eyes."

"You jes' tries tuh keep from workin', John. Out nearly all night proagin' over de Creek and now yuh don't wanta do nothin'."

"Ah done plowed uh acre and uh half tuh yo' one, and nowhere you put yo' foot down but whut 'tain't uh rock dere. Nobody can't make nothin' on dis place—look lak God jus' stood up and throwed uh handful uh rocks. If dis ain't work, 'tain' uh hound dawg in Georgy."

"Jes' you stay from over dat Creek, runnin' after all dem gals and git yo' night rest, dem rocks wouldn't be so worrysome."

"Ah do mo' of it than you right now. Dis ain't no slavery time," John flung back over his shoulder as he started towards the house.

43

"Yuh done got powerful biggity since yuh been on dat Pearson place," Ned muttered to himself, "Can't say uh word, 'thout he got tuh gimme two fuh one."

Amy stood trembling between her son and her husband. The other children were growing up and imitating everything that John did, as closely as possible. Zack and Zeke were already trying on John's hats and ties. Their whole talk was "over de Creek," and "man when us git on dat ole train." Amy had managed to keep things on an even keel by soothing John's feelings and reminding Ned that if John went over to Notasulga to choir practice and meeting, that he was now seventeen and ought to have a little freedom. So it had gone, and now the cotton was knee-high. The crops more than half made. She breathed a little easier. She was at the house putting on a pot of collard greens when John came in for the sweat-rag.

"Mama, better tell Ned tuh leave me be. Tell 'im tuh stop his bulldozia. Ah done heered 'im lyin' tuh Mist' Shelby makin' out Ah don't do nothin'—hard ez Ah works."

"He be's drunk when he keer on lak dat and his likker tell 'im tuh talk. Don't pay 'im no mind."

"But, mama, ev'ry time Ah go cross de Creek he look lak he go crazy and git tuh blasphemin' 'bout no 'count gals. Ah don't keer if he do be peepin' through his likkers he got tuh quit dat. Sho ez gun's iron, he got tuh quit dat. He don't know nothin' 'bout—'bout no gal Ah keeps comp'ny wid."

"Heah de rag yuh wanted, John. Go 'long back tuh work and Ah'll give Ned uh straightenin'. Dat is if he kin stand uh straightenin'."

Ned was sullen when John returned but he said nothing. He took part of his humor out on the mule and held the other inside him. He said to himself as he stumbled along behind his plow, "Damn biggity rascal! Wisht Ah had 'im tied down so he couldn't move! I'd put uh hund'ed lashes on his bare back. He know he got de advantage uh me. He don't even know his pappy and he ought tuh be proud Ah took and married his ma and made somethin' out of 'im. He ought to be humble,

44

but he ain't, and plenty folks right now on account uh his yaller skin will put 'im above me. Wisht Ah knowed somethin' that would crumple his feathers! But he sho' is makin' dis crop, though. Ah oughter clear more'n uh hund'ed dollars. Effen Ah do, Ahm gwine buy me uh hawse and buggy, and ain't gwine 'low nobody tuh hitch it up but me."

That evening the things unsaid laid a steamy blanket over talk. John made the long journey over the creek and Ned fumed.

"Whyn't you tell John whut yuh got tuh say, Ned?" Amy slapped back, "You *been* tellin' 'im."

" 'Cause Ah don't want tuh hafta kill 'im, dat's how come. He must smell hisself—done got so mannish. Some fast 'omanish gal is grinnin' in his face and he tries tuh git sides hisself."

Amy smoked her pipe and went on to bed. The children too. Zeke and Zack were in the woods trying out a new coon dog and came in after moon-up. John came home later.

When Amy brought dinner to the field next day John took his bucket and went off alone to eat. With a huge hickory tree between him and the others, he pulled out the three cornered note and read again and again.

Sweet Notasulga, Chocklit Alabama Date of kisses, month of love Dere John, you is my honey. I won't never love nobody else but you. I love choir practise now. Sugar is sweet, and lard is greasy, you love me, don't be uneasy.

Your darling,
LUCY ANN POTTS

Ned called several times before John heard him.

"John Buddy! You John! Come heah and take holt uh dese plow lines."

"Yes suh," John said at last.

"Don't set dere and answer me. When Ah speak, you move!"

"Ah, Ahm comin', but Ah ain't goin' tuh run fuh nobody."

"Looka heah, John, Ahm sick uh yo' sass. Ah got it in me tuh tell yuh and if Ah don't tell yuh, Ah'll purge when Ah die. Youse uh good fuh nothin' trashy yaller rascal—ain't fit tuh tote guts tuh uh bear." A sudden frenzy took Ned, "Anyhow, Ah done made up mah mind tuh beat you nelly tuh death. You jes' spilin' fuh uh good killin'! Drop dem britches below yo' hocks, and git down on yo' knees. Ah means tuh straighten you out dis day."

As he said this, Ned snatched off the trace-chain from the plow and turned upon John who was still twenty feet or more from his step-father. When Ned whirled about with the doubled trace-chain in his right fist he found not a cowering bulk of a boy but a defiant man, feet spread wide, a large rock drawn back to hurl.

"Don't you vary! Dog damn yuh!" John challenged. "Come uhnother step and Ah'll bust yuh wide open, wid dis rock. You kin cuff and kick Zeke and them around but Ah done promised Gawd and uh couple uh other men tuh stomp yo' guts out nex' time you raise yo' hand tuh me."

For a throbbing space the two stood face to face. Ned turned and hobbled off.

"Stand dere! Jes' you stand dere till Ah go git mah double-barrel britch-loader and Ahm gointer blow yo' brains out!"

Ned limped off towards the house. John held his pose until the older man dipped below the first rise. Then he let fall his arm, and walked back towards the hickory tree.

"Ahm gointer git behind dis tree and if dat ugly-rump nigger come back here wid dat gun, Ahm gointer bust 'im wide open wid uh rock 'fore he know whut hit 'im. Humph! Ah don't b'lieve he gone at no britch-loader nohow. He gone 'cause he got skeered Ah wuz goin' take dat trace-chain 'way from 'im and lay it 'cross his own back."

John waited a long time. Ned could have gone twice the distance and returned with a gun. If he could have looked over the hill he would have seen Ned "proaging" off to the Turk place to get a gallon of red-eye-for-courage. Finally John came out from behind the hickory tree and loosed the mules from

46

the plows and looped up the plow lines on the hames.

"Shucks! Ahm goin' 'way from heah." It came to John like a revelation. Distance was escape. He stopped before the burnt-off trunk of a tree that stood eight or ten feet high and threw the character of Ned Crittenden upon it.

"And you, you ole battle-hammed, slew-foot, box-ankled nubbin, you! You ain't nothin' and ain't got nothin' but whut God give uh billy-goat, and then round tryin' tuh hell-hack folks! Tryin' tuh kill somebody wid talk, but if you wants tuh fight,—dat's de very corn Ah wants tuh grind. You come grab me now and Ah bet yuh Ah'll stop *you* from suckin' eggs. Hit me now! G'wan hit me! Bet Ah'll break uh egg in yuh! Youse all parts of uh pig! You done got me jus' ez hot ez July jam, and Ah ain't got no mo' use fuh yuh than Ah is for mah baby shirt. Youse mah race but you sho ain't mah taste. Jus' you break uh breath wid me, and Ahm goin' tuh be jus' too chastisin'.

"Ahm jus' lak uh old shoe—soft when yuh rain on me and cool me off, and hard when yuh shine on me and git me hot. Tuh keep from killin' uh sorry somethin' like yuh, Ahm goin' way from heah. Ahm goin' tuh Zar, and dat's on de other side of far, and when you see me agin Ahm gointer be somebody. Mah li'l' finger will be bigger than yo' waist. Don't you part yo' lips tuh me no mo' jes' ez long ez heben is happy—do Ah'll put somethin' on yuh dat lye soap won't take off. You ain't nothin' but uh big ole pan of fell bread. Now dat's de word wid de bark on it."

John stepped back a few paces, balanced his rock, hurled it against the stump with all his might and started across the field to the creek.

The involuntary beauty of sunset found him once again upon the plantation of his birth exulting among the herd, and finding Pheemy's cabin good to be in.

CHAPTER 5

❖

H ello, John."

"Hello, Bully."

"Whut you doin' back over here?"

"Come tuh git me uh job uh work again. Whuss de news?"

"Oh de white folks is still in de lead. Seen Mist' Alf yit?"

"Naw, goin' up tuh de big house now."

"Soon's yuh git back tuh de quarters Ah got uh bug tuh put in yo' ear."

"Awright, be back tuhreckly."

There were more used suits in Alf Pearson's clothes closet and John received them.

"My son, Mister Alfred's, clothes don't fit you now as well as they did last year, John. Too tight. Reckon I'll have to give you mine from now on. By the way, John, I've lost two hogs since you've been gone. Get back on your same job. Can you read and write fairly well now, John?"

"Yes suh."

"That's fine. I want you to take this note book and keep up with the groceries and fertilizer and feed that the folks in the quarters draw. It's hard for me to do it with running the bank and watching slick politicians. I had thought my son would have been home by now to help me, but it seems to take quite a long time to finish studying in Paris."

"Yes suh."

"You just take everybody's name on a separate page and put down everything they get the moment you hand it to 'em."

"Yes suh."

"And John, if you've been fooling around Duke's wife, leave her alone. He's been up here to me about it. Don't start no fight about it. There's plenty single girls around here."

"Ah ain't studyin' 'bout his Exie, Mist' Alf. He better talk tuh *her.* She de one come pullin' on me."

Alf Pearson laughed heartily and gave John a playful shove.

"Get along you rascal you! You're a walking orgasm. A living exultation."

"Whut's dat, Mist' Alf?"

"Oh never mind about that. Keep up with the pigs."

That night M'haley and Big 'Oman and Bootsie got up a game of "Hide and Seek" but John counted and let the other boys hide. The game ended fairly early. John had been around behind the house to look at his writing and the chimney and found it all defaced, so he didn't want to play. When the game was over he called Bully aside.

"Bully, Ah wrote some writin' on de back uh An' Pheemy's chimbley."

"Yeah, Ah know you did. Fack is, ev'rybody know yuh did, and dat's de very crow Ah wants tuh pick wid yuh."

"Is you heard who took and scratched it, and put smut out de chimbley all over it and mommucked it all up?"

"You ain't mad, is yuh?"

"Yeah, Ahm mad. Ahm jes' ez hot ez Tucker when de mule kicked his mammy, and any man dat tell me tuh mah face dat he done it he got tuh smell mah fist. You know who done it, Bully?"

"Don't yuh say Ah tole yuh and when you go tuh git atter her, don't you call my name, but M'haley took and done dat when she heered you wuz singin' in de choir. Some of 'em say you jes' done it so you could git a chance tuh see Lucy Potts."

"Whut M'haley got tuh do wid dat? Ah feel lak Ah could take and lam her wid lightnin'."

"Why doncher do it, John? If 'twas me felt bad lak you do, Ah'd beat her jes' ez long ez she last. Anyhow she takin' de under currents on you."

"Naw, Ah don't choose beatin' lady people. Uh man is crazy tuh do dat—when he know he got tuh submit hisself tuh 'em. Ahm gittin' sleepy. B'lieve Ah'll turn in."

Bully went away whistling, and John made to go inside to bed.

"John!" in a soft whisper from around the corner of the house. "Come heah, John."

John stepped to the corner, "Who dat callin' me?"

"Aw, you come see," the voice retreated into the shoulder-high cotton. John followed.

"Whut you want wid me, M'haley?"

"Look lak you ain't glad youse back."

"Yes Ah is, M'haley, but 'tain't lak de fust night Ah come. Ah reckon all de new done wore off de plantation."

" 'Tain't de plantation. Dat's jes' de same. Ah reckon you jes' ain't got time tuh strain wid us quarters niggers now. You sings on de choir at Macedony."

"Whut's singin' notes got tuh do wid it? It jus' 'tain't new no mo'."

"Naw, you jes' stuck on dat li'l' ole Lucy Ann, and she ain't nothin' but uh baby. She ain't but leben years ole."

"She twelve now, goin' on thirteen. She had her birth night de day befo' mines. Her'n on December 31, and mine's January 1. Ain't dat funny?"

"Ahm fifteen, so goody, goody, goody."

John said nothing. After a while M'haley said, "John, Ah thought once me and you wuz gointer make uh wed." He stood stolid and silent.

In the silence she threw her arms about John's passive neck and swung herself off the ground, then lay still against him.

"John."

"Hunh."

"Feel mah heart. Put yo' hand right heah. Ain't it beatin' hard? Dat's 'cause Ahm so glad youse back. Feel it again. My

51

heart is rearin' and pitchin' fur you lak uh mule in uh tin stable. John, Ah loves you, Ah swear Ah does. You so pretty and you ain't color-struck lak uh whole heap uh bright-skin people. John?"

"Hunh."

"John, hug me till mah dress fit tight."

The next day John whitewashed Pheemy's chimney, and wrote Lucy's name in huge letters across it, and on Sunday he was at church far ahead of anybody else, with a three-cornered note in his hymn-book.

"Hope ole big-mouf M'haley don't come pukin' her guts 'round heah," he thought aloud. This was another day and another place. Pearson's quarters and M'haley had no business here. His eye wandered out of the window and down the dusty road. A bunch of girls approached in starchy elegance. "Lawd, dat look lak M'haley now—comin' heah tuh bull-doze and dominize."

John fell to his knees and prayed for cleansing. He prayed aloud and the empty house threw back his resonant tones like a guitar box.

"Dat sho sound good," John exulted. "If mah voice sound *dat* good de first time Ah ever prayed in de church house, it sho won't be de las'." He arose from his knees and before the drove of girls had reached the steps John had forgotten all about his sins and fears, but he retreated to the choir-stand out of M'haley's reach.

As soon as Lucy took her seat before him he leaned forward and thrust his hymn-book into her hand. She coyly dropped hers, and he picked it up and pretended to search for a song. Lucy slyly did the same and read:

Dere Lucy:
>Whin you pass a mule tied to a tree,
>Ring his tail and think of me.

Your sugger-lump,
JOHN

John read:

> Long as the vine grow 'round the stump
> You are my dolling sugar lump.
> Mama whipped me last night, because Bud told her we
> was talking to each other.

Your sweet heart,
LUCY ANN

John was so sweetly distracted by this note that he was blind and deaf to his surroundings. Bud Potts had rapped loudly and importantly and had gestured with his hands as if he were pushing a wash-basket of clothes up on a high shelf for the choir to rise. Everyone was standing but John. He never noticed this until Oral Johnson nudged him.

"Get yo' pitch!" Bud ordered as if he were giving the order to fire on Fort Sumter.

"Basses—duh-h-h-h. Y'all got it? Altos—fah-h-h—Trebles—me-e-e-e—. Pay 'tension dere, Lucy!"

Satisfied in the matter of the pitch, Bud took a full breath and broke out thru his nose—"Duh, duh, duh, duh! Dole la fee so lah so fee." The altos were right behind the basses and fighting in haughty jerks for sound supremacy—"fah! fah! me! sol! fah-so-la-so-lah-so-fah!" The trebles pitched out in full, Ory behind the pack and keened furiously to make up for lost time, "—me, me, ray, do! Me-fah-lah-so-lah-so-fah! Oh me, me, me,—"

It was a hard race and hotly contended at the top of the lungs all the way. The trebles won because while altos, basses and even other trebles forgot their notes in confusion and fell by the wayside, Lucy never missed a note. Bud growled away in the bass but Lucy treed him and held him growling in discomfiture out upon a limb until the end of the piece cut him down.

John beat the bass notes by a vigorous side-to-side motion of his head and everybody in the audience thought they heard him singing them.

53

The preacher arose.

"Ah takes mah tex' and Ah takes mah time." He pursed up his wrinkled black face and glared all over the church. No one accepting the challenge he went on—"Ah takes mah tex' 'tween de lids uh de Bible," and slammed it shut. Another challenging glare about the room. Same results. "Don't you take and meddle wid *whar* Ah takes mah tex'. Long ez Ah gives yuh de word uh Gawd, 'tain't none uh yo' business whar Ah gits it from."

For two hours his voice beat about the ears of the people and the "Amen's" rocked and rolled back to the pulpit.

John heard little of it. He studied the back of Lucy's head and shoulders and the way the white rice buttons ran down her back and found plenty to entertain him the whole while.

When the cotton had been picked and ginned, Alf had John to pick out the hogs for the barbecue. The same elaborate preparations as usual. Same high laughter, but John sat passively in a doorway with Zeke who was getting tall and emitting ram odors.

"Less we dance, John Buddy. Ah wants tuh swing one dem gals."

John laughed scornfully, "Whut you know 'bout swingin' gals? You don't eben know how tuh dance."

"Dat's much ez *you* know. Ah done been tuh four, five frolics 'cross de Creek since you been gone."

Phrony came dashing up, hair wrapped with blue rag strings and reeking of lemon extract used as a perfume.

"John how come you ain't dancin'?"

"Ah got uh bone in mah leg," John bantered.

"Aw come on, John."

"Go head on, Phrony. You got plenty boys 'sides me. Ah tell yuh Ah got uh bone in mah leg."

"Sho 'nuff, John? When did you git it in dere? You wuz walkin' all righ' jes' fo' dark."

"He jes' funnin' wid yuh," Zeke cut in, " 'Course he got uh bone in his leg. How he goin' tuh walk if he ain't? Come on and lemme switch yo' coat."

Zeke grabbed Phrony by the point of her elbow and they plunged into the cauldron of sound.

John sat on, thinking of the words on the chimney back, but soon Exie found him.

"John, how come you ain't in de play party? M'haley dancin' wid Bully."

"She's uh much-right gal. Much right for Bully ez it is for me."

Exie laughed happily, "Big 'Oman huntin' you too and plenty mo'."

"Whut for?"

"Dey say de dance don't go so good 'thout you. Dey say de boys neither de gals don't do 'round when you ain't dere lak dey do when yo' is."

"Dey done 'thout me 'fo' dey seen me. Ah jes' don't feel lak no dancin' and whoopin' and hollerin' t'night."

"Me neither. Less we all jes' set and talk, John."

"Naw, Gawd! Ah don't want Duke pickin' no fight wid me over you. You his'n."

"Us ain't got no courthouse papers. Dat's commissary license us got. Ah kin quit anytime, and then agin effen Ah had courthouse license Ah got divorce in mah heels." She picked up John's hand and pulled it into her lap. Just then M'haley walked up to them.

"Oh 'scuse me," she turned away scornfully, "Ah didn't reckon you wuz so busy, John," she whirled and ran back to the dance.

"You better g'wan back tuh de play party, Exie. M'haley's goin' tuh tell Duke on you."

"Let her tell 'im, tell 'im, turn 'im up and smell 'im."

John rose. "Ah got tuh step off a li'l' piece. Ah'll be right back." He walked off and Exie started on back to the fire. Half way she met Duke, and John could hear the struggle of battle. He turned about and hurried to them.

"Whut you beatin' Exie 'bout? She ain't done nothin'."

"If she wan't doin' nothin', whut y'all doin' up heah in de

dark?" He struck her violently in the face again. John stepped between them.

"Don't lam dis 'oman no mo', Duke. She ain't did a thing wrong. You wanta beat on somebody, hop me. Mah shoulders is broad."

Besides the ones who had heard M'haley say out loud that John and Exie were up the hill in the dark too busy to dance, there were others who had heard what Duke said when he left the fire-lit circle. So the crowd had surrounded the three. Exie, bruised but exultant, John and Duke standing face to face.

"Fight, fight, you no kin. Kill on 'nother 'twon't be no sin," Nunkie shouted.

Old Pheemy stepped between and scattered the crowd.

"Neb mind," Duke threatened as he was led away, "Ah ain't through wid you, John Pearson. Ahm goin' git yuh! Ahm goin' tuh git yuh if Ah have tuh steal yuh! Youse bigger'n me, but mah Barlow knife'll even us up."

The dance went on. John danced a little with Big 'Oman and Bootsie but he wasn't flamboyant.

In the bed with Zeke later he said, "Zeke, Ahm goin' 'way from here."

"You ain't skeered uh Duke, is yuh?"

"Naw, Duke cuts and shoots too, but all de shootin' he do is shoot fuh home if somebody git behind 'im, and cut fuh de nearest way. He don't fight no men-folks. He's uh woman-jessie. Beat up women and run from mens. Ah ain't got him tuh study 'bout, but Ah feel lak Ah weighs uh thousand pounds and it's mah heart make me feel that away."

"How come?"

"Y'know dat li'l' gal dat trebles in de choir at Macedony— de one whut don't wrop her hair, de onliest one up dere dat don't wrop her hair no time wid all dat cord-string lake de rest? Well, Ah loves her, and she say she love me too, and Ah betcha old moufy M'haley uh some uh dese other niggers goin' make out Ahm goin' wid Exie, and dat's whut me and Duke lak tuh fought over, and then agin Mist' Alf done tole me not tuh fool wid Exie and Duke goin' up tuh de big house and tell uh lie on me."

"If yuh go off somewhere, John Buddy, lemme go wid yuh, heah, Please?"

"You too little. Ain't but fourteen, and if Ah go 'way from heah atall, Ahm goin' tuh de tie-camp and cut cross ties. Man asted me tuh go yistiddy in Notasulga. Yuh makes good money too."

"John Buddy, please. Heah?"

"Naw, you stay 'round heah and watch out for Lucy. Git word tuh me iffen any ole mullet-head tries tuh cut me out. Ahm gointer write tuh you and you way-lay her and git her tuh read it fuh yuh."

"Aw, Ah kin read too. Ah kin read some."

"Whut kin you read?"

"In de fust reader it say, 'This is Ned. He has a dog,' Ah kin read dat lak anything. Dat's uh heap, ain't it?"

"Dat'll do, but Ah ain't goin tuh write 'bout no Ned in de fust reader, and neither no dawg. You do lak Ah tell yuh, and if she say she don't pay dese niggers' talk no mind, you git de word tuh me quick ez yuh kin, heah, Zeke?"

"Unhunh."

"Yuh see, she got de advantage uh me 'cause she knows Ah love her, but Ah don't know whether she love me or not. Lots uh folks makes 'miration at her. You stay 'round heah and back mah fallin', and then nex' time Ah'll take you 'long."

"Aw right, John Buddy."

The next morning John was gone—walked to Opelika and on to the tie-woods on the Alabama River.

CHAPTER 6

✦

It was dusk-dark when John walked into the tie-camp. At some distance away he could see a group of men bunched on the ground beside a small fire. Gaming. They were so intent that John was right on them before they knew. When somebody saw him, there was a breathy cry, "De buckra!" Somebody grabbed up the dice and everyone made to run. John laughed and stepped up among them.

"Ha, ha! Y'all thought Ah wuz white, didn't yuh?"

Everyone laughed except Coon Tyler. He was every bit as large as John and several years older. He looked up at John out of red, angry eyes and growled, "You oughter quit goin' 'round skeering folks. You better hail fo' you tuh walk up on *me* agin."

John kept on laughing. "Lawd, y'all sho wuz snatchin' and grabbin'. Ah ought not tuh uh said nothin' and some uh y'all would uh been to Selma in five minutes."

Coon would not be amused, "You scoundrel-beast, you git from over de game!"

John stepped back a little, not in fear but in surprise.

"You ain't mad, is yuh?" he asked.

One of the men said, "Don't pay Coon no mind, he jes' funnin' wid yuh."

Seeing the passive attitude in John, Coon blazed, "Funnin'?

59

Y'all know Ah don't joke and Ah don't stand no jokin'. 'Tain't nothin' in de drug store'll kill yuh quick ez me."

"Mah name is Ezeriah Hill, but de lady people calls me Uncle Dump," the oldest man in the group said to John, "Whuss yo' name, boy?"

"John. Where de boss at?"

"He gone intuh town. Be back tuhreckly. He goin' hiah yuh 'cause us needs help. Come on lemme show yuh uh place tuh sleep."

John followed him into the bunk house. "Heah whar you sleep at. Eve'ybody scorch up dey own grub. Be ready tuh hit de grit by daylight."

"Yes suh."

"Chaw tuhbacker uh smoke?"

"Naw suh."

"Wall you gwine learn 'cause you can't keep dis camp grub on yo' stomach lessen yuh do. Got tuh learn how tuh cuss too. Ah kin see you ain't nothin' but uh lad of uh boy. Mens on dese camps is full uh bulldocia 'til dey smell uh good size fist. Den dey dwindles down tuh nelly nothin'."

All next day John wielded a broad axe, a maul and pestle with the rest. He found that he liked the rhythmic swing, the chant "Cuttin' timber!" with the up stroke of the axe. Then the swift, sure descent, "Hanh!" Up again, "Cuttin' ties! Hanh." All day long, "Cuttin' timber! Hanh! Cuttin' ties, hanh!"

A boy called Do-dirty because of his supposed popularity with and his double-crossing of women, took John to town with him Saturday night. John was eager to go so he could buy writing paper and a pencil. He got it and then Do-dirty proudly showed him the town, and the town's women. It was late Sunday evening when they returned to camp and from one thing to another it was two weeks before John wrote to Ezekiel.

And when a month passed and he got no answer he began to feel that there would never be a word from Lucy. He went to town often. On the nights that he stayed in camp he was the center of camp life. He could chin the bar more times than anyone there. He soon was the best shot, the fastest runner and in wrestling no man could put his shoulders to the ground. The boss began to invite his friends out to watch the fun. John won his first match by pinning Nelse Watson from another camp to the ground, but his greatest stunt was picking up an axe by the very tip end of the helve and keeping the head on a level with his shoulders in his out-stretched arm. Coon could muscle out one axe, but John could balance two. He could stand like a cross, immobile for several seconds with an axe muscled out in each hand. Next to showing muscle-power, John loved to tell stories. Sometimes the men sat about the fire and talked and John loved that. One night Do-dirty began, "Y'all wanta heah some lies?"

"Yeah," said Too-Sweet, "Ah evermore loves lies but you can't tell none. Leave John tell 'em 'cause he kin act 'em out. He take de part uh Brer Rabbit and Brer B'ar and Brer Fox jes' ez natche'l."

"Aw, 'tain't nothin' tuh 'im," Coon grumbled, "y'all make me sick."

Saturday afternoon Do-dirty looked off towards the West and cried, "Looka yonder! Who dat comin' runnin'?"

Everybody looked but John. He was inside getting ready to go to town.

"Do John Buddy work at dis heah camp?" he heard and recognized Zeke's voice.

"Come inside, Zeke!" he called out quickly.

Zeke came in and sat down on the bunk beside John. No words. Happiness radiated from one to the other.

"You seen Lucy?"

"Yeah, two times."

"Whut she say?"

Zeke tugged at a letter inside his clothes.

"She writ dis tuh yuh and tole me tuh mail it, but Ah run off and bring it tuh yuh. Yuh see Ah ain't got yo' letter till day befo' yestiddy. 'Cause pappy wouldn't leave me go tuh town

61

tuh de Post Office. John Buddy, you goin' tuh leave me stay wid yuh? Hunh?"

John spelled slowly thru his letter and smiled, "Yeah, you kin stay whut li'l' time Ahm goin' tuh be heah. Two mo' pay days and Ahm gone. Got tuh take uh birthday gif' tuh Lucy. Wisht Ah could give her Georgy under fence."

"John Buddy, Ahm hongry. Feel lak Ah ain't dirtied uh plate dis week."

"Wait uh minute. Ah'll stir yuh up uh Ash-cake and you kin sop it in some syrup. Maybe Ah ain't goin' tuh town nohow now."

John went outside and fixed the fire and put the bread in the hot ashes and covered it up.

"Reckon Ah better git uh bucket uh water, Zeke. You watch de bread. It's uh good li'l' piece tuh de spring."

Zeke watched the bread and took it out of the ashes when it was thoroughly brown. John had not returned. Most of the men lounged about outside. Finally Coon said to Zeke, "You better run down de hill dere and see whut's de matter wid yo' big buddy. Pant'er got 'im, maybe."

All alarm, Ezekiel leaped up and flew down the path he had seen John take. In a few minutes he saw John coming.

"Where you goin', Zeke?"

"Huntin' yuh. Skeered uh brute-beast had done kotched yuh."

When they got back to the bunk house, John gave Zeke his tin plate and set the gallon jug of syrup before him.

"He'p yo'self, Zeke, and grow hair on yo' chest."

Zeke poured a plate full of syrup and looked for the Ash-cake. "Whar at de bread is?" he asked John.

"You seen it since me," John answered. He looked about and seeing the suppressed laughter on the men's faces he asked, "Where de bread Ah took and cooked fuh mah li'l' bubber?"

General laughter. John got angry. "Ah say, who took and done 'way wid mah bread? Whoever done it mus' be skeered tuh own it."

Coon first, laughing instantly, "Ah et yo' damn bread. Don't you lak it, don't yuh take it, heah mah collar, come and shake it."

"Yeah and Ahm gointer shake it too dis day and year of our Lawd, and if Ah don't, Gawd knows, Ahm gointer give it uh common trial. My gal don't 'speck me tuh run."

They flew at each other and the others scrambled out of the way. Coon was too wise to clinch. He stayed his distance and slugged, but his wariness wore him out. Trying to hit and duck at the same time, he struck out ten or twelve times and landed one high on the enemy's head. John ran in and landed one smack in his enemy's mouth, and while Coon was spitting out his teeth, he ripped a mule-kicking right to the pit of Coon's stomach and the fight was over and done.

John felt good. His first real fight. Something burned inside him. He tasted blood in his mouth, but there was none actually. He wished somebody else would hit him. He wanted to feel himself taking and giving blows.

"You be keerful how you hit folks, Jawn," Uncle Dump cautioned, "you don't know yo' own strength. Dat man (indicating Coon) is hurt bad."

"He been pickin' on me ever since Ah been heah, and Ah been takin' and takin' 'til mah guts is full."

An hour before Lucy's letter had arrived Coon might have eaten John's Ash-cake and offered other insults safely. Now John was different. There was something about Lucy that stuck another and stiffer bone down his back.

He walked over and looked upon the fallen Coon. His surly black face was relaxed in a vacuous manner—blowing bloody foam out thru his swollen lips at every breath.

"Nex' time he fool wid me, Ah bet Ah'll try mah bes' tuh salivate 'im. He try tuh be uh tush hawg—puttin' out his brags everywhere."

He cooked Zeke more bread and soon the camp had settled down to normal. Somebody put Coon in his bunk, and he never spoke a word until after John had taken Zeke to town.

"Know whut," he lisped to the others, "dat boy slipped up

63

on me, but Ahm gwine git even wid him. 'Tain't too late. Seben years ain't too long fuh uh coudar tuh wear uh ruffled bosom shirt. Ahm gwine gently chain-gang fuh dat same nigger."

"Aw," Dump disparaged, "you got uh belly full uh John. You ain't wantin' no mo' uh him."

"Yeah Ah wants tuh fight 'im, but not wid no fist. Ah flies hot quick but Ahm very easy cooled when de man Ahm mad wid is bigger'n me."

CHAPTER 7

❖

J ohn and Zeke got back to Notasulga in time for the
Christmas tree at Macedony, and John put a huge China
doll on the tree for Lucy. She didn't know he had re-
turned until he walked in during the singing and sat across the
aisle from her.

At home, Emmeline Potts pounced upon the large package.
"Dis is uh stray bundle dat didn't come from de Sunday
School and it didn't come from dis house." She opened it.
"Lucy Ann, read dis piece uh paper and tell me who give you
dis great big play-pritty."

Lucy faltered. She turned the paper around two or three
times.

"John Pearson."

"Dat big yaller boy from cross de Creek?"

"Yes ma'am."

"Whut he doin' givin' *you* uh present?"

"Ah don't know'm."

"Yes you do, madam. Dere's uh bug under dat chip. Mind
yuh now, mah young lady; Ah ketch you foolin' wid boys,
'specially uh yaller bastard, Ahm uh goin' tuh put hick'ries tuh
yo' back tuh set, Miss Potts. Ah done tole Artie Mimms he kin
have yuh when yuh git sixteen."

CHAPTER 8

✦

Alf Pearson welcomed John back with a bluff cursing out.

"I told you to leave Duke's woman alone. I didn't tell you to leave the place. Don't gimme excuses nor back talk. G'wan to work. I'll be glad when some good girl grabs you and makes something out of you. Stop running away. Face things out."

That Sunday Mehaley got two of her friends to go to Macedony with her, though they all belonged to Shiloh.

"Less go slur dat li'l' narrer-contracted Potts gal," she urged. "Somebody say John put uh great big doll-baby on de tree fuh her and den agin he bought her gold hoop ear-rings fuh her birthday. Course Ah don't believe he done no sich uh hot-do, but she fool wid me tuhday Ah means tuh beat her 'til she rope lak okra, and den agin Ah'll stomp her 'til she slack lak lime."

They crowded near Lucy after preaching, but old Emmeline was ever at Lucy's elbow. John had written Lucy to meet him at the spring, but Lucy was not permitted the liberty.

"Naw, you ain't goin' lolly-gaggin' down tuh no spring wid all dese loose gals. You goin' git in dis road 'head uh me and g'wan home."

Emmeline was most emphatic, but while she said her good

67

byes to her friends, John came up and tipped his hat.

"How yuh do, Mis' Potts."

"Howdy John," she glared like noon.

"Mis' Potts, kin Ah scorch Mis' Lucy home?"

"Lucy ain't takin' no comp'ny yit. She ain't but fourteen and Ah don't turn mah gals loose tuh take comp'ny 'til dey sixteen, and when Ah does Ah picks de comp'ny mahself. Ah ain't raisin' no gals tuh throw 'way on trash."

Richard Potts spoke up. "Whut make you got tuh plow so deep, Emmeline? Ack lak 'tain't nobody got feelings but you. All right, son, Ah reckon it won't hurt nothin' if yuh walk 'long wid Lucy jes' ahead uh us. But she too young tuh court."

The world turned to red and gold for Lucy. She had read the jealousy and malice in Mehaley's face, and John had asked for her company right in front of Mehaley and her crowd! He had faced her hard-to-face mama! She stretched up another inch. There was little to say on the way home, but she had made those big girls stand back. There was one moment when they reached the bend in the road a moment before Richard and Emmeline and John had squeezed her arm. The whole world took on life. Lucy gave no sign that she noticed the touch but in one flash she discovered for herself old truths.

John noted the prosperous look of the Potts place. It was different from every other Negro's place that he had ever seen. Flowers in the yard among whitewashed rocks. Tobacco hanging up to dry. Peanuts drying on white cloth in the sun. A smoke-house, a spring-house, a swing under a china-berry tree, bucket flowers on the porch.

"Stay and have dinner wid us," Richard Potts invited.

John stayed but ate little, and in his presence Lucy cut peas in two and split grains of rice, for which she was coarsely teased by her brothers until John left her, shamefaced.

Another look from his gray eyes that Lucy knew was her look and nobody else's, and John loped on off to Pearson's.

The next morning Lucy found a hair upon her body and exulted.

"Ahm uh woman now."

The following Saturday when she stripped to bathe in the wooden wash tub, she noted that tiny horizontal ridges had lifted her bust a step away from childhood.

She wrote John a long letter and granted him her special company.

CHAPTER 9

❖

You Lucy!" Emmeline scolded as she struggled along
behind John and Lucy on the way from church, "Ain't
Ah done tole yuh and tole yuh not tuh let no boys be
puttin' dey hand all over yuh? You John! You stay arm-length
from dat gal and talk it out. You got uh tongue."

Lucy and John sniggered together slyly and walked an inch
or two farther apart.

"Good Gawd, dey could drive uh double team between us
now," John complained.

"Talk loud, Ah don't 'low no whisperin' tuh no gal uh
mine."

They talked about the preaching and the new hymn-books
and the proposed church organ. Some were for the innovation
but the majority of the congregation thought that kind of
music in a church would be sinful to the extreme. Emmeline
stayed close enough to hear every word.

At home Lucy's married sister, Dink, sympathetically invei-
gled Emmeline into the kitchen where she was dishing up
dinner. Lucy and John sat in the parlor with the crayon en-
largements on easels and the gilded moustache-cups and sau-
cers on wire props and the religious mottoes on the wall.

John cleared his throat to speak, but Emmeline popped in
at that moment and took her seat beside the center table. John

71

was on one side of the room behind her and Lucy was on the other side facing her.

"Ah been keepin' comp'ny wid you uh long time, ain't Ah, Lucy?"

"Yeah, mighty nigh uh year now."

"And you ain't never had manners 'nough tuh ast *me* fuh her comp'ny reg'lar," Emmeline snapped.

Conversation died. On the lower shelf of the center table John spied Lucy's double slate with the slate-pencil suspended from it by a string.

"Dis de same slate you use in school, ain't it, Lucy?"

"Unhunh."

John opened the slate and wrote a few words in it as softly as possible. Emmeline seemed neither to see nor hear the scratching of the pencil, but when John leaned forward and tried to hand the slate past Emmeline to Lucy, Emmeline's hand flew out like a cat's paw and grabbed the slate. She looked on both sides and saw no writing, then she opened it and looked hard at the message, "I got something to tell you. Less go for a walk." Emmeline couldn't read a word and she was afraid that no one would read it correctly for her, but one thing she was sure of, she could erase as well as the world's greatest professor. She spoiled out the words with a corner of her apron, and put the slate back under the table. Not a word was passed.

"Mama!" from the kitchen.

"Whut you want, Dink?"

"Come turn dis sweet bread out on uh plate. Ahm skeered Ah'll make it fall uh tear it, tryin' tuh git it out de pan."

Emmeline went grumbling to the rear.

"Less set on de piazza," John suggested, "Maybe us kin git uh word in edgeways 'fo' she git back."

"Aw right."

They went out on the porch and sat slyly side by side—Lucy in the old red rocker, and John on a cow-hided straight chair.

"Lucy, Ah loves yuh."

Emmeline burst out of the parlor.

"Lucy! Whut you doin' settin' on top uh dat boy?"

"Ah ain't settin' on top of 'im. Uh milk cow could git between us."

"Don't you back talk *me.* When Ah speak you *move.* You hear me Lucy?"

"Yessum."

"How come you ain't movin'? Mah orders is five feet apart. Dink know befo' she married Ah never 'lowed her tuh set closer dan five feet and you know it and when Ah don't 'low tuh one, Ah ain't gwine 'low tuh de other. Heifer! Move dat chear 'way from dat boy!"

Silence.

"Lucy!"

"Yessum."

"Is you deef?"

"No'm."

Richard came in from the barn at that moment and called his wife.

"Aw, Emmeline, don't plow so deep. You puts de shamery on folks. Come on inside and hep Dink fix de dinner. Ahm hongry."

"Naw, Ah see she done got hard-headed, and Ahm gwine pray fuh her. Hard-headed chillun never come tuh no good end. Mind whut Ah say! Ahm gwine tell God about *you,* madam."

She pulled back the curtain in the parlor so that she could see every move on the porch and prayed.

"O Lawd and our Gawd, You know Ah tries tuh raise mah chillun right and lead 'em in de way dat dey should go, and Lawd You know it 'tain't right fuh boys and gals tuh be settin' on top one 'nother; and Lawd You know You said You'd strike disobedient chillun dead in dey tracks, and Lawd make mine humble and obedient, and tuh serve Thee and walk in Thy ways and please tuh make 'em set five feet apart, and when Ah done sung mah last song, done prayed mah last prayer, please suh, Jesus, make up mah dyin' bed and keep mah chillun's feet p'inted tuh de starry pole in glory and make

73

'em set five feet 'part. Dese and all other blessin's Ah ast in Jesus name, Amen, and thang Gawd."

"Aw Emmeline, dat prayer uh yourn ain't got out de house," Richard commented, "it's bumblin' 'round 'mong de rafters right now and dat's fur as it'll ever git."

Out on the porch John said softly, "Meet me tuhmorrer 'cross de branch by dat swee' gum tree 'bout fo' o'clock."

"Aw right. Aincha goin' tuh stay and have some dinner wid us?"

"Naw, Ah don't choose none. Dey got baked chicken at de big house and Ah eats from dere whenever Ah wants tuh. You gointer be sho' tuh be at our tree?"

"Unhunh."

"Sho now?"

"Unhunh."

"S'pos'n yo' mah uh some of de rest of 'em ketch yuh?"

Lucy threw herself akimbo. "Humph, dey can't do nothin' but beat me, and if dey beat me, it sho won't kill me, and if dey kill me dey sho can't eat me. Ah'll be dere jus' as sho as gun's iron."

" 'Bye den, Lucy. Sho wisht Ah could smack yo' lips."

"Whut's dat you say, John?"

"Oh nothin'. 'Bye. Doan let de booger man ketch yuh."

"Don't let ole Raw-Head-and-Bloody-Bones waylay yuh neither."

John was at the tree long before Lucy. He was sitting on the knurly-roots tying his handkerchief into a frogknot when he saw her coming diffidently down the hill on the Potts side of the branch. Presently she was standing before him.

" 'Lo, Lucy."

"Hello, John. Ah see you fixin' tuh make soap."

"Whut make you say dat, Lucy?"

"Ah see yuh got yo' bones piled up."

She pointed to his crossed legs and they both laughed immoderately.

"Miss Lucy, uh Lucy, whyn't yuh have some set down?"

"Unrack yo' bones den and make room."

Lucy sat down. John untied his handkerchief and Lucy plaited rope-grass. John attempted another knot but fumbled it nervously. Lucy caught hold of the handkerchief also.

"Lemme he'p yuh wid dat, John. Ah know how tuh tie dat. Heah, you take dem two corners and roll 'em whilst Ah git dese fixed."

They both held the handkerchief taut between them. But before the knot could be tied John pulled hard and made Lucy lean towards him.

"Lucy, something been goin' on inside uh me fuh uh long time."

Diffidently, "Whut, John?"

"Ah don't know, Lucy, but it boils up lak syrup in de summer time."

"Maybe you needs some sassafras root tuh thin yo' blood out."

"Naw, Lucy, Ah don't need no sassafras tea. You know whuss de matter wid me—but ack lak you dumb tuh de fack."

Lucy suddenly lost her fluency of speech. She worked furiously at the love-knot.

"Lucy, you pay much 'tention tuh birds?"

"Unhunh. De jay bird say 'Laz'ness will kill you,' and he go to hell ev'ry Friday and totes uh grain uh sand in his mouf tuh put out de fire, and den de doves say, 'Where you *been* so long?'"

John cut her short. "Ah don't mean dat way, Lucy. Whut Ah wants tuh know is, which would you ruther be, if you had yo' ruthers—uh lark uh flyin', uh uh dove uh settin'?"

"Ah don't know whut you talkin' 'bout, John. It mus' be uh new riddle."

"Naw 'tain't, Lucy. Po' me, Lucy. Ahm uh one wingded bird. Don't leave me lak dat, Lucy."

Suddenly Lucy shouted, "Look, John, de knot is tied right, ain't it pretty?"

"Yeah, Lucy iss sho pretty. We done took and tied dis knot, Miss Lucy, less tie uh 'nother one."

"You got mo' han'kerchiefs in yo' pocket?"

"Naw. Ah ain't studyin' 'bout no hankechers neither. De knot Ah wants tuh tie wid you is de kind dat won't come uh loose 'til us rises in judgment. You knows mah feelings."

"How Ah know whut you got inside yo' mind?"

"Yeah yuh do too. Y'all lady people sho do make it hard fuh us men folks. Look me in de eye Lucy. Kiss me and loose me so Ah kin talk."

There was an awkward bumping of mouths. Lucy had had her first kiss.

"Lucy, Ah looked up intuh Heben and Ah seen you among de angels right 'round de throne, and when Ah seen *you,* mah heart swole up and put wings on mah shoulders, and Ah 'gin tuh fly 'round too, but Ah never would uh knowed yo' name if ole Gab'ull hadn't uh whispered it tuh me."

He extended his hands appealingly.

"Miss Lucy, how 'bout changin' frum Potts tuh Pearson?"

"Yeah, John."

"When?"

"Whenever you ready fuh me. You know mo' 'bout dat dan Ah do."

"How 'bout on yo' birthday, Lucy? Us kin make merry fuh uh heap uh things den at de same time."

"Aw right, John."

It was coldish on the December night, as Lucy made ready to meet John at the church. She had only finished her wedding-dress the day before, and only her father had seemed to care whether she had one or not. Now the puffed and laced little dress of light gray cashmere lay across the bed with her new shoes and six starchy petticoats loaded down with lace of her own making.

"Lucy Ann!" Emmeline bawled from the kitchen.

"Whut, mama?"

"Don't you answer *me* no 'whut'! Ah'll come in dere and stomp yo' guts out. Whut you got all dis fiah goin' fuh?"

"Mama, you know Ah got tuh bath mah self 'fo' Ah put on dese clothes."

"Ah keers nothin' 'bout no bathin'. 'Nother thing, you

done kilt up fo' uh mah fryin'-size chickens, madam, and got 'em all cooked."

"No'm, Ah ain't kilt none uh yo' chickens. Dem wuz mah own Ah kilt fuh mah weddin'."

"How come dey yourn? You stinkin' li'l' heifer you!"

" 'Cause dem is some uh Lay-over's biddies dat Ah raised. Papa gimme dat hen las' year, and tole me tuh start raisin' mahself some chickens, so's Ah have uh good start when Ah git married, and you know Ah got twenty odd from her now."

"Youse uh lie, madam. Eve'y chicken on dis place is mines. Ah woulda give yuh uh few fuh seed if you wuz marryin' anybody. Here Artie Mimms is wid sixty acres under plow and two mules and done ast me fuh yuh ever since yuh wuz ten years old and Ah done tole 'im he could have yuh and here you is jumpin' up, goin' over mah head, and marryin' uh nigger dat ain't hardly got changin' clothes."

"He is got changin' clothes."

"Hush up! Maybe he got clothes, but he ain't got uh chamber pot tuh his name nor uh bed tuh push it under. Still he kin take you outa uh good home and drag yuh off tuh Pearson's quarters."

"Mama, yuh been hell-hackin' me eve' since us tole yuh us wuz gointer git married. Whut Ah keer 'bout ole Artie Mimms?"

"He ain't ole!"

"He is so ole, too. Ah looked at 'im good last big meetin'. His knees is sprung and his head is blossomin' fuh de grave. Ah don't want no ole springy-leg husband."

"You better want one dat kin feed yuh! Artie got dat farm and dem mules is paid fuh. He showed me and yo' paw de papers las' week."

"Whut Ah keer how many mules he got paid fuh? Ah ain't speckin' tuh live wid no mules. You tryin' tuh kill me wid talk. Don't keer whut yuh say, Ahm gointer marry John dis night, God bein' mah helper."

Lucy had been fixing her bath all during the talk. She now closed the room door, flung off her clothes with a savage

77

gesture and stepped into the tub.

Instantly Emmeline's angry hand pushed against the latched door. "Whose face you slammin' uh door in, madam? Ah means tuh bring you down offa yo' high horse! Whar dem peach hick'ries? Somebody done done 'way wid mah switches. Aaron! You go cut me five uh six good peach switches and don't bring me nothin' dat ain't long ez mah arm. Dis gal done provoked me. Ah been tryin' tuh keep offa her back 'til dat trashy yaller bastard git her outa dis house, but she won't lemme do it. Go git dem hick'ries so Ah kin roast 'em in dis fiah. Ah birthed her, she didn't birth me, and Ah'll show her she can't run de hawg over me."

"Yessum, mama, Ahm gwine."

"Make haste, Aaron. Go in uh speedy hurry!"

Lucy spoke from the wash-tub, "Mama, 'tain't no use in you sendin' Aaron out tuh be cuttin' and ruinin' papa's peach trees, 'cause Ahm tellin' anybody, ole uh young, grizzly or gray, Ah ain't takin' no whippin' tuhnight. All mah switches done growed tuh trees."

"Whuss dat you say in dere, madam?"

Richard drove 'round to the front and hitched the horse and buggy at that moment.

"Whut's all dis racket gwine on in heah?" he demanded.

"Dat youngest gal uh your'n done sassed me out, and dared me tuh hit uh. Ah birthed uh but now she's older'n me. She kin marry dat yaller wretch, but Ah means fuh her tuh tote uh sore back when he gits uh."

"Aw dry up, Emmeline, dry up! She done done her pickin', now leave her be. If she make her bed hard, she de one got tuh lay on it. 'Tain't you. Git yo' clothes on fuh de weddin'. Us Potts can't leave our baby gal go off tuh git married by herself."

"Me! Ah ain't gointer put mah foot in de place. Ahm gointer let folks see whar Ah stand. Ah sho ain't gwine squench mah feelin's fuh Lucy and dat John and you and nobody else—do Ah'll purge when Ah die."

Richard tucked Lucy into the buckboard and drove the

silent little bundle to the church huddled against him. His arm about her gave his blessing but he knew that she would have gone anyway. He but made the way easier for her little feet.

To Lucy, Macedony, so used to sound and fervor, seemed cold and vacant. Her family, her world that had been like a shell about her all her life was torn away and she felt cold and naked. The aisle seemed long, long! But it was like climbing up the stairs to glory. Her trembling fear she left on the climb. When she rode off beside John at last she said, "John Buddy, look lak de moon is givin' sunshine."

He toted her inside the house and held her in his arms infant-wise for a long time. "Lucy, don't you worry 'bout yo' folks, hear? Ahm gointer be uh father and uh mother tuh you. You jes' look tuh me, girl chile. Jes' you put yo' 'pendence in me. Ah means tuh prop you up on eve'y leanin' side."

CHAPTER 10

❖

A month after he was married John had moved up into the house-servants' quarters just back of the big house. John had achieved a raise in his wages. Alf Pearson had given them among other things a walnut bed with twisted posts, as a wedding present, and Lucy loved it above all else. She made it a spread and bolster of homemade lace.

After a few months Mehaley began to waylay John at the pig pens and in devious ways to offer herself. John gradually relaxed and began to laugh with her. She grew bolder. The morning after Lucy's first son was born, when he found her at the chicken house before him, he said, "Mehaley, Ah ain't gonna say Ah ain't laked you 'cause youse soft and nice, but Ah got Lucy, and Ah don't keer how she feel uh nothin', Ah'll want her right on. Ah tastes her wid mah soul, but if Ah didn't take holt uh you Ah'd might soon fuhgit all 'bout yuh. Pomp love you—you go marry Pomp. He'll do fuh yuh lak uh man. You better take and marry 'im."

"Ah don't want no Pomp! John Buddy, you know'd me 'fo' yuh knowed Lucy. If y'all wuz ever tuh quit would yuh marry me, John Buddy?"

"Us ain't never gonna do no quittin' 'til one uh us is six feet in de ground, and if you git de notion tuh run tell her a whole mess tuh back her feelin's and tear up peace, you better take

81

wings and fly 'fo' Ah find it out. You hear me? Nothin' ain't gointer part us."

So when Pomp Lamar, the new hoe hand, fell beneath Mehaley's mango call—exotic, but fibrous and well-bodied— she answered "Yes" quickly with a persuasive kiss.

"But Ahm got tuh be married real, Pomp."

"And dat's whut Ah means tuh do, M'haley, come nex' pay-day."

"And less we g'wan off dis farm, Pomp. You know is too much back-bendin' and mule-smellin' on cotton plantations. Less go on some public works, lak uh sawmill uh sumpin'. Ah kin git 'long wid anybody any whar so long ez you half-way treat me right."

"M'haley, you might not know it, but youse gittin' uh do-right man. Whenever you needs somebody tuh do uh man's part Ah'll be 'round dere walkin' heavy over de floor."

Next pay-day the quarters was gathered at Mehaley's mother's cabin. Quantities of sweet biscuits had been cooked up along with the chickens. The wedding was set for eight o'clock and the crowd was there—all except Pomp. People began to ask questions that had no answers. Mehaley didn't get dressed. She was asked why she was still in her working clothes.

"Humph! Y'all think Ahm gwine put mah trunk on mah back and de tray on mah head, and dat man don't never come? Naw indeed! Ah ain't gwine tuh dress tuh marry no man 'til unless he be's in de house."

"You reckon he done run off?" Nunkie asked.

"Aw naw," Duke dissented. "He tole me he wuz crazy tuh marry Haley. He jus' keepin' colored folks time. When white folks say eight o'clock dey mean eight o'clock. When uh colored person say eight o'clock, dat jes' mean uh hour ago. He'll be heah in plenty time."

It was after nine when the bridegroom arrived. "Where you been at all dis time?" Mehaley's mother wanted to know.

"Ah couldn't stand on de flo' wid M'haley in dem ole

sweaty britches. Ah been off tuh borry me some clothes tuh git married in."

Mehaley began to dress with the interference of ten or more ladies. Finally she was ready, but a quarrel arose as to who was to perform the ceremony. Mehaley's father wanted to do it, but her mother had invited the pastor.

"Ah don't keer if you *is* her pappy," the mother stated, "you ain't nothin' but uh stump-knocker and Ah wants dis done real. Youse standin' in uh sho 'nuff preacher's light. G'wan set down and leave Elder Wheeler hitch 'em right. You can't read, no-how."

"Yes, Ah kin too."

"Naw, you can't neither. G'wan sit down. If us wuz down in de swamp whar us couldn't git tuh no preacher, you'd do, but here de pastor is. You ain't nothin' but uh jack-leg. Go set in de chimbley corner and be quiet."

"You always tryin' tuh make light uh mah preachin'," the husband defended, "but Gawd don't. Dis de fust one uh mah chillun tuh jump over de broomstick and Ah means tuh tie de knot mah own self."

Around eleven o'clock, the pastor, worn out by the stubbornness of the father, retired from the field, and the couple stood upon the floor.

"Whar yo' shoes, Pomp?" Mehaley asked. "You ain't gwine marry me barefooted, is yuh?"

"Dey over dere under de bed. Yo' paw and the preacher argued so long and dem new shoes hurted mah foots so bad, Ah took 'em off. Now Ah can't git 'em back on. Dat don't make uh bit uh diff'rence. You goin' tuh see mah bare foots uh whole heap after dis."

So Mehaley Grant stood up to marry Pomp Lamar and her father Woody Grant, who had committed the marriage ceremony to memory anyway, grabbed an almanac off the wall and held it open pompously before him as he recited the questions to give the lie to the several contentions that he could not read.

"Ah now puhnounce you man and wife."

"Bus' her, Pomp, bus' her rat in de mouf. She's yourn now, g'wan Pomp. Les see yuh kiss her!"

After many boisterous kisses, the women took Mehaley by the arm and led her off.

"Us goin' and bath M'haley fuh huh weddin'-night. Some uh y'all men folks grab Pomp, and give him uh washin' off."

Mehaley got out of bed that night after the guests had all gone home.

"Whar yuh gwine, Haley?"

"Huntin' fuh mah box uh snuff."

"Yo' box uh snuff? Gal, don't you know you jes' got done married tuh uh husband? Put out dat light and come git back under dese kivvers."

"Naw, Pomp, not 'til Ah gits uh dip uh snuff. Ah wants it real bad."

She hunted about until she found it. "Lawd," she cried, "you see some dem women done messed 'round and spilt soap suds in mah snuff!"

She sat down before the fireplace and wept, hard racking sobs. Pomp's assurance that she would have a dozen boxes from the Commissary first thing in the morning did not comfort her, and it was only when her stormy tears had exhausted her that she let her new husband lead her back to bed. In his arms, she said, "Pomp, don't fuhgit you said you wuz gwine take me 'way fuhm heah."

"Cose Ah is, Haley. Nex' pay-day, sho." He kept his word.

At sundown on the evening of their leaving, Lucy was on her knees at the praying ground, telling God all her feelings.

"And oh, Ah know youse uh prayer-hearin' God. Ah know you kin hit uh straight lick wid uh crooked stick. You heard me when Ah laid at hell's dark door and cried three long days and nights. You moved de stumblin' stone out my way, and now, Lawd, you know Ahm uh po' child, and uh long ways from home. You promised tuh be uh rock in uh weary land— uh shelter in de time uh storm. Amen."

Lucy and John raced around their house in the later afternoons playing "Hail Over" and "Hide the Switch," and Lucy grew taller. The time came when she could no longer stand under John's outstretched arm. By the time her third son was born she weighed ninety-five pounds.

John had added weight to his inches and weighed two hundred and fifteen pounds, stripped. There was no doubt about it now. John was foreman at Pearson's. His reading and writing had improved to the degree where Alf could trust him with all the handling of supplies.

"John," Alf said to him one day, "you damn rascal! that girl you married is as smart as a whip and as pretty as a speckled pup. She's making a man of you. Don't let her git away."

"Oh good Lawd, naw! Mist' Alf, she even nice. Don't talk 'bout her never partin' from me. Dat sho would put de affliction on me."

"Well, John, you'd better keep Big 'Oman out of that Commissary after dark. Aha! You didn't think I knew, did you? Well, I know a lot of things that would surprise folks. You better clean yourself up."

The hand of John's heart reached out and clutched on fear. Alf Pearson shoved him on out of his office and returned to work, chuckling. Two days later Big 'Oman was gone. It got said that she was shacked up with somebody in a tie-camp on the Alabama River.

A month later John said, "Lucy, somebody done wrote Mist' Alf 'bout uh drove uh cows dey wants tuh sell 'im. He say fuh me tuh go look over 'em and see whut dey worth. Be back Sad'day."

"Iss been rainin' uh lot fuh you tuh be goin' uh long way, John."

"Goin' on horse-back, Lucy. De water ain't goin' bother me."

Lucy said no more. John didn't notice her silence in the haste of his departure, but a few miles on down the road he said, "Humph! Lucy ain't frailed me none wid uh tongue. Wonder how come dat?"

On Thursday John was cheerfully riding away from Lucy,

but at daybreak on Saturday he was dressed and ready to ride back.

"John, you ain't gwine leave me, is yuh?" Big 'Oman sobbed, "thought you come to stay. De big boss say you kin git uh job right heah."

"Ah got uh job, Big 'Oman. Done been off too long now."

The weeping girl clung to his stirrup. "When you comin' back tuh me, John?"

"In times and seasons, Big 'Oman. Lemme go now. All at rain yistiddy and las' night makes bad travelin'. Bad 'nough when Ah wuz comin'. De later it gits, de higher de river."

He dashed off quickly and rode hard, counting the miles as he went.

"Eighteen miles from home. 'Leben mo' miles. Heah 'tis de river—eight mo' miles."

The river was full of water and red as judgment with chewed-up clay land. The horse snorted and went mincing down to the bridge. Red water toting logs and talking about trouble, wresting with timber, pig-pens, and chicken coops as the wind hauls feathers, gouging out banks with timber and beating up bridges with logs.

"Git up, Roxy! Us got tuh cross dis river, don't keer if she run high ez uh bell-tower, us got tuh cross. Come on up dere. Let de damn bridge shake, bofe us kin swim."

Midway over, a huge log struck the far end of the bridge and tore it loose from the shore and it headed down stream. The whole structure loosened, rolled over and shot away.

John freed himself and struck out for shore. Fifty feet or more down stream Roxy landed, snorting her loss of faith in the judgment of man. John felt himself being carried with the stream in spite of his powerful stroke, but inch by inch he was surely gaining land. The neighing of Roxy had attracted the attention of a white squatter on the farther shore and John saw people looking on his fight with the Alabama.

There was a cry from the shore, a thud at the back of his head and he sank.

86

John strode across infinity where God sat upon his throne and looked off towards immensity and burning worlds dropped from his teeth. The sky beneath John's tread crackled and flashed eternal lightning and thunder rolled without ceasing in his wake.

Way off he heard crying, weeping, weeping and wailing—wailing like the last cry of Hope when she fled the earth. Where was the voice? He strained his eye to see. None walked across the rim bones of nothingness with him, but the wailing wailed on. Slowly John saw Lucy's face. Lucy wept at a far, far distance, but the breath of her weeping sent a cold wind across the world. Then her voice came close and her face hung miserably above his, weeping. She brought the world with her face and John could see without moving his head the familiar walls of their house.

Gradually things came closer. The gourd dipper, the water-bucket, the skillets and spiders, and his wife so close above him, forearm across her face, retching in tears.

"Whuss de matter, Lucy? You thought Ah wuzn't never comin' back? Don't you know nothin' couldn't keep me 'way from you?"

"John! Ah thought you wuz dead."

"Naw, Ah ain't dead. Whatever give you de idea Ah wuz dead, Lucy?"

"Dey brought yuh home fuh dead dis mawnin' and iss nelly sundown now and you ain't moved, and you ain't spoke 'til jus' now."

"Who brung me home?"

"De Bickerstaffs. Say de bridge washed uhway wid yuh and de hawse on it, and you got hit by de timber. Yo' lip is cut deep and yo' head is hurted in de back and uh bad place right dere side yo' nose."

"Umph, umph, umph! Lawd have mussy. Ah thought Ah been sleep. So dat's how come Ahm all wet up and mah face hurt me so, eh?"

"Yeah, and John, Ahm so glad you ain't dead 'way from me and mah li'l' chillun, and then agin Ah hated tuh think 'bout you herded tuh judgment in yo' sins."

A silent wait.

"You can't lay on dis floor all night. Ah got tuh git yuh in de bed some way uh 'nother. Lemme go call somebody tuh he'p me muscle yuh. Ah sent fuh mah folks but 'tain't been nobody from dat side yet."

The next day John called Lucy to him.

"Lucy."

"Yeah, John."

"Dey done tole you 'bout Big 'Oman and me?"

"Yeah, John, and some uh yo' moves Ah seen mahself, and if you loves her de bes', John, you gimme our chillun and you go on where yo' love lie."

"Lucy, don't tell me nothin' 'bout leavin' you, 'cause if you do dat, you'll make two winters come in one year."

There was a feeling silence.

"Lucy, Ah loves you and you alone. Ah swear Ah do. If Ah don't love you, God's gone tuh Dothan."

"Whut make yuh fool wid scrubs lak Big 'Oman and de rest of 'em?"

"Dat's de brute-beast in me, but Ah sho aim tuh live clean from dis on if you 'low me one mo' chance. Don't tongue-lash me—jes' try me and see. Here you done had three younguns fuh me and fixin' have uh 'nother. Try me Lucy."

The next big meeting John prayed in church, and when he came to his final:

> You are de same God, Ah
> Dat heard de sinner man cry.
> Same God dat sent de zigzag lightning tuh
> Join de mutterin' thunder.
> Same God dat holds de elements
> In uh unbroken chain of controllment.
> Same God dat hung on Cavalry and died,
> Dat we might have a right tuh de tree of life—

We thank Thee that our sleeping couch
Was not our cooling board,
Our cover was not our winding sheet . . .
Please tuh give us uh restin' place
Where we can praise Thy name forever,

                         Amen.

"Uh prayer went up tuhday," Deacon Moss exulted to Deacon Turl. "Dat boy got plenty fire in 'im and he got uh good strainin' voice. Les' make 'im pray uh lot."

Deacon Turl agreed and went on home to his chicken dumplings.

John never made a balk at a prayer. Some new figure, some new praise-giving name for God, every time he knelt in church. He rolled his African drum up to the altar, and called his Congo Gods by Christian names. One night at the altar-call he cried out his barbaric poetry to his "Wonder-workin'" God so effectively that three converts came thru religion under the sound of his voice.

"He done more'n de pastor," Moss observed. "Dat boy is called tuh preach and don't know it. Ahm gwine tell him so."

But Moss never did. Lucy's time was drawing nigh and a woman named Delphine drifted into town from Opelika. John was away from both home and church almost continually in the next month.

Alf went to see Lucy.

"Lucy Ann, where's that husband of yours?"

"He's out 'round de barn somewheres, ain't he, Mist' Alf?" Lucy asked. She knew he was not there. She knew that Alf Pearson knew he was not there and that Alf Pearson knew that she knew he was not there, but he respected her reticence.

"Lucy, you oughta take a green club and flail John good. No matter what I put in his way to help him along, he flings it away on some slut. You take a plow-line and half kill him."

When Alf was gone Lucy looked drearily up the path for her husband and saw her oldest brother coming with his double team.

89

"Lawd a mussy!" she groaned and dropped into a chair. A heavy knocking at the door.

"Who dat?"

"Iss me, Bud. Lemme come in right now. Ahm in uh big hurry."

Lucy opened the door feebly and Bud's stumpy figure thrust itself inside aggressively as if it said in gestures, "Who you tryin' tuh keep out?"

"Lucy, Ah come tuh git dat three dollars you borried offa me."

"Well, Bud, tuh tell yuh de truth, Ah ain't got it right dis minute. Mah husband ain't here, but he'll be here pretty soon, then he'll pay yuh sho, Bud."

"Who don't know he ain't here? How he gointer be here, and layin' all 'round de jook behind de cotton gin wid Delphine?"

"You better come back, Bud, when he's here and tell 'im all dat tuh his face."

"And whut it takes tuh tell 'im, Ah got it! He ain't nothin' but uh stinkin' coward or he wouldn't always be dodgin' back uh yuh. Ah'll tell 'im all right. 'Tain't no fight in him."

"G'wan home, Bud. If papa wuzn't dead you wouldn't come heah lak dis—and me in mah condition."

"Ah know you done wished many's de time you had married Artie Mimms."

"Naw. Not nary time."

"Gimme mah money and lemme go 'fo' Ah git mad agin."

"Ah tole you Ah ain't got no money and won't have none till John come."

"You ain't gonna git none den—dat is if he ever come. Some folks say he done quit you fuh dat Delphine. She strowin' it herself all over Macon County and laffin' at yuh. You jes' dumb tuh de fact."

"You can't pay no 'tention tuh talk. Dey's talkin' everywhere. De folks is talkin' in Georgy and dey's talkin' in Italy. Ah don't pay dese talkers no mind."

"Gimme de money, Lucy, and lemme go."

"Done tole yuh Ah ain't got no money. Come back heah when John is home."

"Naw, Ah ain't gonna do nothin' lak dat. Ah come heah wid de determination tuh git mah money uh satisfaction, one."

"But, don't you see Ah ain't in no fix tuh be fretted all up this uh way? G'wan leave me uh lone."

Bud looked around him contemptuously. "Humph! Here mah sister is cooped up wid three li'l' chillun in uh place ain't big uhnough tuh cuss uh cat in 'thout gittin yo' mouf full uh hair."

"G'wan way from me, Bud. Ahm too sick tuh be worried."

"Naw, Ah means tuh have something fuh mah money. Gimme dat bed."

"Dat big one wid de knobs on it?"

"Yep. Who you reckon want de tother one dat dem chillun done wet in? Move! Don't you git in mah way. Move! If you wuz married tuh anybody you wouldn't be in no sich uh fix."

The bed was down in a twinkling, the feather mattress and bolster heaped upon the floor, while Bud dragged out the head and foot pieces. Lucy sank down upon the mattress and fought the lump in her throat. When her brother returned for the rails and slats, Lucy was crumpled in a little dark ball in the center of the deep mound of feathers.

"Bud, you ought'n tuh take dat bed. Mist' Alf give it tuh us. Dat's our weddin' bed."

"He oughta give 'im mo'. Git up offa dat air mattress!"

"Ah ain't, and if you don't git offa dis place Ah'll call Mist' Alf. Ah bet you'll leave here then."

"Aw Ah ain't skeered uh no white man. Ah been free ever since Grant took Richmond."

But in a few moments Bud was gone and Lucy was shivering and weeping upon the feather mattress.

"Hezekiah," she called to her oldest boy, "run down tuh de quarters lak uh li'l' man and tell An' Pheemy tuh come quick. Run on, son. Youse five years ole now, youse uh great big boy. Hurry up."

"Mama, Ahm hungry."

"Mama know it too. Run on now. Run fast, Hezekiah! Show mama how fas' you kin run. Oh Gawd have mussy on me! Have mussy in uh mos' puhticular manner. Have mussy on mah ever-dyin' soul!"

Before midnight Lucy in awful agony upon her pallet on the floor had given birth to her first daughter.

The odor of airless childbirth hung over the stuffy room. Pheemy with the help of Old Edy and Della performed the ancient rites.

Edy and Della sweetened the mother and put a clean meal-sack sheet beneath Lucy, but only Pheemy could handle the after-birth in the proper way, so that no harm could come to Lucy. That is she buried it shoulder deep to the east of the house beneath a tree, then she returned and attended to the navel string of the baby and adjusted the belly-band.

"Della, you and Edy kin go 'long now. Ah kin see after Lucy."

They went reluctantly. As soon as the sound of their feet died away Pheemy asked, "How you feelin' inside, honey?"

"Lawd, An' Pheemy, Ah got somethin' in mah heart ain't got no name. Ah layin' here right now tryin' tuh find some words for feelin's. Look lak mah right heart ain't beatin' no mo'."

"Neb mine, Lucy, 'bout de words. You needs sleep and rest and some chicken gruel. Ah gwine bring yuh some. Ahm gwine find some sheep pills so de baby kin have some sheep shadney."

That night Pheemy fell asleep in a chair before the fire. The children full of corn pone and buttermilk had been asleep since early night. Lucy alone saw John when he crept in towards morning. She shut her eyes and pretended sleep. John stood looking down upon her for a long time. Lucy, later, thru the crack of her eye saw him examining the new-born baby, and felt him timidly tucking the covers under her feet, and heard him stretching himself on the floor beside the mattress; heard the deep breathing of his sleep. She raised herself upon her elbows and looked at him hard. She looked at the flickering fire, the rude dingy walls and everything in the room and knew that she'd never lose the picture as long as she lived. She stretched out her hand nearest her husband and rested the fingers on his tousled head. With her other arm she cuddled her baby close, and fell into a deep, healthful sleep.

When Lucy woke up, old Hannah was riding high. The light was strong in her face. She looked about and asked Pheemy, "Where John?"

"He at de barn—done chopped up uh tree for wood. Oughter be 'bout through wid his work by now. You better suckle dat chile."

John crept in and stood before Lucy while her fat daughter searched hungrily for the nipple.

"Lucy, whut you doin' sleepin' on de floor?"

"Dat's all Ah got tuh sleep on, John Buddy."

"Where de weddin' bed at?"

"Bud come took it fuh dat li'l' change us owe 'im fuhm las' year."

"When he come got it?"

"Yistiddy."

He hung his head a moment.

"Lucy, kin Ah see de baby?"

"She nussin' now, John. Soon's she git through."

"Dat ain't no trouble." He stooped and picked up mother and child and sat with them in his lap. "Lucy, Ahm sho proud uh dis li'l' girl chile you done had. Dat's jus' whut Ah wanted—uh girl so us could have it fuh uh doll-baby. An' Pheemy, don't Lucy have de biggest babies? Dis chile it almost big as her. She so little Ah hafta shake de sheets tuh find her in de bed."

She slapped him feebly.

"Ain't you got no better sense dan tuh set in uh man's lap and box his jaws? He's liable tuh let yuh fall thru his legs." He stopped laughing abruptly. "An' Pheemy you fed mah wife and slopped mah three li'l' pigs?"

"Look in de meal-barrel and see."

John didn't look. Pheemy's words told him. He laid Lucy

again upon the pallet and left. As he stepped thru the wire fence gap at Bud's place he saw Bud riding up the path behind him on his mule, his huge bull whip coiled upon his saddle-horn.

"Gid up dere, Sooky!" Bud Potts held his eyes stubbornly before him. John Pearson's hand flung out, grasped the mule's bridle close to the bit, and shoved the animal back upon its haunches.

"Gid down, Bud. You might kin beat me, but if you do, eve'ybody goin tuh know you been in uh fight. So good uh man, so good uh man."

"Whut you mean, John, comin' here pickin' uh fuss lak dat?"

"Ah ain't come tuh pick no fuss, Ahm come tuh fight. God bein' mah helper Ah means tuh teach yuh how tuh go proagin' 'round takin' folkses weddin' beds when dey ain't home and flinging dey wives on de floor. Gid down!"

"If you wuz any kind uh man, all dis wouldn't come tuh pass. De white folks and eve'ybody is sick and tiahed uh de way you keerin' on. Nohow you can't beat *me*. Ahm uh *man*."

"Maybe Ah can't, but Ahm so goin' tuh give it uh common trial. Hit de ground! If Ah don't beat yuh, you kin go and tell de word Ah give it uh po' man's trial."

Bud tried to ride off, but he was snatched scuffling to the ground and hammered to his knees time and time again. When he swore no more, when he begged for mercy no more, John picked him up and heaved him across the rump of the mule and recrossed the branch.

Almost home he remembered the empty meal-barrel and swerved off into the Weens' wood lot where droves of piney wood rooters nosed for ground nuts. John laid a shoat by the heels and stuck it expertly before it had squealed more than three or four times. Looking all about to see if he was seen, he swung the hog over his shoulder and took the back way home.

By that time the sun was washing herself in the bloody sea and splashing her bedclothes in red and purple. John built a fire under the washpot, and dressed his meat before he came inside the house. When Lucy opened her eyes from a nap, crude slabs of pork steak were sizzling in the skillets.

"Where you git all dat fresh meat from, John?"

"Neb' mind where Ah got de meat from. You jes' eat 'til you git plenty. Ah'll get out and throw uh natural fuh you any time. You got uh *man* tuh fend fuh yuh."

"Lawd knows Ah do needs one. Me and mah po' li'l' chillun been singin' mighty low 'round here."

"Now, Lucy, don't start dat talk 'bout breakin' up and quittin' 'cause Ah ain't goin' tuh hear dat. Youse mah wife and all Ah want you tuh do is gimme uh chance tuh show mah spunk."

"Good Lawd, John, dat's all justice been beggin' righteous tuh do—be uh *man*. Cover de ground you stand on. Jump at de sun and eben if yuh miss it, yuh can't help grabbin' holt uh de moon."

"Li'l' Bit, please don't tongue lash me," there was a short pause, " 'cause Ah done beat Bud nelly tuh death, and dat's plenty tuh think uhbout—by rights Ah oughta kilt 'im." He rubbed his swollen knuckles.

"Oh mah Gawd! When?"

"Dis evenin'—jus' 'fo' Ah come home, Lucy. Ah wouldn't be no man atall tuh let yo' brother uh nobody else snatch uh bed out from under you, mo' special in yo' condition."

"John dat's goin' tuh cause trouble and double, Bud hate you and now you done hit 'im he ain't goin' tuh let his shirt-tail touch 'im till he tell it tuh de white folks. Lawd, me and mah po' chilluns. If dey ever git yuh on dat chain-gang Ah never speck tuh see you live no mo'."

"Ah ain't goin' tuh no chain-gang. If dey ever git in behind me, Ah'll tip on 'cross de good Lawd's green. Ah'll give mah case tuh Miss Bush and let Mother Green stand mah bond."

"Dey liable tuh grab yuh, 'fo' yuh know it."

"Aw les' squat dat rabbit and jump uh 'nother one. You ack lak you done cut loose."

"Naw, Ah ain't cut loose but look lak wese tied tuhgether

95

by uh long cord string and youse at one end and Ahm at de other. Way off."

"You kin take in some de slack."

"Don't look lak it."

"Aw, lemme see de caboose uh dat. Less eat dis hog meat and hoe-cake. Jes' 'cause women folks ain't got no big muscled arm and fistes lak jugs, folks claims they's weak vessels, but dass uh lie. Dat piece uh red flannel she got hung 'tween her jaws is equal tuh all de fistes God ever made and man ever seen. Jes' take and ruin a man wid dey tongue, and den dey kin hold it still and bruise 'im up jes' ez bad."

"Say whut yuh will or may, you tryin' tuh loud talk me, but, John, you gives mah folks too much tuh go on. Ah wants mah husband tuh be uh great big man and look over 'em all so's Ah kin make 'em eat up dey talk. Ah wants tuh uphold yuh in eve'ything, but yuh know John, nobody can't fight war wid uh brick."

96

CHAPTER 11

❖

Duke came panting up to Lucy's late the next afternoon. Lucy was propped up in a rocker and Pheemy was washing baby rags.

"Hates tuh tell yuh, Lucy, but dey done got 'im."

"Do, Jesus."

"Yassum, de high sheriff put his hand on his shoulder down dere by de deepo' 'bout uh hour uh go. Bud Potts swo' out de warrant, and den Weens say he goin' have 'im bound over tuh de big cote. Sho is bad, and you in yo' condition."

"Where dey got 'im, Duke?"

"In de big jail. Cy Perkins, Jestice uh de Peace, goin' tuh bind 'im over. Den Judge Pearson'll set on de case nex' cote day."

Lucy rose abruptly, "Ahm goin', Pheemy. You take keer mah chillun."

"Lucy, yo' body ain't healed up yit. You can't go."

"Ah specks tuh be back 'fo' dark, An' Pheemy."

"Gal, you ain't but three days out uh labor. De elements is pizen tuh yuh, and effen yuh git lated 'til after sundown, de pizen night air sho will be de last uh you."

Lucy flung the plaid shawl about her head and shoulders. "And, An' Pheemy, if de baby cries tuh nuss 'fo' Ah git back, jus' give her uh sugar-tit tuh suck on and keep her pacified."

Lucy stepped out of the cabin door and was gone. In due time she stood in Cy Perkins' office where he was holding court. She saw her brother's bruised and beaten face. She saw her husband handcuffed and humble, his eyes turned away from the world.

The court had not set. She still had time if she worked fast. She held her shawl under the chin with the frail fingers of one hand as she went and stood before her brother.

"Don't come puttin' up no po' mouf tuh me, Lucy. Git out mah face," Bud shouted before she could speak. "Dis case ain't uh goin' tuh be nol prossed uh nothin' else. Ah wouldn't squash it fuh mah mammy. You made yo' bed now lay in it."

She turned away. Cy Perkins called her.

"Howdy, Lucy."

"Well, Ah thankee, Mist' Perkins. Ah come tuh see 'bout mah husband."

"Got any bail money, Lucy? That's what you need."

"Naw suh. Ah come wid jus' whut Ah stand in, 'cause Ah ain't got nothin' else, but Ah come."

Cy Perkins looked hard at the forlorn little figure. Lucy stood before him with her large bright eyes staring and not knowing she stared. Suddenly she sat down because she couldn't stand any more.

"Look like you're sick, Lucy."

"Mah troubles is inward. Mist' Perkins."

"Her new baby ain't but three days old," Duke volunteered.

Perkins fumbled with his papers, never looking at Lucy the while. John remained with head hung down and face averted except for one begging glance at Lucy. Finally the Justice of the Peace arose and beckoned Lucy into his back office.

"Don't try to stand up, Lucy. Set down before you fall down. It's too bad that you are out at a time like this. Listen, Lucy, this is serious. Your family is well thought of 'round here and lots of folks think John needs a good whipping before he goes to the gang. If he's got any friends he better call on 'em now. Tell you the truth, Lucy, if it wasn't for you,

98

and me knowing your papa so well, I wouldn't have parted my lips, but your husband is in a mess of trouble."

"Thankee, Mist' Perkins. Ah got fo' li'l' chillun 'round mah feet; if dey send John off Ah don't know whut'll 'come uh us all."

"Have you been to Judge Alf yet?"

"Naw suh. Ah hates tuh go 'cause he done cautioned John good tuh behave hisself, but Ah reckon Ah better."

"Hurry across there to his office. I won't set court until you get back."

Lucy didn't come back. She all but collapsed on the steps of Pearson's office, and he sent her home in his buggy. Alf Pearson strode across to Perkins' office and asked that the prisoner be released in his charge and it was done. Weens was paid for his hog, but John was bound over to the big court for the assault upon his brother-in-law. There was a great deal of loud whispering about night-riders and the dark of midnight, but nobody touched John as he drove Judge Pearson home.

"John, I'm not going to ask you why you've done these things, partly because I already know, and partly because I don't believe you do."

"If Ah had uh knowed 'twuz gointer raise all dis rukus."

Alf laughed sardonically, "Of course you did not know. Because God has given to all men the gift of blindness. That is to say that He has cursed but few with vision. Ever hear tell of a happy prophet? This old world wouldn't roll on the way He started it if men could see. Ha! In fact I think God Himself was looking off when you went and got yourself born."

"Yes suh, Ah speck so."

They turned into the cedar-lined drive that led up to the big, columned veranda.

"John, distance is the only cure for certain diseases. Here's fifty dollars. There are lots of other towns in the world besides Notasulga, and there's several hours before midnight. I know a man who could put lots of distance between him and this place before time, even wearing his two best suits—one over the other. He wouldn't fool with baggage because it would hold him back. He would get to a railroad twenty-five or thirty miles off."

John assisted Alf Pearson to alight.

"Good bye, John. I know how to read and write and I believe Lucy does too."

He strode up the steps of his veranda very straight and stiff, as if he had an extra backbone in his back.

In the early black dark John was gone. Lucy feverishly peeped thru first one crack then another, watching up the big road after him.

"Lucy, whyn't you stay in dat bed?" Pheemy grumbled. "You look lak youse jes' determined tuh be down sick and Ah already got mah hands full wid dese chilluns."

"An' Pheemy, Ahm standin' on de watch wall. Reckon de patter rollers'll ketch 'im?"

"Lawd naw. He pitched out towards Chehaw and dem folks is in Notasulga waitin' fuh midnight."

The hours went past on their rusty ankles and midnight stood looking both ways for day.

"Hush!" said Lucy, "dey's comin'!"

Pheemy listened hard but couldn't hear a thing.

"Dat's all right, An' Pheemy, Ah don't zakly hear nothin' neither, but uh far uhway whisper look lak it's puttin' on flesh."

They stood peering for a quarter of an hour or more at the narrow slit of the big road visible from the cabin. Then sure enough as silently as horsemen can, rode twenty or thirty men in the cloud-muddied moonlight. Slowly, watchfully, as they passed the big gate that led to the quarters and on past the stately cedar drive.

"How come dey ain't turned in?" Lucy asked, a tremble.

"Dey ain't gwine set foot on Judge Alf Pearson's place, if dey run on 'im outside dey'd grab 'im. Dey might go in some folks' quarters, but 'tain't never no patter roller set foot on dis place. Dey know big wood from brush."

Pheemy told the truth, but she was only embolden to speak

100

after the last rider had passed the big gate, and faded into the distance.

"Maybe dey already got 'im."

"Aw naw, gal, g'wan tuh rest. Dey jes' bluffin' tuh skeer us black folks."

The next day Chuck Portlock met Alf Pearson and tried to say casually, "Say, Judge dey tell me dat nigger run off. You got any notion which way he went?"

"Afraid not, Chuck. I've treed many a coon in my time, but I don't believe I've got a drop of bloodhound in me."

CHAPTER 12

❖

John's destination was purely accidental. When he came
out upon the big road to Chehaw, he overtook another
Negro. They hailed each other gladly in the early dawn.

"Where you bound fuh?" John asked.

"Tuh ketch me uh high henry."

"Whuss dat?"

"Uh railroad train, man, where you been all yo' days you
don't know de name of uh train?"

"Oh, 'bout in spots and places. Where you bound fuh when
you git on de train?"

"Tuh Florida, man. Dat's de new country openin' up. Now
git me straight, Ah don't mean West Florida, Ah means de real
place. Good times, good money, and no mules and cotton."

"B'lieve Ah'll go 'long wid yuh."

"Man, dat calls fuh more'n talk. Dat calls fuh money."

"How much?"

"Twenty odd dollars. 'Cordin' tuh where at you goin'."

"Where you goin'?"

"Tuh uh town called Sanford. Got uh sister dere. She keep-
in' uh boardin' house," he looked John over, "she's uh fine
lookin', portly 'oman; you better come 'long."

"Um already married, thankee jes' de same. Man, Ah got
uh putty 'oman. Li'l' bitsa thing. Ahm sho tuh send fuh her

soon ez Ah git settled some place."

"Aw shucks man, you ain't lak me. Ah don't take no women no place. Ah lets every town furnish its own."

They bought their tickets and John sat in a railway coach for the first time in his life, though he hid this fact from his traveling mate. To him nothing in the world ever quite equalled that first ride on a train. The rhythmic stroke of the engine, the shiny-buttoned porter bawling out the stations, the even more begilded conductor, who looked more imposing even than Judge Pearson, and then the red plush splendor, the gaudy ceiling hung with glinting lamps, the long mournful howl of the whistle. John forgot the misery of his parting from Lucy in the aura of it all. That is, he only remembered his misery in short snatches, while the glory lay all over him for hours at the time. He marvelled that just anybody could come along and be allowed to get on such a glorified thing. It ought to be extra special. He got off the train at every stop so that he could stand off a piece and feast his eyes on the engine. The greatest accumulation of power that he had ever seen.

CHAPTER 13

❖

As John and his mate stepped off the train at Sanford, they were met by a burly, red-faced white man who looked them over sharply—which gave them both the fidgets. Finally he asked, "Where y'all come from?"

"Up de road uh piece in Wes' Florduh," John's partner answered, much to his relief.

"Want work?"

"Ah kinda got uh job promised tuh me already," John's mate answered again.

"How 'bout you, Big Yaller?"

"Nawsuh, Ah ain't got no job. Ah would love tuh hear tell uh one."

"Come along then. Ever done any work on uh railroad?"

"Nawsuh, but Ah wants tuh try."

"Git yo duds then. We going over to Wildwood. Dollar a day. Seaboard puttin' thru uh spur."

That night John slept in the railroad camp and at sun-up he was swinging a nine-pound hammer and grunting over a lining bar.

The next day he wrote Lucy and sent her all of his ready money.

All day long it was strain, sweat and rhythm. When they were lining track the water-boy would call out, "Mr. Dugan!"

105

The straining men would bear down on the lining bars and grunt, "Hanh!"

"Hanh!"

"Got de number ten!"

"Hanh!"

"Got de pay-car!"

"Hanh!"

"On de rear end."

"Hanh!"

"Whyncher pick 'em up!"

"Hanh!"

"Set it over."

"Hanh!"

And the rail was in place. Sometimes they'd sing it in place, but with the same rhythm.

> When Ah get in Illinois
> Ahm gointer spread de news about de Floriduh boys
> Sho-ove it over
> Hey, hey, can't you live it?

Then a rhythmic shaking of the nine-hundred-pound rail by bearing down on the bars thrust under it in concert.

"Ahshack - uh - lack - uh - lack - uh - lack - uh - lack - uh - lack - uh - hanh!"

Rail in place.

"Hey, hey, can't you try?"

He liked spiking. He liked to swing the big snub-nosed hammer above his head and drive the spike home at a blow. And then the men had a song that called his wife's name and he liked that.

"Oh Lulu!"

"Hanh!" A spike gone home under John's sledge.

"Oh, oh, gal!"

"Hanh!"

"Want to see you!"

"Hanh!"

106

"So bad."

"Hanh!"

And then again it was fun in the big camp. More than a hundred hammer-muscling men, singers, dancers, liars, fighters, bluffers and lovers. Plenty of fat meat and beans, women flocking to camp on pay-day.

On Sunday John and his breaster went into town to church. The preacher snatched figure after figure from the land of images, and the church loved it all. Back in camp that night, John preached the sermon himself for the entertainment of the men who had stayed in camp and he aped the gestures of the preacher so accurately that the crowd hung half-way between laughter and awe.

"You kin mark folks," said Blue. "Dass jes' lak dat preacher fuh de world. Pity you ain't preachin' yo'self."

"Look, John," said his breaster, "dey's uh colored town out 'cross de woods uh piece—maybe fifteen tuh twenty miles, and dey's uh preacher—"

"You mean uh whole town uh nothin' but colored folks? Who bosses it, den?"

"Dey bosses it deyself."

"You mean dey runnin' de town 'thout de white folks?"

"Sho is. Eben got uh mayor and corporation."

"Ah sho wants tuh see dat sight."

"Dat's jes' whar Ah wants tuh take yuh nex' Sunday. Dey got uh Meth'dis' preacher over dere Ah wants yuh tuh mark. He talk thru his nose and he preaches all his sermons de same way. Sho would love tuh hear you mark 'im."

"Ah'll sho do it. Whut's de name uh dat town?"

"Eatonville, Orange County."

The Negro mayor filled John with almost as much awe as the train had. When he was leaving town that Sunday night he told his friend, "Ahm comin' back tuh dis place. Uh man kin be sumpin' heah 'thout folks tramplin' all over yuh. Ah wants mah wife and chillun heah."

There were many weeks between John and the little Negro village. He would resolve to move there on next pay-day, but trips to town, and visitors to camp defeated his plans.

But a letter from Lucy nerved him and he found work pruning orange trees in Maitland, the adjacent white town, and went to live in Eatonville.

He had meant to send for Lucy within the month, but one thing and another delayed him. One day, however, in a fit of remorse he went and drew down a month's wages in advance and sent the money to Judge Pearson for his wife because he was ashamed to write to her.

He was working for Sam Mosely, the second most prosperous man in Eatonville, and borrowed his team to meet Lucy at the train.

He wouldn't let her walk down the coach steps, but held wide his arms and made her jump into his bosom. He drove the one mile from the depot in Maitland to the heart of Eatonville with a wagon full of laughter and shouts of questions.

"Glad tuh see me, Lucy?" John asked as soon as he had loaded the battered tin trunk and the feather bed on the wagon and sprung into the driver's seat.

" 'Course, John."

"Is you only mouf glad or yuh sho nuff glad?"

"Sho nuff, but one time Ah thought you sho took uh long time tuh write tuh me and send fuh us."

"You looks lak new money 'round heah, honey. Ah'd send fuh you, if Ah didn't had bread tuh eat. Look how our li'l' gal done growed."

"Yeah she walkin' and talkin'. You been 'way from us might nigh uh yeah."

The children exclaimed at the fruit clustered golden among the dark glistening foilage.

"Ah got y'all plenty oranges at de house, y'all chaps. Yo' papa lookin' out fuh yuh."

"You got us uh house, John?" Lucy asked happily.

"Ah mean where Ah been stayin' at. Ah reckon us all kin git in dere."

" 'Tain't no mo' houses in town?"

"Yeah, two, three vacant, but us ain't got much money.

108

Sendin' fuh y'all and all, and den us ain't got nothin' tuh go in uh house but ourselves."

"Dat ain't nothin'. You go git us house of our own. 'Tain't nothin' lak being yo' own boss. Us kin sleep on de floor 'til we kin do better."

Lucy sniffed sweet air laden with night-blooming jasmine and wished that she had been born in this climate. She seemed to herself to be coming home. This was where she was meant to be. The warmth, the foliage, the fruits all seemed right and as God meant her to be surrounded. The smell of ripe guavas was new and alluring but somehow did not seem strange.

So that night John and his family were housekeeping again. John went to the woods at the edge of town and filled three crocus sacks with moss and each of the larger children had a sack apiece for a mattress. John and Lucy took the baby girl upon the feather mattress with them.

Next morning Lucy awoke at daylight and said to John in bed, "John, dis is uh fine place tuh bring up our chillun. Dey won't be seein' no other kind uh folks actin' top-superior over 'em and dat'll give'em spunk tuh be bell cows theyselves, and you git somethin' tuh do 'sides takin' orders offa other folks. Ah 'bominates dat."

"Whut's it goin' tuh be, Lucy?"

"You knows how tuh carpenter. Go ast who want uh house built, and den you take and do it. You kin prop up shacks jus' as good as some uh dem dat's doin' it."

And to John's surprise people wanted houses built all over Orange County. Central Florida was in the making.

"And now less don't pay Joe Clarke no mo' rent. Less buy dis place, John."

"Dat's uh bigger job than Ah wants tuh tackle, Lucy. You so big-eyed. Wese colored folks. Don't be so much-knowin'."

But the five acre plot was bought nevertheless, and John often sat on Joe Clarke's store porch and bragged about his determination to be a property owner.

"Aw, 'tain't you, Pearson," Walter Thomas corrected, "iss dat li'l' handful uh woman you got on de place."

"Yeah," Sam Mosely said earnestly, "Anybody could put hisself on de ladder wid her in de house. Dat's de very 'oman Ah been lookin' fuh all mah days."

"Yeah, but Ah seen uh first, Sam, so you might jus' ez well quit lookin'," John said and laughed.

"Oh Ah knows dat, John. 'Twon't do me no good tuh look, but yet and still it won't hurt me neither. You might up and die uh she might quit yuh and git uh sho nuff husband, and den she could switch uh mean Miss Johnson in dat big house on Mars Hill."

"Hold on dere uh minute, Sam," John retorted half in earnest amid the general laughter, "less squat dat rabbit and jump uhnother one. Anyhow mah house liable tuh be big ez your'n some uh dese days."

"Aw, he jes' jokin' yuh, Pearson," Joe Clarke, the mayor intervened, "I god, you takin' it serious."

When John got home that night Lucy was getting into bed. John stopped in the hallway and took his Winchester rifle down from the rack and made sure that it was loaded before he went into the bedroom, and sat on the side of the bed.

"Lucy, is you sorry you married me instid uh some big nigger wid uh whole heap uh money and titles hung on tuh him?"

"Whut make you ast me dat? If you tired uh me, jus' leave me. Another man over de fence waitin fuh yo' job."

John stood up, "Li'l' Bit, Ah ain't never laid de weight uh mah hand on you in malice. Ain't never raised mah hand tuh yuh eben when you gits mad and slaps mah jaws, but lemme tell you somethin' right now, and it ain't two, don't you never tell me no mo' whut you jus' tole me, 'cause if you do, Ahm goin' tuh kill yuh jes' ez sho ez gun is iron. Ahm de first wid you, and Ah means tuh be de last. Ain't never no man tuh breathe in yo' face but me. You hear me? Whut made you say dat nohow?"

"Aw, John, you know dat's jus' uh by-word. Ah hears all de women say dat."

"Yeah, Ah knows dat too, but *you* ain't tuh say it. Lemme

110

tell you somethin'. Don't keer whut come uh go, if you ever start out de door tuh leave me, you'll never make it tuh de gate. Ah means tuh blow yo' heart out and hang fuh it."

"You done—"

"Don't tell me 'bout dem trashy women Ah lusts after once in uh while. Dey's less dan leaves uh grass. Lucy do you still love me lak yuh useter?"

"Yeah John, and mo'. Ah got mo' tuh love yuh fuh now."

John said, "Neb mine mah crazy talk. Jus' you hug mah neck tight, Ah'd sweat in hell fuh yuh. Ah'd take uh job cleaning out de Atlantic Ocean jus' fuh yuh. Look lak Ah can't git useter de thought dat you married me, Lucy, and you got chillun by *me!*"

And he held Lucy tightly and thought pityingly of other men.

The very next Sunday he arose in Covenant Meeting and raised the song, "He's a Battle-Axe in de Time Uh Trouble," and when it was done he said, "Brothers and Sisters, Ah rise befo' yuh tuhday tuh tell yuh, God done called me tuh preach."

"Halleluyah! Praise de Lawd!"

"He called me long uhgo, but Ah wouldn't heed tuh de voice, but brothers and sisters, God done whipped me tuh it, and like Peter and Paul Ah means tuh preach Christ and Him crucified. He tole me tuh go, and He'd go with me, so Ah ast yo' prayers, Church, dat Ah may hold up de blood-stained banner of Christ and prove strong dat Ah may hold out tuh de end."

The church boiled over with approval, "Ah knowed it! Tole 'im long time uhgo dat's whut he wuz cut out fuh. Thang God. He's goin' tuh be uh battle-axe sho 'nuff—Hewin' down sinners tuh repentance."

His trial sermon had to be preached in a larger church—so many people wanted to hear him. He had a church to pastor before the hands had been laid on his head. The man who preached his ordination sermon was thrown in deep shadow by the man who was to be ordained.

The church he pastored at Ocoee did all they could to hold him, but the membership was less than a hundred. Zion Hope, of Sanford, membership three hundred, took him to her bosom, and her membership mounted every month.

John dumped a heavy pocketbook into Lucy's lap one Monday morning before he took off his hat.

Lucy praised him. "We goin' tuh finish payin' fuh dis place wid dis money. De nex' time, us buy de chillun some changin' clothes. You makin' good money now, John. Ah always knowed you wuz goin' tuh do good."

He wore the cloak of a cloud about his shoulders. He was above the earth. He preached and prayed. He sang and sinned, but men saw his cloak and felt it.

"Lucy, look lak Ah jus' found out whut Ah kin do. De words dat sets de church on fire comes tuh me jus' so. Ah reckon de angels must tell 'em tuh me."

"God don't call no man, John, and turn 'im loose uh fool. Jus' you handle yo' members right and youse goin' tuh be uh sho 'nuff big nigger."

"Ain't Ah treatin' 'em good, Lucy? Ah ain't had no complaints."

"Naw, you wouldn't hear no complaints 'cause you treatin' 'em too good. Don't pomp up dem deacons so much. Dey'll swell up and be de ruination of yuh. Much up de young folks and you got somebody tuh strain wid dem ole rams when dey git dey habits on. You lissen tuh me. Ah hauled de mud tuh make ole Cuffy. Ah know whuts in 'im.

"Don't syndicate wid none of 'em, do dey'll put yo' business in de street." Lucy went on, "Friend wid few. Everybody grin in yo' face don't love yuh. Anybody kin look and see and tell uh snake trail when dey come cross it but nobody kin tell which way he wuz goin' lessen he seen de snake. You keep outa sight, and in dat way, you won't give nobody uh stick tuh crack yo' head wid."

As he swaggered up to Joe Clarke's store porch in his new clothes, putting and taking with his yellow cane, Sam Mosely teased, "Well, John done got tuh be uh preacher."

"Yeah Ah is, and Ah ain't no stump-knocker neither. Ah kin go hard."

"Maybe so, John, but anybody kin preach. Hard work and hot sun done called uh many one. Anybody kin preach."

"Naw dey can't neither. Take you for instance."

"Don't want tuh. Ahm de mayor."

"You ain't goin' tuh be it after de 18th day of August. Watch and see."

"Who gointer be it; Joe Clarke? He said he wuzn't runnin'."

"Naw, Ahm gointer be de mayor."

"You runnin' fuh mayor?"

"Not now but Ahm goin' tuh run when de time come, and if you want tuh be mayor agin you better *run.* Don't fool wid it—run! Go hard uh go home. You and Clarke ain't had nobody tuh run against, but dis time big Moose done come down from de mountain. Ahm goin' tuh run you so hard 'til they can't tell yo' run-down shoe from yo' wore out sock."

General laughter.

"I God," Joe Clarke declared, "Ah never seen two sworn buddies dat tries tuh out do on 'nother lak y'all do. You so thick 'til one can't turn 'thout de other one, yet and still you always buckin' 'ginst each other."

" 'Tain't me," Sam Mosely defended, "Iss him, but he can't never ekal up tuh me 'cause Ah come heah from Wes' Flordah uh porpoise, but look whut Ah got now. Ahm uh self-made man."

"Ah come heah right out de tie woods in uh boot and uh shoe, but Ah got proppity too. Whut you goin' tuh call *me?*" He thrust out his chest.

"Uh wife-made man," Mosely retorted amid boisterous laughter, "if me and him wuz tuh swap wives Ah'd go past 'im so fast you'd think it wuz de A.C.L. passin' uh gopher."

"Better say joe, 'cause you don't know. Anyhow when you run for mayor next time git ready tuh take yo' whippin'. De time done come when big britches goin' tuh fit li'l' Willie."

And Rev. Pearson did win. He was swept into office by the

113

overwhelming majority of seventeen to three.

"Tell yuh how yuh beat me, John," Mosely said on the store porch that night, "course 'twan't fair, but it wuz de way you and Lucy led de gran' march night 'fo' las' at de hall, but by rights uh preacher ain't got no business dancin'."

"Grand marchin' ain't dancin'. Ah never cut uh step."

"Dat's right too, y'all," Joe Lindsay put in, "you ain't dancin' 'til yuh cross yo' feet, but Rev. John, no sinner man couldn't uh led dat march no better'n you and Lucy. Dat li'l' 'oman steps it lightly, slightly and politely."

"Tuh make short talk outa long," added Walter Thomas, "Sam, youse uh good man. Ah don't know no better conditioned man in dese parts. Yo' morals is clean ez uh fish—and he been in bathin' all his life, but youse too dry fuh de mayor business. Jes' lak it 'twuz wid Saul and David."

Lucy was going to have another baby and in her condition she missed John a lot. Now that he was called here and there over the state to conduct revivals, she knew that he must go. She was glad to see him in new suits that his congregation proudly bestowed upon him without his asking. She loved to see him the center of admiring groups. She loved to hear him spoken of as "The Battle-Axe." She even loved his primitive poetry and his magnificent pulpit gestures, but, even so, a little cold feeling impinged upon her antennae. There was another woman.

Time and time over the dish-pan, she'd find herself talking aloud.

"Lawd lemme quit feedin' on heart meat lak Ah do. Dis baby goin' tuh be too fractious tuh live." And then again, "Lawd, if Ah meet dat woman in heben, you got tuh gimme time tuh fight uh while. Jus' ruin dis baby's temper 'fo' it git tuh dis world. 'Tain't mah fault, Lawd, Ahm jus' ez clean ez yo' robes."

This was her second baby since coming to Florida, and she remembered how happy he had been at the coming of the fourth boy. A new baby might change things, perhaps, and she was right. When the new little girl was a month old, he

114

took the lacy, frilly little bundle out of Lucy's arms and carried it out to the waiting horse and buggy.

"You ain't got time tuh fool wid dat youngun, John. You goin' up tuh Sanford tuh preach, ain't yuh?"

"Yeah, and de church got tuh see dis baby. Dis is sho mah work. De very spit uh me. 'Cep'n—"

" 'Cep'n what? Dem sho yo' gray eyes."

"Dey ain't whut Ah wuz fixin' tuh say. Dat's mah eye color alright but her eyes look at yuh lak she know sumpin. Anybody'd think she's grown. Wonder whut she thinkin' 'bout?"

"Take uh God tuh tell. Ah toted de rest uh de chillun in mah belly, but dat one wuz bred in mah heart. She bound tuh be diffunt."

"Git yo' things on, Lucy, and come on tuh Sanford wid me. De church ain't seen mah wife in six months. Put on dat li'l' red dress and come switchin' up de aisle and set on de front seat so you kin be seen. Ahm goin' tuh tote de baby, lessen you want me tuh tote bofe of yuh."

"Go 'way, Ah don't hafta wear dat ole red dress 'cause Ah got uh brand new princess, laced down de back wid uh silk cord wid tassels on it."

With her bangs above her shining eyes and the door-knob knot of hair at the back, Lucy sat on that front seat in church and felt a look strike her in the back and slide off helplessly. Her husband's glance fell on her like dew. Her look and nobody else's was in his gray eyes, and the coldness melted from the pit of her stomach, and at the end of the sermon John came down from the pulpit and took the baby from her arms and standing just before the pulpit proudly and devotedly called, "Come heah eve'ybody, one at de time and pass by and look on yo' pastor's baby girl chile. Ah could shout tuhday." And they came.

There came other times of cold feelings and times of triumphs. Only the coldnesses grew numerous.

Once she had sent him off to Alabama when she felt such a coldness that it laid her in a sick-bed. She knew that the glory of his broadcloth and Stetson would humble Bud, chagrin old

Ned and make Amy happy, and in his present glory the "leaf of grass" would wither. Lucy prayed often now, but sometimes God was tired and slept a little and didn't hear her. Maybe He had other Johns somewhere that needed His ear, but Lucy didn't get too tired. She didn't worry God too much. She had her husband and seven children now and her hands were kept busy. John had to be pushed and shoved and there was no one to do it but Lucy.

There came the day, with Lucy's maneuvering, when John stood up in the State Association and was called Moderator. "Wisht ole Ned and Bud could see me now," John gloated, "always makin' out Ah wuzn't goin' tuh be nothin'. Ah uh big nigger now. Ain't Ah Lucy?"

"You sho is. All you got tuh do now is tuh *ack* lak one."

"Don't you reckon Ah know how tuh ack, Lucy? You ain't out dere wid Brown and Battle and Ford and all dem big mens, lak Ah is. You always tryin' tuh tell me whut tuh do. Ah wouldn't be where Ah is, if Ah didn't know no more'n you think Ah do. You ain't mah guardzeen nohow."

John strode off in his dark blue broadcloth, his hand-made alligator shoes, and his black Stetson, and left Lucy sitting on their porch. The blue sky looked all wrinkled to Lucy thru the tears.

And soon Lucy knew who the woman was, and once or twice the thought troubled her that John knew she knew, but didn't care.

One night as she sang the sleep song to the younger children she noticed a sallow listlessness in Isis, her younger girl. The next day she knew it was typhoid. For a week she fought it alone. John was down the East Coast running a revival and didn't come at once. When he did come, the doctor said, "Well, Reverend, I'm glad you're here. If she can last 'til midnight she's got a chance to get over it, but—but I doubt if she will live 'til dark."

The restrained Lucy stood at the far side of the bed looking at her child, looking at John. The agony of the moment sweated great drops from his forehead. He would have fallen

116

on the bed but Lucy led him outside.

"Ah can't stand 'round and see mah baby girl die. Lucy! Lucy! God don't love me. Ah got tuh go 'way 'til it's all over. Ah jus' can't stay."

So John fled to Tampa away from God, and Lucy stayed by the bedside alone. He was gutted with grief, but when Hattie Tyson found out his whereabouts and joined him, he suffered it, and for some of his hours he forgot about the dying Isis, but when he returned a week later and found his daughter feebly recovering, he was glad. He brought Lucy a new dress and a pineapple.

CHAPTER 14

❖

People in Sanford began to call Lucy aside. There was much under-voice mention of Hattie Tyson, Oviedo and shame, Gussie, Tillie, Della, church court, making changes in the pulpit and monthly conference.

"John," Lucy began abruptly one day, "you kin keep from fallin' in love wid *anybody,* if you start in time."

"Now whut you drivin' at?"

"You either got tuh stop lovin' Hattie Tyson uh you got tuh stop preachin'. Dat's whut de people say."

"Ah don't love no Hattie Tyson. De niggers lyin' on me."

"Maybe so, but if you don't you oughta stay from 'round her. Ah done seen de green tree ketch on fire, so you know uh dry one will burn."

"Lawd how some folks kin lie! Dey don't wait tuh find out a thing. Some of 'em so expert on mindin' folks' business dat dey kin look at de smoke comin' out yo' chimbley and tell yuh whut yuh cookin'."

"Yo' church officers is talkin' it too, John."

"Sho 'nuff, Lucy?"

"Dey talkin' 'bout settin' you down."

"Lawd have mussy! You ain't 'ginst me too, is yuh Lucy?"

"Naw, Ah'll never be 'ginst yuh, John, but Ah did thought you done strayed off and don't love me no mo'."

"You musta thought it, Lucy, 'cause nobody sho didn't tell yuh. If you don't know, ast somebody."

"John, now don't you go 'round dat church mealy-moufin 'round dem deacons and nobody else. Don't you break uh breath on de subjick. Face 'em out, and if dey wants tuh handle yuh in conference, go dere totin' uh high head and Ah'll be right dere 'long side of yuh."

Conference night came and the church was full. It was evident that the entire congregation was keyed up. The routine business was gotten out of the way quickly. Beulah Tansill flung her low look at the pastor and then at Deacon Tracy Patton. Deacon Patton cleared his throat and did a great deal of head scratching. The look on the pastor's face didn't seem to belong there. It was bold and unusual. It sort of dared him and the words he had brought there with him wouldn't slide off his tongue. He scratched his head some more. He had stirred up the side front the first time, he tried the opposite side back.

"Uh, ruh, uh ruh, any onfinished business?" prompted Deacon Harris.

Deacon Patton almost rose that time. Another look at Pearson and Lucy and he laid down his hat and scratched with both hands. Gave his entire head a thorough scratching and held his mouth open in sympathy.

"Shet yo' mouf, Tracy Patton!" Sister Berry cautioned. "De flies will blow yo' liver tuhreckly."

"Shet your'n. You tries tuh be so much-knowin'. You got tuh learn how tuh speak when you spokin to, come when youse called."

"Ah ain't got tuh do but two things—stay black and die," Sister Berry snapped.

"Less stand adjourned," Deacon Harris hurried, "us don't want no fight."

That was as far as the conference went. The Chairman realized that the Chief spokesman was not going to speak, hastily adjourned, hoping that Beulah and Tracy wouldn't implicate him if they talked it. He made it his business to walk home

120

with the pastor and drop a defensive suggestion in his ear in advance.

"Rev. Ahm diggin' mah sweet pitaters tuhmorrer. Goin' tuh bring you some too."

"Thanks, Aleck. Mah wife and chillun all loves dem good ole yeller yams, good ez Ah do."

"Dey sho gointer git some. Look heah, Elder Pearson Ah reckon you done heard dat some dese niggers is throwin' lies 'bout you and some woman over 'bout Oviedo. Ah ain't tole yuh nothin', and you be keerful uh dese folks dat totes yuh news. Uh dog dat'll bring uh bone will keep one. You know dat's de truth. Good night."

John had read the hostility in the meeting and his relief at his temporary deliverance was great. He said nothing to his wife, but he bought a dozen mangoes and thrust the bag into her hand.

As they undressed for bed Lucy asked in a matter of fact tone, "Whut tex' you goin' tuh preach on Sunday comin'?"

"Iss Communion so Ah reckon Ah'll preach de Passover Supper in de upper room."

"Don't you preach it. Dis thing ain't thru wid yit. 'Tain't never goin' tuh be finished 'til you tackle dey feelings and empty out dey hearts—do, it'll lay dere and fester and after while it would take God hisself tuh clean up de mess."

"Whut mo' kin Ah do? Ah wuz dere fuh dem tuh handle me and dey didn't do it."

"Dat wuz 'cause de folks didn't have no leader. They wuz plenty fight in dere. All dey needed wuz uh lead hound. You git yo'self out dey mouf and stay out of it, hear me?"

"Whut mus' Ah do?"

"You preach uh sermon on yo'self, and you call tuh they remembrance some uh de good things you done, so they kin put it long side de other and when you lookin' at two things at de same time neither one of 'em don't look so big, but don't tell uh lie, John. If youse guilty you don't need tuh git up dere and put yo' own name on de sign post uh scorn, but don't say you didn't do it neither. Whut you say, let it be de truth. Dat what comes from de heart will sho reach de heart agin."

"Mah chillun, Papa Pearson don't feel lak preachin' y'all tuhday," he began on Sunday after he had sung a song, "y'all been looking at me fuh eight years now, but look lak some uh y'all been lookin' on me wid unseein' eye. When Ah speak tuh yuh from dis pulpit, dat ain't me talkin', dat's de voice uh God speakin' thru me. When de voice is thew, Ah jus' uhnother one uh God's crumblin' clods. Dere's seben younguns at mah house and Ah could line 'em all up in de courthouse and swear tuh eve'yone of 'em, Ahm uh natchel man but look lak some uh y'all is dumb tuh de fack.

"Course, mah children in Christ, Ah been here wid y'all fuh eight years and mo'. Ah done set by yo' bedside and buried de dead and joined tuhgether de hands uh de livin', but Ah ain't got no remembrance. Don't keer if Ah laugh, don't keer if Ah cry, when de sun, wid his blood red eye, go intuh his house at night, he takes all mah remembrance wid 'im, but some yuh y'all dat got remembrance wid such long tangues dat it kin talk tuh yuh at a distance, when y'all is settin' down and passin' nations thew yo' mouf, look close and see if in all mah doin's if dere wuz anything good mingled up uhmoungst de harm Ah done yuh. Ah ain't got no mind. Y'all is de one dat is so much-knowin' dat you kin set in judgment.

"Maybe y'all got yo' right hand uh fellership hid behind yuh. De Lawd's supper is heah befo' us on de table. Maybe mah hands ain't tuh break de bread fuh yuh, maybe mah hands ain't tuh tetch de cup no mo'. So Ahm comin' down from de pulpit and Ah ain't never goin' back lessen Ah go wid yo' hearts keepin' comp'ny wid mine and yo' fire piled on mah fire, heapin' up."

He closed the great Bible slowly, passed his handkerchief across his face and turned from the pulpit, but when he made to step down, strong hands were there to thrust him back. The church surged up, a weeping wave about him. Deacons Hambo and Harris were the first to lay hands upon him. His

122

weight seemed nothing in many hands while he was roughly, lovingly forced back into his throne-like seat.

After a few minutes of concerted weeping, he moved down to the Communion table and in a feeling whisper went thru the sacrifice of a God.

CHAPTER 15

�֎

An' Dangie Dewoe's hut squatted low and peered at the road from behind a mass of Palma Christi and elderberry. The little rag-stuffed windows hindered the light and the walls were blackened with ancient smoke.

She had thrown several stalks of dried rabbit tobacco on the fire for power and sat with her wrinkled old face pursed up like a black fist, watching the flames.

Three quick sharp raps on the door.

"Who come?"

"One."

"Come on in, Hattie." As the woman entered An' Dangie threw some salt into the flame without so much as a look at her visitor. "Knowed you'd be back. Set down."

Hattie sat a moment impatiently, then she looked anxiously at An' Dangie and said, "He ain't been."

"He will. Sich things ez dat takes time. Did yuh feed 'im lak Ah tole yuh?"

"Ain't laid eyes on 'im in seben weeks. How Ahm goin' do it?"

"Hm-m-m." She struggled her fatness up from the chair and limped over to an old tin safe in the corner. She fumbled with the screw top of a fruit jar and returned with a light handful of wish-beans. "Stan' over de gate whar he sleeps and eat dese

125

beans and drop de hulls 'round yo' feet. Ah'll do de rest."

"Lawd, An' Dangie, dere' uh yard full uh houn' dawgs and chillun. Eben if none uh dem chillun see me, de dawgs gwine bark. Ah wuz past dere one day 'thout stoppin'."

"G'wan do lak Ah tell yuh. Ahm gwine hold de bitter bone in mah mouf so's you kin walk out de sight uh men. You bound tuh come out more'n conquer. Jes' you pay me whut Ah ast and 'tain't nothin' built up dat Ah can't tear down."

"Ah know you got de power."

"Humph! Ah reckon Ah is. Y' ever hear 'bout me boilin' uh wash-pot on uh sail needle?"

"Yas ma'am and mo' besides."

"Well don't come heah doubtin' lak you done jes' now. Aw right, pay me and g'wan do lak Ah tell yuh."

Hattie took the knotted handkerchief out of her stocking and paid. As she reached the door, the old woman called after her, " 'Member now, you done started dis and it's got tuh be kep' up do hit'll turn back on yuh."

"Yas'm."

The door slammed and An' Dangie crept to her altar in the back room and began to dress candles with war water. When the altar had been set, she dressed the coffin in red, lit the inverted candles on the altar, saying as she did so, "Now fight! Fight and fuss 'til you part." When all was done at the altar she rubbed her hands and forehead with war powder, put the catbone in her mouth, and laid herself down in the red coffin facing the altar and went into the spirit.

CHAPTER 16

❖

Lucy was lying sick. The terrible enemy had so gnawed away her lungs that her frame was hardly distinguishable from the bed things.

"Isie?"

"Yes ma'am."

"Come give mama uh dose uh medicine."

"Yes'm."

The skinny-legged child of nine came bringing a cheap glass pitcher of water. "Ah pumped it off so it would be cool and nice fuh yuh."

"Thankee, Isie. Youse mah chile 'bove all de rest. Yo' pa come yet?"

"Yes'm, he out 'round de barn somewhere."

"Tell 'im Ah say tuh step heah uh minute."

John Pearson crossed the back porch slowly and heavily and entered the bedroom with downcast eyes.

"Whut you want wid me, Lucy?"

"Here 'tis Wednesday and you jus' gittin' home from Sanford, and know Ahm at uh mah back too. You know dat Hezekiah and John is uhway in school up tuh Jacksonville, and dese other chillun got tuh make out de bes' dey kin. You ought tuh uh come on home Monday and seen after things."

127

He looked sullenly at the floor and said nothing. Lucy used her spit cup and went on.

"Know too Ahm sick and you been home fuh de las' longest and ain't been near me tuh offer me uh cup uh cool water uh ast me how Ah feel."

"Oh you sick, sick, sick! Ah hates tuh be 'round folks always complainin', and then again you always doggin' me 'bout sumpin'. Ah gits sick and tired uh hearing it!"

"Well, John, you puts de words in mah mouf. If you'd stay home and look after yo' wife and chillun, Ah wouldn't have nothin' tuh talk uhbout."

"Aw, yes you would! Always jawin' and complainin'."

Lucy said, "If you keep ole Hattie Tyson's letters out dis house where mah chillun kin git holt of 'em and you kin stop folkses mouf by comin' on home instid uh layin' 'round wid her in Oviedo."

"Shet up! Ahm sick an' tired uh you' yowin' and jawin'. 'Tain't nothin' Ah hate lak gittin' sin throwed in mah face dat done got cold. Ah do ez Ah please. You jus' uh hold-back tuh me nohow. Always sick and complainin'. Uh man can't utilize hisself."

He came to the bed and stood glaring down upon her. She seemed not to notice and said calmly after a short pause, "Ahm glad tuh know dat, John. After all dese years and all dat done went on dat Ah ain't been nothin' but uh stumblin'-stone tuh yuh. Go 'head on, Mister, but remember—youse born but you ain't dead. 'Tain't nobody so slick but whut they kin stand uh 'nother greasin'. Ah done told yuh time and time uhgin dat ignorance is de hawse dat wisdom rides. Don't git miss-put on yo' road. God don't eat okra."

"Oh you always got uh mouf full uh opinions, but Ah don't need you no mo' nor nothing you got tuh say, Ahm uh man grown. Don't need no guardzeen atall. So shet yo' mouf wid me."

"Ah ain't going' tuh hush nothin' uh de kind. Youse livin' dirty and Ahm goin' tuh tell you 'bout it. Me and mah chillun got some rights. Big talk ain't changin' whut you doin'. You can't clean yo'self wid yo' tongue lak uh cat."

There was a resounding smack. Lucy covered her face with her hand, and John drew back in a sort of horror, and instantly strove to remove the brand from his soul by words, "Ah tole yuh tuh hush." He found himself shaking as he backed towards the door.

"De hidden wedge will come tuh light some day, John. Mark mah words. Youse in de majority now, but God sho don't love ugly."

John shambled out across the back porch, and stood for an unknowing time among the palmetto bushes in a sweating daze feeling like Nebuchadnezer in his exile.

Lucy turned her face to the wall and refused her supper that her older daughter Emmeline cooked and that Isis brought to her.

"But mama, you said special you wanted some battercakes."

"You eat 'em, Isie. Mama don't want uh thing. Come on in when you thru wid yo' supper lak you always do and read mama something out yo' reader."

But Isis didn't read. Lucy lay so still that she was frightened. She turned down the lamp by the head of the bed and started to leave, but Lucy stopped her.

"Thought you was sleep, mama."

"Naw, Isie, been watchin' dat great big ole spider."

"Where?"

"Up dere on de wall next tuh de ceilin'. Look lak he done took up uh stand."

"Want me tuh kill 'im wid de broom?"

"Naw, Isie, let 'im be. You didn't put 'im dere. De one dat put 'im dere will move 'im in his own time."

Isis could hear the other children playing in the back room.

"Reckon you wanta go play wid de rest, Isie, but mama wants tuh tell yuh somethin'."

"Whut is it, mama?"

"Isie, Ah ain't goin' tuh be wid yuh much longer, and when Ahm dead Ah wants you tuh have dis bed. Iss mine. Ah sewed fuh uh white woman over in Maitland and she gimme dis bedstead fuh mah work. Ah wants you tuh have it. Dis mah feather tick on here too."

"Yes'm mama, Ah—"

"Stop cryin', Isie, you can't hear whut Ahm sayin', 'member tuh git all de education you kin. Dat's de onliest way you kin keep out from under people's feet. You always strain tuh be de bell cow, never be de tail uh nothin'. Do de best you kin, honey, 'cause neither yo' paw nor dese older chillun is goin' tuh be bothered too much wid yuh, but you goin' tuh git 'long. Mark mah words. You got de spunk, but mah po' li'l' sandy-haired chile goin' suffer uh lot 'fo' she git tuh de place she kin 'fend fuh herself. And Isie, honey, stop cryin' and lissen tuh me. Don't you love nobody better'n you do yo'self. Do, you'll be dying befo' yo' time is out. And, Isie, uh person kin be killed 'thout being stuck un blow. Some uh dese things Ahm tellin' yuh, you wont understand 'em fuh years tuh come, but de time will come when you'll know. And Isie, when Ahm dyin' don't you let 'em take de pillow from under mah head, and be covering up de clock and de lookin' glass and all sich ez dat. Ah don't want it done, heah? Ahm tellin' you in prefer-ence tuh de rest 'cause Ah know you'll see tuh it. Go wash yuh face and turn tuh de Twenty-Sixth Chapter of de Acts fuh me. Den you go git yo' night rest. If Ah want yuh, Ah'll call yuh."

Way in the night Lucy heard John stealthily enter the room and stand with the lamp in his hand peering down into her face. When she opened her eyes she saw him start.

"Oh," he exclaimed sharply with rising inflection. Lucy searched his face with her eyes but said nothing.

"Er, er, Ah jus' thought Ah'd come see if you wanted anything," John said nervously, "if you want anything, Lucy, all you got tuh do is tuh ast me. De favor is in me."

Lucy looked at her husband in a way that stepped across the ordinary boundaries of life and said, "Jus' have patience, John, uh few mo' days," and pulled down her lids over her eyes, and John was glad of that.

John rushed from Lucy's bedside to the road and strode up

130

and down in the white moonlight. Finally he took his stand beneath the umbrella tree before the house and watched the dim light in Lucy's room. Nothing came to him there and he awoke Emmeline at daybreak, "Go in yo' ma's room Daught' and come back and tell me how she makin' it."

"She say she ain't no better," Daught' told him.

The spider was lower on the wall and Lucy entertained herself by watching to see if she could detect it move.

She sent Isis to bed early that Thursday night but she herself lay awake regarding the spider. She thought that she had not slept a moment, but when in the morning Isis brought the wash basin and tooth brush, Lucy noted that the spider was lower and she had not seen it move.

That afternoon Mrs. Mattie Clarke sat with her and sent Isis out to play.

"Lucy, how is it 'tween you and God?"

"You know Ah ain't never been one to whoop and holler in church, Sister Clarke, but Ah done put on de whole armor uh faith. Ah ain't afraid tuh die."

"Ahm sho glad tuh hear dat, Sister Pearson. Yuh know uh person kin live uh clean life and den dey kin be so fretted on dey dyin' bed 'til dey lose holt of de kingdom."

"Don't worry 'bout me, Sister Clarke. Ah done been in sorrow's kitchen and Ah done licked out all de pots. Ah done died in grief and been buried in de bitter waters, and Ah done rose agin from de dead lak Lazarus. Nothin' kin touch mah soul no mo'. It wuz hard tuh loose de string-holt on mah li'l' chillun." Her voice sank to a whisper, "But Ah reckon Ah done dat too."

"Put whip tuh yo' hawses, honey. Whip 'em up."

Despite Lucy's all-night vigil she never saw the spider when he moved, but at first light she noted that he was at least a foot from the ceiling but as motionless as a painted spider in a picture.

The evening train brought her second son, John, from Jacksonville. Lucy brightened.

"Where's Hezekiah?" she asked eagerly.

"He's comin'. His girl is gointer sing uh solo at de church on Sunday and he wants to hear her. Then he's coming right on. He told me to wire him how you were."

"Don't do it, John. Let 'im enjoy de singin'."

John told her a great deal about the school and the city and she listened brightly but said little.

After that look in the late watches of the night John was afraid to be alone with Lucy. His fear of her kept him from his bed at night. He was afraid lest she should die while he was asleep and he should awake to find her spirit standing over him. He was equally afraid of her reproaches should she live, and he was troubled. More troubled than he had ever been in all his life. In all his struggles of sleep, the large bright eyes looked thru and beyond him and saw too much. He wished those eyes would close and was afraid again because of his wish.

Lucy watched the spider each day as it stood lower. And late Sunday night she cried out, "O Evening Sun, when you git on de other side, tell mah Lawd Ahm here waitin'."

And God awoke at last and nodded His head.

In the morning she told Emmeline to fry chicken for dinner. She sent Isis out to play. "You been denyin' yo' pleasure fuh me. G'wan out and play wid de rest. Ah'll call yuh if Ah want yuh. Tell everybody tuh leave me alone. Ah don't want no bother. Shet de door tight."

She never did call Isis. Late in the afternoon she saw people going and coming, coming and going. She was playing ball before the house, but she became alarmed and went in.

The afternoon was bright and a clear light streamed into the room from the bare windows. They had turned Lucy's bed so that her face was to the East. The way from which the sun comes walking in red and white. Great drops of sweat stood out on her forehead and trickled upon the quilt and Isis saw a pool of sweat standing in a hollow at the elbow. She was breathing hard, and Isis saw her set eyes fasten on her as she came into the room. She thought that she tried to say some-

132

thing to her as she stood over her mother's head, weeping with her heart.

"Get her head offa dat pillow!" Mattie Mosely ordered. "Let her head down so she kin die easy."

Hoyt Thomas moved to do it, but Isis objected. "No, no, don't touch her pillow! Mama don't want de pillow from under her head!"

"Hush Isie!" Emmeline chided, "and let mama die easy. You makin' her suffer."

"Naw, naw! she said *not* tuh!" As her father pulled her away from her place above Lucy's head, Isis thought her mother's eyes followed her and she strained her ears to catch her words. But none came.

John stood where he could see his wife's face, but where Lucy's fixed eyes might not rest upon him. They drew the pillow from beneath Lucy's head and she gulped hard once, and was dead. "6:40" someone said looking at a watch.

"Po' thing," John wept. "She don't have tuh hear no mo' hurtin' things." He hurried out to the wood pile and sat there between two feelings until Sam Mosely led him away.

"She's gone!" rang out thru the crowded room and they heard it on the porch and Mattie Mosely ran shouting down the street, "She's gone, she's gone at last!"

And the work of the shrouding began. Little Lucy, somewhat smaller in death than she had been even in life, lay washed and dressed in white beneath a sheet upon the cooling board when her oldest son arrived that evening to break his heart in grief.

That night a wind arose about the house and blew from the kitchen wall to the clump of oleanders that screened the chicken house, from the oleanders to the fence palings and back again to the house wall, and the pack of dogs followed it, rearing against the wall, leaping and pawing the fence, howling, barking and whining until the break of day, and John huddled beneath his bed-covers shaking and afraid.

CHAPTER 17

❖

T hey put Lucy in a little coffin next day, the shiny coffin that held the beginning and the ending of so much. And the September woods were ravished by the village to provide tight little bouquets for the funeral. Sam Mosely, tall, black and silent, hitched his bays to his light wagon and he bore Lucy from her house and children and husband and worries to the church, while John, surrounded by his weeping family, walked after the wagon, shaking and crying. The village came behind and filled the little church with weeping and wild-flowers. People were stirred. The vital Lucy was gone. The wife of Moderator Pearson was dead.

"There is rest for the weary" rose and fell like an organ. Harmony soaked in tears.

"She don't need me no mo' nohow," John thought defensively.

"On the other side of Jordan, in the sweet fields of Eden— where the tree of life is blooming—"

And the hot blood in John's veins made him deny kinship with any rider of the pale white horse of death.

"Man born of woman has but a few days."

Clods of damp clay falling hollowly on the box. Out of sight of the world, and dead men heard her secrets.

That night they sat in the little parlor about the organ and the older children sang songs while the smaller ones cried and whimpered on. John sat a little apart and thought. He was free. He was sad, but underneath his sorrow was an exultation like a live coal under gray ashes. There was no longer guilt. But a few days before he had shuddered at the dread of discovery and of Lucy's accusing eye. There was no more sin. Just a free man having his will of women. He was glad in his sadness.

The next day John Pearson and Sam Mosely met on Clarke's porch. Sam remarked, "Funny thing, ain't it John—Lucy come tuh town twelve years uhgo in mah wagon and mah wagon took her uhway."

"Yeah, but she b'longed tuh me, though, all de time," John said and exulted over his friend.

CHAPTER 18

Deacons Hambo, Watson, Hoffman and Harris waited on Rev. Pearson in his study at the parsonage.

"No mealy-moufin', Harris. No whippin' de Devil 'round de stump. He got tuh be told." Hambo urged.

"Ahm goin' tuh tell 'im how we feel. You too hot tuh talk. You ain't in yo' right mind."

"Oh yes, Ah is too, Ahm hot, though. Ahm hot ez July jam. Jee-esus Christ!"

John entered the room radiating cheer.

"Hello, boys. How yuh do?"

"Don't do all dey say, but Ah do mah share," said Hambo quickly, "and damned if you don't do yourn."

Pearson didn't know whether it was one of the bluff Hambo's jokes or not. He started to laugh, then looked at the men's faces and quit.

"Oh."

"Now lemme handle dis, Hambo, lak we said," begged Harris.

"Naw, lemme open mah mouf 'fo' Ah bust mah gall. John, is you married tuh dat Hattie Tyson?"

"Yeah."

"DeG—D—hell you is, man! Yo' wife ain't been dead but

three months, and you done jumped up and married befo' she got col' in her grave!''

"Ah got dese li'l' chillun and somebody got tuh see after 'em.''

"Well de somebody you got sho ain't seein' after 'em. They's 'round de streets heah jes' ez raggedy ez jay-birds in whistlin' time. Dey sho ain't gittin' uh damn bit uh 'tention.''

"Course Ah didn't marry her jus' tuh wait on de chillun. She got tuh have some pleasure.''

"Course she is! Dat strumpet ain't never done nothin' but run up and down de road from one sawmill camp tuh de other and from de looks of her, times was hard. She ain't never had nothin'—not eben doodly-squat, and when she gits uh chance tuh git holt uh sumpin de ole buzzard is gone on uh rampage. She ain't got dis parsonage and dem po' li'l' motherless chillun tuh study 'bout.''

"Hold on dere, Hambo, y'all. Dat's mah wife.''

"Sh-h-ucks! Who don't know dat Hattie Tyson! Ah ain't gonna bite mah tongue uh damn bit and if you don't lak it, you kin jus' try me wid yo' fist. Ahm three times seben and uh button! And whut makes me mad 'nough tuh fight uh circle-saw is, you don't want uh yo'self. You done got trapped and you ain't got de guts tuh take uh rascal-beater and run her 'way from here. She done moved you 'way from Eatonville 'cause 'tain't 'nough mens and likker dere tuh suit her.''

"Wait uh minute, Hambo.''

"Ain't gonna wait nothin' uh de kind. Wait broke de wagon down. Ah jes' feel lak takin' uh green club and waitin' on dat wench's head until she acknowledge Ahm God and besides me there's no other! Gimme lief, John, and Ah'll make haste and do it. Ah feels lak stayin' wid yo' head uh week. Dey tell me you eben drawed uh knife on yo' son John, 'cause he tried tuh keep dah strumpet out his mama's feather bed dat she give tuh li'l' Isis on her death-bed, and nobody but uh lowdown woman would want you scornin' yo' name all up lak dat.''

Pearson hung his head.

"If y'all come heah tuh 'buke me, g'wan do it."

Hoffman spoke up.

"We ain't come to 'buke you, Reverend, but de church sho is talkin' and gittin' onrestless 'bout yo' marriage."

"Yeah, dat's jus' whut Ah come fuh—tuh 'buke yuh. Ah ain't come tuh make yuh no play-party. Stoopin' down from where you stand, fuh whut?" Hambo broke out again, "Jus 'cause you never seen no talcum powder and silk kimonos back dere in Alabama."

Harris and Hoffman took him by the arms and led him forth, and John went back upstairs and wept.

Hattie had heard it all, but she stayed out of sight until the rough tongued Hambo was gone. She went to John, but first she combed her hair and under-braided the piece of John-de-conquer root in her stiff back hair. "Dey can't move me—not wid de help Ah got," she gloated and went in to John where he lay weeping.

"Thought you tole me dat Hambo wuz yo' bosom friend?"

"He is, Hattie. Ah don't pay his rough talk no mind."

"Ah don't call dat no friend—comin' right in yo' house and talkin' 'bout yo' wife lak she wuz uh dog. If you wuz any kind of uh man you wouldn't 'low it."

"Uh preacher can't be fightin' and keerin' on. Mo' special uh Moderator. Hambo don't mean no harm. He jus' 'fraid de talk might hurt me."

"Him and them sho treats me lak uh show man treats uh ape. Come right in mah house and run de hawg over me and tryin' tuh put you 'ginst me. Youse over dem and you ought not tuh 'low 'em tuh cheap, but 'stid uh dat they comes right to yo' face and calls yo' wife uh barrel uh dem things. Lawd knows Ah ain't got no puhtection uh tall! If Miss Lucy had tuh swaller all Ah does, Ah know she glad she dead."

"Lucy ain't never had nobody to call her out her name. Dey better not. Whut make *you* call her name? Hambo is de backbone uh mah church. Ah don't aim to tear de place tuh pieces fuh nobody. Put dat in yo' pipe and smoke it."

Hattie heard and trembled. The moment that John left town to conduct a revival meeting, she gathered what money she could and hurried to the hut of An' Dangie Dewoe.

CHAPTER 19 ·

✦

The Lord of the wheel that turns on itself slept, but the world kept spinning, and the troubled years sped on. Tales of weakness, tales of vice hung about John Pearson's graying head. Tales of wifely incontinence which Zion Hope swallowed hard. The old ones especially. Sitting coolly in the shade of after-life, they looked with an utter lack of tolerance upon the brawls of Hattie and John. They heard her complaints often and believed her and only refused action because they knew the complaint to be equally guilty, but less popular than the man against whom she cried. Besides, the younger generation winked at what their elders cried over. Lucy had counselled well, but there were those who exulted in John's ignominious fall from the Moderatorship after nine years tenure, and milled about him like a wolf pack about a tired old bull—looking for a throat-hold, but he had still enough of the former John to be formidable as an animal and enough of his Pagan poesy to thrill. The pack waited. John knew it and was tired unto death of fighting off the struggle which must surely come. The devouring force of the future leered at him at unexpected moments. Then too his daily self seemed to be wearing thin, and the past seeped thru and mastered him for increasingly longer periods. He whose pres-

141

ent had always been so bubbling that it crowded out past and future now found himself with a memory.

He began to remember friends who had lain back on the shelf of his mind for years. Now and then he surprised them by casual visits, but the pitying look would send him away and it would be a long time before he made such a call again.

He began to see a good deal of Zeke who had moved with his family to Florida, a year or two before Lucy died. He loved seeing Zeke because he was just as great a hero in his brother's eyes as he had been when he was the biggest Negro Baptist in the State and when Zion Hope had nine hundred members instead of the six hundred now on its roll. Zeke talked but always spared him.

Yes, John Pearson found himself possessed of a memory at a time when he least needed one.

"Funny thing," he said sitting in Zeke's kitchen with his wife, "things dat happened long time uhgo used to seem way off, but now it all seems lak it wuz yistiddy. You think it's dead but de past ain't stopped breathin' yet."

"Eat supper wid us, John Buddy, and stay de night."

"Thankee, Zeke. B'lieve Ah will fuh uh change." He went to bed at Zeke's after supper. Slept a long time. He awoke with a peculiar feeling and crept out of the house and went home.

"Hattie, whut am Ah doin' married tuh you?" John was standing in his wife's bedroom beside her bed and looking down on her, a few minutes later.

Hattie sat up abruptly, pulling up the shoulder straps of her nightgown.

"Is dat any way fuh you tuh do? Proagin' 'round half de night lak uh damn tom cat and den come heah, wakin' me up tuh ast uh damn fool question?"

"Well, you answer me den. Whut is us doin' married?"

"If you been married tuh uh person seben years and den come ast sich uh question, you mus' be crazy uh drunk one. You *is* drunk! You oughta know whut us doin' married jus' ez well ez Ah do."

"But Ah don't. God knows Ah sho don't. Look lak Ah been sleep. Ah ain't never meant tuh marry you. Ain't got no recollection uh even tryin' tuh marry yuh, but here us is married, Hattie, how come dat?"

"Is you crazy sho 'nuff?"

"Naw, Ah ain't crazy. Look lak de first time Ah been clothed in mah right mind fuh uh long time. Look lak uh whole heap uh things been goin' on in mah sleep. You got tuh tell me how come me and you is married."

"Us married 'cause you said you wanted me. Dat's how come."

"Ah don't have no 'membrance uh sayin' no sich uh thing. Don't b'lieve Ah said it neither."

"Well you sho said so—more'n once too. Ah married yuh jes' tuh git rid of yuh."

"Aw naw. Ah ain't begged you tuh marry me, nothin' uh de kind. Ah ain't said nothing' 'bout lovin' yuh tuh my knowin', but even if Ah did, youse uh experienced woman—had plenty experience 'fo' Ah ever seen yuh. You know better'n tuh b'lieve anything uh man tell yuh after ten o'clock at night. You know so well Ah ain't wanted tuh marry you. Dat's how come Ah know it's uh bug under dis chip."

"Well—if you didn't want me you made lak yuh did," Hattie said doggedly.

"Dat sho is funny, 'cause Ah know Ah wanted Miss Lucy and Ah kin call tuh memory eve'y li'l' thing 'bout our courtin' and 'bout us gittin' married. Couldn't fuhgit it if Ah wuz tuh try. Mo' special and particular, Ah remember jus' how Ah felt when she looked at me and when Ah looked at her and when we touched each other. Ah recollect how de moon looked de night us married, and her li'l' bare feets over de floor, but Ah don't remember nothin' 'bout *you*. Ah don't know how de moon looked and even if it rained uh no. Ah don't 'call to mind making no 'rangements tuh marry yuh. So you mus' know mo' 'bout it than Ah do."

Hattie pulled her long top lip down over the two large chalky-white false teeth in front and thought a while. She sank

143

back upon her pillow with an air of dismissal. "Youse drunk and anybody'd be uh fool tuh talk after yuh. You know durned well how come you married me."

"Naw, Ah don't neither. Heap uh things done went on Ah ain't meant tuh be. Lucy lef' seben chillun in mah keer. Dey ain't here now. Where is mah chillun, Hattie? Whut mah church doin' all tore up? Look at de whiskey bottles settin' 'round dis house. Dat didn't useter be."

"Yeah, and you sho drinks it too."

"But Ah didn't useter. Not in Lucy's time. She never drunk none herself lak you do, and she never brought none in de house tuh tempt me."

"Aw g'wan out heah! Don't keer if Ah do take uh swaller uh two. You de pastor uh Zion Hope, not me. You don't hav' to do lak me. Youse older'n me. Hoe yo' own row. De niggers fixin' tuh put yuh out dat pulpit 'bout yo' women and yo' likker and you tryin' tuh blame it all on me."

"Naw it's jus' uh hidden mystery tuh me—what you doin' in Miss Lucy's shoes."

And like a man arisen, but with sleep still in his eyes, he went out of the door and to his own bedroom.

Hattie lay tossing, wondering how she could get to An' Dangie Dewoe without arousing suspicion.

"Wonder is Ah done let things go too long, or is de roots jus' done wore out and done turn'd back on me?"

There was no sleep in either bedroom that night.

Hattie crept into John's bed at dawn and tried her blandishments but he thrust her rudely away.

"Don't you want me tuh love yuh no mo'?"

"Naw."

"How come?"

"It don't seem lak iss clean uh sumpin."

"Is you mad cause Ah learnt tuh love yuh so hard way back dere 'fo' Miss Lucy died?"

"Ah didn't mind you lovin' me, but Ah sho is mad wid yuh fuh marryin' me. Youse jus' lak uh blowfly. Spoil eve'y thing yuh touch. You sho ain't no Lucy Ann."

144

"Naw, Ah ain't no Miss Lucy, 'cause Ah ain't goin' tuh cloak yo' dirt fuh yuh. Ah ain't goin' tuh take offa yuh whut she took so you kin set up and be uh big nigger over mah bones."

" 'Tain't no danger uh me bein' no big nigger wid *you* uhround. Ah sure ain't de State Moderator no mo'."

"And dat ain't all. You fool wid me and Ah'll jerk de cover offa you and dat Berry woman. Ah'll throw uh brick in yo' coffin and don't keer how sad de funeral will be, and Ah dare yuh tuh hit me too. Ah ain't gonna be no ole man's fool."

"You know Ah don't beat no women folks. Ah married Lucy when she wuzn't but fifteen and us lived tuhgether twenty-two years and Ah ain't never lifted mah hand—"

Suddenly a seven-year-old picture came before him. Lucy's bright eyes in the sunken face. Helpless and defensive. The look. Above all, the look! John stared at it in fascinated horror for a moment. The sea of the soul, heaving after a calm, giving up its dead. He drove Hattie from his bed with vile imprecations.

"You, you!" he sobbed into the crook of his arm when he was alone, "you made me do it. And Ah ain't never goin' tuh git over it long ez Ah live."

During breakfast they quarreled over the weak coffee and Hattie swore at him.

"No woman ain't never cussed me yet and you ain't gonna do it neither—not and tote uh whole back," he gritted out between his teeth and beat her severely, and felt better. Felt almost as if he had not known her when Lucy was sick. He panged a little less. So after that he beat her whenever she vexed him. More interest paid on the debt of Lucy's slap. He pulled the crayon enlargement of Hattie's out of its frame and belligerently thrust it under the wash-pot while she was washing and his smoking eyes warned her not to protest.

"Rev'und," she began at breakfast one morning, "Ah needs uh pair uh shoes."

"Whyn't yuh go git 'em den?"

"Where Ahm goin' tuh git 'em from?"

"Speer got plenty and J. C. Penney swear he sells 'em."

"Dat ain't doin' me no good lessen Ah got de money tuh buy 'em wid."

"Ain't yuh got no money?"

"You ain't gimme none, is yuh? Not in de last longest."

"Oh you got shoes uh plenty. Ah see yuh have five uh six pairs 'round out under de dresser. Miss Lucy never had nothin' lak dat."

"Miss Lucy agin! Miss Lucy dis, Miss Lucy dat!"

"Yeah Miss Lucy, and Ahm gointer put uh headstone at her grave befo' anybody git shoes 'round heah—eben me."

"Mah shoes is nelly wore out, man. Dat headstone kin wait."

"Naw, Hattie, 'tain't gonna wait. Don't keer if youse so nelly barefooted 'til yo' toes make prints on de ground. She's gointer git her remembrance-stone first. You done wore out too many uh her shoes already. Here, take dis two bits and do anything you wanta wid it."

She threw it back viciously. "Don't come lounchin' me out no two bits when Ah ast you fuh shoes."

Hattie reported this to certain church officers and displayed her general shabbiness. Harris sympathized.

"Iss uh shame, Sister. Ah'd cut down dat Jonah's gourd vine in uh minute, if Ah had all de say-so. You know Ah would, but de majority of 'em don't keer whut he do, some uh dese people stands in wid it. De man mus' is got roots uh got piece uh dey tails buried by his door-step. Know whut some of 'em tole me? Says he ain't uh bit worse dan de rest uh y'all 'round de altar dere. Y'all gits all de women yuh kin. He jus' de bes' lookin' and kin git mo' of 'em dan de rest. Us pays him tuh preach and he kin sho do dat. De best in de State, and whut make it so cool, he's de bes' lookin'. Eben dem gray hairs becomes 'im. Nobody don't haft do lak he *do,* jus' do lak he *say* do. Yes ma'am, Sister Pearson 'twon't do fuh us tuh try tuh handle 'im. He'd beat de case. De mo' he beat you de better some of 'em laks it. Dey chunkin stones at yo' character and sayin' you ain't fit. Pot calling de kittle black. Dey points de finger uh scorn at yuh and say yo' eye is black. All us kin do is tuh lay low and wait on de Lawd."

"Sho wisht Ah could he'p mahself," Hattie whimpered.

"They *is* help if you knows how tuh git it. Some folks kin hit uh straight lick wid uh crooked stick. They's sich uh thing ez two-headed men."

"You b'lieve in all dat ole stuff 'bout hoodoo and sich lak, Brer Harris?" Hattie watched Harris's face closely.

"Yeah, Ah do, Mrs. Rev'und. Ah done seen things done. Why hit's in de Bible, Sister! Look at Moses. He's de greatest hoodoo man dat God ever made. He went 'way from Pharaoh's palace and stayed in de desert nigh on to forty years and learnt how tuh call God by all his secret names and dat's how he got all dat power. He knowed he couldn't bring off all dem people lessen he had power unekal tuh man! How you reckon he brought on all dem plagues if he didn't had nothin' but human power? And then agin his wife wuz Ethiopian. Ah bet she learnt 'im whut he knowed. Ya, indeed, Sister Pearson. De Bible is de best conjure book in de world."

"Where Ahm goin' ter fin' uh two-headed doctor? Ah don't know nothin' 'bout things lak dat, but if it kin he'p mah condition—"

"An' Dangie Dewoe wuz full uh power, but she dead now, but up t'wards Palatka is uh 'nother one dat's good. He calls hisself War Pete."

The old black woman of the sky chased the red-eyed sun across the sky every evening and smothered him in her cloak at last. This had happened many times. Night usually found John at his brother's house until late or at the bluff Deacon Hambo's who kept filthy epithets upon his tongue for his pastor, but held down the church with an iron hand.

A fresh rumor spread over the nation. It said war. It talked of blood and glory—of travel, of North, of Oceans and transports, of white men and black.

And black men's feet learned roads. Some said good bye cheerfully . . . others fearfully, with terrors of unknown dangers in their mouths . . . others in their eagerness for distance said nothing. The daybreak found them gone. The wind said North. Trains said North. The tides and tongues said North, and men moved like the great herds before the glaciers.

Conscription, uniforms, bands, strutting drum-majors, and the mudsills of the earth arose and skipped like the mountains of Jerusalem on The Day. Lowly minds who knew not their State Capitals were talking glibly of France. Over there. No man's land.

"Gen'l Pushin', Gen'l Punishin', Gen'l Perchin', Gen'l Pershin'. War risk, war bread, insurance, Camp dis-and-dat. Is you heard any news? Dead? Lawd a mussy! Sho hope mah boy come thew aw-right. De black man ain't got no voice but soon ez war come who de first man dey shove in front? De nigger! Ain't it de truth? Bet if Ole Teddy wuz in de chear he'd straighten out eve'ything. Wilson! Stop dat ole lie. Wilson ain't de man Teddy Roosevelt wuz. De fightin'est man and the rulin'est man dat God ever made. Ain't never been two sho 'nuff smart mens in dese United States—Teddy Roosevelt and Booger T. Washington. Nigger so smart he et at de White House. Built uh great big ole school wuth uh thousand dollars, maybe mo'. Teddy wuz allus sendin' fuh 'im tuh git 'im tuh he'p 'im run de Guv'ment. Yeah man, dat's de way it 'tis—niggers think up eve'ything good and de white folks steal it from us. Dass right. Nigger invented de train. White man seen it and run right off and made him one jes' lak it and told eve'ybody he thought it up. Same way wid 'lectwicity. Nigger thought dat up too. DuBois? Who is dat? 'Nother smart nigger? Man, he can't be smart ez Booger T.! Whut did dis DuBois ever do? He writes up books and papers, hunh? Shucks! dat ain't nothin', anybody kin put down words on uh piece of paper. Gimme da paper sack and lemme see dat pencil uh minute. Shucks! Writing! Man Ah thought you wuz talkin' 'bout uh man whut had done sumpin. Ah thought maybe he wuz de man dat could make sidemeat taste lak ham."

Armistice. Demobilized. Home in khaki. "Yeah man, parlez vous, man, don't come bookooin' 'round heah, yuh liable tuh git hurt. Ah could uh married one uh dem French

148

women but shucks, gimme uh brown skin eve'y time. Blacker de berry sweeter de juice. Come tuh mah pick, gimme uh good black gal. De wine wuz sour, and Ah says parlez vous, hell! You gimme mah right change! Comme telly vous. Nar, Ah ain't goin' back tuh no farm no mo'. Ah don't mean tuh say, 'Git up' tuh nary 'nother mule lessen he's setting down in mah lap. God made de world but he never made no hog outa me tuh go 'round rootin' it up. Done done too much bookoo plowing already! Woman quick gimme mah sumpin t' eat. Toot sweet."

World gone money mad. The pinch of war gone, people must spend. Buy and forget. Spend and solace. Silks for sorrows. Jewels to bring back joy. The factories roared and cried, "Hands!" and in the haste and press white hands became scarce. Scarce and dear. Hands? Who cares about the color of hands? We need hands and muscle. The South—land of muscled hands.

"George, haven't you got some relatives and friends down South who'd like a job?"

"Yes, suh."

"Write 'em to come."

Some had railroad fare and quickly answered the call of the North and sent back for others, but this was too slow. The wheels and marts were hungry. So the great industries sent out recruiting agents throughout the South to provide transportation to the willing but poor.

"Lawd, Sanford gettin' dis Nawth bound fever lak eve'y-where else," Hambo complained one Sunday in church. "Elder, you know we done lost two hund'ed members in three months?"

"Co'se Ah knows it, Hambo. Mah pocketbook kin tell it, if nothing else. Iss rainin' in mah meal barrel right uh long."

"Dat's awright. De celery farms is making good. All dese folks gone Nawth makes high wages 'round heah. Less raise de church dues," and it was done.

But a week later Hambo was back. "Looka heah, John, dis thing is gittin' serious sho 'nuff. De white folks is gittin' worried too. Houses empty eve'ywhere. Not half 'nough people tuh work de farms—crops rotting in de ground. Folks plantin' and ain't eben takin' time tuh reap. Mules lef' standin' in de furrers. Some de folks gone 'thout lettin' de families know, and dey say iss de same way, only wurser, all over de South. Dey talkin' 'bout passin' laws tuh keep black folks from buying railroad tickets. Dey tell me dey stopped uh train in Georgy and made all de colored folks git off. Up dere iss awful, de pullman porters tell me. Ride half uh day and see nothin' but farms wid nobody on 'em."

"Yeah," Pearson answered, "had uh letter from mah son in Tennessee. Same way. In some parts de white folks jails all them recruitin' agents so dey hafta git de word uhround in secret. Folks hafta slip off. Drive off in cars and ketch trains further up de line."

"Tell yuh whut Ah seen down tuh Orlando. De man wuz skeered tuh git offa de train, but he seen uh colored man standin' 'round de deepo', so he took and called 'im and he says, 'Ahm uh labor agent, wanta work?' He tole him, 'Yes suh.' 'Well git some mo' men and have 'em down heah tuh meet de Nawth bound train at 2:40 o'clock. Ah'll stick mah hand out de winder and show wid mah fingers how many Ah got transportation for. Y'all watch good and count mah fingers right,' and he done it. Wanted sixteen. He beckoned one of 'em onto de train and fixed up wid him fuh de rest and dey all went wid 'im. Dat's all yuh kin heah. On de streets—in de pool-room—pickin' beans on de farm—in de cook kitchen—over de wash board—before dey go in church and soon ez dey come out, tellin' who done already went and who fixin' tuh go."

"Yeah," agreed Rev. Pearson, "we preachers is in uh tight fix. Us don't know whether tuh g'wan Nawth wid de biggest part of our churches or stay home wid de rest."

"Some of 'em done went. Know one man from Palatka done opened up uh church in Philadelphy and most of 'em is his ole congregation. Zion Hope sho done lost uh many one. Most of 'em young folks too."

"Well maybe they won't stay Nawth. Most of 'em ain't useter col' weather fuh one thing."

"Yeah, but dey'll git used tuh it. Dey up dere now makin' big money and livin' in brick houses. Iss powerful hard tuh git uh countryman outa town. He's jus' ez crazy 'bout it ez uh hog is 'bout town swill. Dey won't be back soon."

Do what they would, the State, County and City all over the South could do little to halt the stampede. The cry of "Goin' Nawth" hung over the land like the wail over Egypt at the death of the first-born. The railroad stations might be watched, but there could be no effective censorship over the mails. No one could keep track of the movements of cars and wagons and mules and men walking. Railroads, hardroads, dirt roads, side roads, roads were in the minds of the black South and all roads led North.

Whereas in Egypt the coming of the locust made desolation, in the farming South the departure of the Negro laid waste the agricultural industry—crops rotted, houses careened crazily in their utter desertion, and grass grew up in streets. On to the North! The land of promise.

CHAPTER 20

✦

H attie was rubbing in the first water and dropping the white things into the wash-pot when Deacon Harris hurried up to her back gate.

"Mawnin', Sister Pearson," opening the gate.

"Howdy do, Deacon?"

"Ain't got no right tuh grumble. How you?"

"Not so many, dis mawnin'. You look lak you in uh kinda slow hurry."

"Nope, jes' anxious tuh tell yuh uh thing uh two."

"If is sumpin tuh better mah condition, hurry up and tell it. God knows Ah sho needs somebody tuh give aid and assistance. Reverend and his gang sho is gripin' me. Ah feels lak uh cat in hell wid no claws."

"First thing, Ah got uh man Ah b'lieve, if de crowd ever git tuh hear 'im, dey'd lak 'im better'n de Rev'und."

"Where he come from?"

"Wes' Floriduh. Man he kin cold preach! Preached over in Goldsborough las' night and strowed fire all over de place. Younger man dan Pearson too."

"Can't you fix it fuh 'im tuh speak at Zion Hope?"

"Sho. Done 'bout got it fixed fuh de fourth Sunday night. Dat ain't Pastoral Sunday, but its de nex' bes'. De crowd'll be almos' ez big."

153

"Dat's fine! Some uh dem niggers don't b'lieve nobody kin preach but John Pearson. Let 'em see. Den maybe dey'll set 'im down. Ah don't keer whut dey do wid 'im. Ah do know one thing, Ah sho got mah belly full. Whus de other things you wuz goin' tuh tell me 'bout?"

"Well, in looking over de books, I saw where mos' of the folks whut would stand up for Rev'und so hard, is gone. If we wuz tuh bring de thing tuh uh vote Ah b'lieve we kin dig up de hidden wedge. Ah been sorta feelin' 'round 'mong some de members and b'lieve de time done come when we kin chop down dis Jonah's gourd vine."

"Dat sho would be all de heben Ah ever want to see. How kin we bring it uhbout? You got tuh have plenty tuh show do some uh dat crowd won't hear it."

"You git uh divorce from 'im. You kin git plenty witnesses tuh bear yuh out in dat. Ah'll be one mahself."

"Chile, he wouldn't keer nothin' 'bout dat. He'd be glad, Ah speck, so he kin run loose wid dat Gertie Burden. Dat's de one he sho 'nuff crazy 'bout."

"Who you tellin'? Ever since she wuz knee high. Us knowed it all de time, but thought yuh didn't."

"He don't try tuh keep it out mah sight. He washes mah face wid her night and day."

"You jokin'!"

"Know whut he told me las' time Ah got 'im 'bout her? Says, 'Don't be callin' dat girl all out her name, Miss Lucy didn't call *you* nothin'.' Deacon Harris, Ah wuz so mad Ah could uh lammed 'im wid lightnin', but how de divorce goin' set 'im down?"

"Yuh see de church punishes fuh things de law don't chastize fuh, and if iss so bad 'til de law'll handle it, de church is bound tuh. Don't need no mo' trial."

"But Ah can't eben start uh divorce trial jus' dry long so."

"You kin pick uh fight outa Sister Beery uh Gertie Burden, can't yuh? Dat'll th'ow de fat in de fiah, and bring eve'ything out in de day light, and when iss all over wid, he'll be uh lost ball in de high grass. Ah sick and tiahed uh all dese so-called

154

no-harm sins. Dis ain't no harm, and dat ain't no harm, and all dese li'l' no-harm sins is whut leads folks straight to hell.''

"De one Ah wants tuh beat de worse is dat ole Beery Buzzard. Right on de church ground she ast me one Sunday, if Miss Lucy's bed wudden still hot when Ah got in it.''

"Jump on her, den.''

"She's rawbony, but she look real strong tuh me. Ole long, tall, black huzzy! Wisht Ah could hurt 'er.''

"She don't eat iron biscuits and she don't sop cement gravy. She kin be hurt, and den agin, you kin git help—not open, yuh know, but on de sly. Somebody tuh hand yuh sumpin jes' when you need it bad.''

"When mus' Ah tackle de slut?''

"De very nex' time Rev'und goes off somewhere tuh preach. If he's dere he'd git it stopped too quick. Befo' it make uhnough disturbment.''

Two incidents nerved Hattie's hand. The first, that same evening Rev. Pearson came in from some carpentry work he had been doing out around Geneva, obviously crestfallen, but nothing she did succeeded in making him tell her the reason.

If she could have seen her husband at noon time of that very same day she would have seen him seated beside the luscious Gertie on a cypress log with her left hand in his and his right arm about her waist.

"John, Ah b'lieve Ahm goin' ter marry.''

"Please, Gertie, don't say dat.''

"You married, ain'tcha? Ahm twenty-two. Papa and mama spectin' me tuh marry some time uh other and dey think Ah oughter take dis chance. You know he got uh big orange grove wid uh house on it and seben hund'ed dollars in de bank.''

"Dat's right, Gertie. Take yo' chance when it comes. Don't think—don't look at me. Ahm all spoilt now. Kiss me one mo' time. Den Ah got tuh go back tuh work. Lawd, Ah hope you be happy. Iss wonderful tuh marry somebody when you wants tuh. You don't keer whut you do tuh please 'em. Some women you wouldn't mind tearin' up de pavements uh hell tuh built 'em uh house, but some you don't give 'em nothin'. You jes' consolate 'em by word uh mouf and fill 'em full uh melody.''

Therefore the next morning at breakfast when John grumbled about the scorched grits and Hattie threatened to dash hot coffee in John's face, he beat her soundly. The muscular exercise burnt up a portion of his grief, but it urged Hattie on. A few days later, when she learned of Gertie's engagement, she was exultant. "Now maybe, it'll hurt 'im, if Ah quit 'im. Gittin' loose from me might gripe 'im now—anyhow it sho ain't gwine he'p 'im none wid Gertie.''

Hattie knew, as do other mortals, that half the joy of quitting any place is the loneliness we leave behind.

CHAPTER 21

✦

The fourth Sunday came shining with the dangerous beauty of flame. Between Sunday School and the 11:00 o'clock service, Andrew Berry called Rev. Pearson aside.

"Is de deacon board tole yuh?"

" 'Bout whut?"

"De new preacher dey got here tuh try out tuhnight?"

"Naw, but Hambo did tell me tuh strow fire dis mawnin'. Reckon he wuz throwin' me uh hint right den."

"Ahm sho he wuz. De Black Herald got it dat dey got *you* on de let-loose and de onliest thing dat keeps some of 'em hangin' on is dey don't b'lieve nobody kin preach lak you, but if dis man dey got here tuhday kin surpass yuh, den dere'll be some changes made. Harris and de Black Dispatch say he kin drive all over yuh."

"Maybe he kin, Andrew. Ain't dat him over dere, talkin' tuh Sister Williams?"

"Yeah. He'll be tuh de service tuh hear *you* so he kin know how tuh do tuhnight when he gits up tuh preach."

John Pearson shook hands politely when he was introduced to Rev. Felton Cozy when he entered the church. Rev. Cozy was cordially invited to sit in the pulpit, which he did very pompously. All during the prayer service that led up to the

157

sermon he was putting on his Oxford glasses, glaring about the church and taking them off again.

Rev. Pearson preached his far-famed, "Dry Bones" sermon, and in the midst of it the congregation forgot all else. The church was alive from the pulpit to the door. When the horse in the valley of Jehoshaphat cried out, "Ha, ha! There never was a horse like me!" He brought his hearers to such a frenzy that it never subsided until two Deacons seized the preacher by the arms and reverently set him down. Others rushed up into the pulpit to fan him and wipe his face with their own kerchiefs.

"Dat's uh preachin' piece uh plunder, you hear me?" Sister Hall gloated. "Dat other man got tuh go some if he specks tuh top dat."

"Can't do it," Brother Jeff avowed, "can't be done."

"Aw, you don't know," contended Sister Scale. "Wait 'til you hear de tother one."

"Elder Pearson ain't preached lak dat in uh long time. Reckon he know?"

"Aw naw. Dey kep' it from 'im. When he know anything, de church'll be done done whut dey going tuh do."

When Rev. Cozy arose that night the congregation slid forward to the edge of its seat.

"Well, y'all done heard one sermon tuhday, and now Ah stand before you, handlin' de Alphabets." He looked all about him to get the effect of his statement. "Furthermo', Ah got uhnother serus job on mah hands. Ahm a race man! Ah solves the race problem. One great problem befo' us tuhday is whut is de blacks gointer do wid de whites?"

After five minutes or more Sister Boger whispered to Sister Pindar, "Ah ain't heard whut de tex' wuz."

"Me neither."

Cozy had put on and removed his glasses with the wide black ribbon eight times.

"And Ah say unto you, de Negro has got plenty tuh feel proud over. Ez fur back ez man kin go in his-to-ree, de black man wuz always in de lead. When Caesar stood on de Roman forum, uccordin' tuh de best authority, uh black man stood beside him. Y'all say 'Amen.' Don't let uh man preach hisself tuh death and y'll set dere lak uh bump on uh log and won't he'p 'im out. Say 'Amen'!!

"And fiftly, Je-sus, Christ, wuz uh colored man hisself and Ah kin prove it! When he lived it wuz hot lak summer time, all de time, wid de sun beamin' down and scorchin' hot—how could he be uh white man in all dat hot sun? Say 'Amen'! Say it lak you mean it, and if yuh do mean it, tell me so! Don't set dere and say nothin'!

"Furthermo' Adam musta been uh colored man 'cause de Bible says God made 'im out de dust uh de earth, and where is anybody ever seen any white dust? Amen! Come on, church, say 'Amen'!

"And twelfth and lastly, all de smartest folks in de world got colored blood in 'em. Wese de smartest people God ever made and de prettiest. Take our race—wese uh mingled people. Jes' lak uh great bouquet uh flowers. Eve'y color and eve'y kind. Nobody don't need tuh go hankerin' after no white womens. We got womens in our own race jes' ez white ez anybody. We got 'em so black 'til lightnin' bugs would follow 'em at twelve o'clock in de day—thinkin' iss midnight and us got 'em in between.

"And nothin' can't go on nowhere but whut dere's uh nigger in it! Say 'Amen'!"

"Amen! He sho is tellin' de truth now!"

At the close of the service, many came forward and shook Cozy's hand and Harris glowed with triumph. He was dry and thirsty for praise in connection with his find so he tackled Sisters Watson and Boger on the way home.

"How y'all lak de sermon tuhnight?"

"Sermon?" Sister Boger made an indecent sound with her lips, "dat wan't no sermon. Dat wuz uh lecture."

"Dat's all whut it wuz," Sister Watson agreed and switched on off.

Harris knew that he must find some other weapon to move the man who had taken his best side-girl from him.

CHAPTER 22

✣

Harris, Hattie and one-eyed Fred Tate went on with their plans for the complete overthrow of Rev. Pearson thru the public chastisement of Sister Berry, but things began to happen in other directions.

While she held a caucus one afternoon with supporters, Hambo sat at Zeke's house and sent one of Zeke's children to find John.

"John, youse in boilin' water and tuh you—look lak 'tain't no help fuh it. Dat damn 'oman you got b'lieves in all kinds uh roots and conjure. She been feedin' you outa her body fuh years. Go home now whilst she's off syndicatin' wid her gang—and rip open de mattress on yo' bed, de pillow ticks, de bolsters, dig 'round de door-steps in front de gate and look and see ain't some uh yo' draws and shirt-tails got pieces cut offa 'em. Hurry now, and come back and let us know whut you find out. G'wan! Don't stop tuh race yo' lip wid mine, and don't try tuh tell me whut you think. Jes' you g'wan do lak Ah tell yuh."

John Pearson went and returned with a miscellany of weird objects in bottles, in red flannel, and in toadskin.

"Lawd, Hambo, here's uh piece uh de tail uh—uh shirt Ah had 'fo' Lucy died. Umph! Umph! Umph!"

"Ha! Ah wuz spectin' dat!"

161

"Whut kin Ah do 'bout it, Hambo?"

"Give it here. Less take it tuh uh hoodoo doctor and turn it back on her, but whut you got tuh do is tuh beat de blood outa her. When you draw her wine dat breaks de spell—don't keer whut it is."

"Don't you fret 'bout dat. Ah 'bominates sich doings. She gointer git her wine drawed dis day, de Lawd bein' may helper. Ahm goin' on home and be settin' dere when she come."

Hattie saw the hole at the gate and the larger one at the front steps before she entered the yard. Inside, the upturned rugs, the ripped-up beds, all had fearful messages for her. Who had done this thing? Had her husband hired a two-headed doctor to checkmate her? How long had he been suspecting her? Where was he now?

"Hattie," John called from the dining-room. She would have bolted, but she saw he made ready to stop her. She stood trembling in the hallway like a bird before a reptile.

"Whut you jumpin' on me fuh?" she cried out as he flung himself upon her.

"You too smart uh woman tuh ast dat, and when Ah git th'ew wid you, you better turn on de fan, and make me some tracks Ah ain't seen befo' do Ahm gointer kill yuh. Hoodooin' me! Stand up dere, 'oman, Ah ain't hit you yet."

And when the neighbors pulled him from her weakening body he dropped into a chair and wept hard. Wept as he had not wept since his daughter's serious illness, emptying out his feelings.

Hattie fled the house, not even waiting to bathe her wounds nor change her clothes. When John's racking sobs had ceased, the stillness after the tumult soothed him. He bathed and slept fourteen hours. In the morning he wrote to each of his children a shy letter. On the third day Hattie struck. He was sued for divorce.

"Ahm sho glad," he told Zeke and Hambo, "she made me

jes' ez happy by quittin' ez Lucy did when she married me."

"Yeah, but if she prove adultery on you in de cotehouse, you sho goin' tuh lose yo' church," Hambo warned. "You got tuh fight it."

CHAPTER 23

✦

Time is long by the courthouse clock.

John Pearson sat restlessly in his seat. Sitting alone
except for Zeke's oldest son. Zeke had to work that day
and his sister-in-law excused herself on the grounds that she
"never had been to any courthouse and she didn't want no
bother with it. Courthouses were bad luck to colored peo-
ple—best not to be 'round there." Many of the people John
had approached for witnesses had said the same thing. "Sho,
sho," they wanted him to win, but "you know dese white
folks—de laws and de cotehouses and de jail houses all
b'longed tuh white folks and po' colored folks—course, Ah
never done nothin' tuh be 'rested 'bout, but— Ah'll be prayin'
fuh yuh, Elder. You bound tuh come out more'n conquer."

So John sat heavily in his seat and thought about that other
time nearly thirty years before when he had sat handcuffed in
Cy Perkins' office in Alabama. No fiery little Lucy here, thrust-
ing her frailty between him and trouble. No sun of love to rise
upon a gray world of hate and indifference. Look how they
huddled and joked on the other side of the room. Hattie, the
destroyer, was surrounded by cheer. Sullen looks his way. Oh
yes, she had witnesses!

Mule-faced, slew-foot Emma Hales was there—rolling her
cock-eye triumphantly at him. Why should she smite out at his

165

head? He remembered the potato pones, the baked chicken with corn-bread dressing, the marble cake, the potato pies that he had eaten in her house many times. He had eaten but never tarried. Never said a word out of the way to her in all his life. He wondered, but Emma knew. She remembered too well how often he had eaten her dinners and hurried away to the arms of the gray-eyed Ethel.

Deacon Harris now outwardly friendly, but he had been told weeks before of Harris's activity against him. Harris should not be hostile, he had taken no woman who loved Harris, for none had wanted him. His incompetence was one of the behind-hand jokes of the congregation. He was blind to human motives but Harris hated him with all the fury of the incompetent for the full-blooded loins.

The toadies were there. Armed with hammers. Ever eager to break the feet of fallen idols. Contemptuous that even the feet of idols should fall among them. No fury so hot as that of a sycophant as he stands above a god that has toppled from a shrine. Faces of gods must not be seen of him. He has worshipped beneath the feet so long that if a god but lowers his face among them, they obscene it with spit. "Ha!" they cried, "what kind of a divinity is this that levels his face with mine? Gods show feet—not faces. Feet that crush—feet that crumble—feet that have no eyes for men's suffering nor ears for agony, lest indeed it be a sweet offering at God's feet. If gods have no power for cruelty, why then worship them? Gods tolerate sunshine, but bestir themselves that men may have storms. From the desolation of our fireplaces, let us declare the glory. If he rides upon the silver-harnessed donkey, let us cry 'hosanna'. If he weeps in compassion, let us lynch him. The sky-rasping mountain-peak fills us with awe, but if it tumbles into the valley it is but boulders. It should be burst asunder. Too long it has tricked us into worship and filled our souls with envy. Crush! Crush! Crush! Lord, thou hast granted thy servant the boon of pounding upon a peak."

So the toadies were there. Vindictively setting the jaw-muscles. Taking folks for fools! But, yes they would testify.

Their injury was great. Let his silk-lined broadcloth look to itself. They meant to rip it from his back today. Think of it, folks! We rip up broadcloth and step on Stetsons. Costly walking-sticks can be made into wood for the cook stove.

Hattie was a goddess for the moment. She sat between the Cherubim on the altar of destruction. She chewed her gum and gloated. Those who held themselves above me, shall be abased. Him who pastored over a thousand shall rule over none. Even as I. His name shall be a hissing, and Hattie's shall be the hand that struck the harp. Selah. Let the world hiss with Hattie. If he but looked with longing! But no, only hurt and scorn was in his eyes. Hurt that so many of his old cronies surrounded her and scorn of herself. Let him ache! If she could but ache him more!

Court was set. The waves of pang that palpitated in the room did not reach up to the judge's bench. No. His honor took his seat as a walrus would among a bed of clams. He sat like a brooding thought with his eyes outside the room. It was just another day with the clerk and the stenographer.

"Hattie Pearson, pwop wah blah!"

John saw the smirking anticipation on the faces of the lawyers, the Court attendants, the white spectators, and felt as if he had fallen down a foul latrine.

"Now, how was it, Hattie?" The look around the room at the other whites, as if to say, "Now listen close. You're going to hear something rich. These niggers!"

"So you wanta quit yo' husband, do you, Hattie? How come? Wasn't he all right? Is *that* him? Why he looks like he oughta be okeh. Had too many women, eh? Didn't see you enough, is that it? Ha! ha! couldn't you get yo'self another man on the side? What you worrying about a divorce for? Why didn't you g'wan leave him and get yourself somebody else? You got divorce in yo' heels, ain't you? You must have the next one already picked out. Ha! ha! Bet he ain't worth the sixty dollars."

So it went on with each of the witnesses in turn. John laughed grimly to himself at the squirming of prospective witnesses who would have fled but found it too late. One by one he saw four of his erstwhile intimates take the stand against him.

Finally the Clerk cast about for defense witnesses, "Say, Reverend, where's *yo'* witnesses?"

"Ain't got none."

"Why? Couldn't you find anybody to witness for you?"

"Yes suh, but who kin tell de truth and swear dat he know uh man ain't done nothin' lak dat?"

The Court laughed, but sobered with a certain respect.

"You want to enter a plea of denial?"

"Naw suh. Ahm goin' tuh say Ah did it all."

"You don't care, then, if Hattie has her freedom?"

"Naw suh, Ah sho don't. Matters uh difference tuh me whut she do, uh where she go."

The fun was over in the Court. Whisperings. Formalities. Papers. It was all over. He saw former friends slinking off to avoid his eye. Hattie was outside, flourishing her papers with over-relish. Loud talking and waving them as if they were a certificate of her virtue.

Hambo's short sturdy legs overtook John as he went down the marble steps, and Hambo's big hand smacked his shoulders.

"Well, you, ole mullet-headed tumble-bug, you!"

John eyed him wearily, "How come didn't but four uh y'all testify aginst me? Ah thought Ah had five friends."

"You ———!" Hambo went into a fit of most obscene swearing, "why didn't you call me fuh uh witness? Didn't Ah tell yuh to?"

"Yeah, but—"

"Take yo' but out my face. Ah wanted tuh git up dere and talk some chat so bad 'til de seat wuz burning me. Ah wanted tuh tell 'bout de mens Ah've knowed Hattie tuh have. She could make up uh 'scursion train all by herself. Ah wanted tuh tell de judge 'bout all dat conjure and all dem roots she been workin' on you. Feedin' you outa her body—."

"And dat's how come Ah didn't have 'em tuh call yuh. Ah

didn't want de white folks tuh hear 'bout nothin' lak dat. Dey knows too much 'bout us as it is, but dey some things dey ain't tuh know. Dey's some strings on our harp fuh us tuh play on and sing all tuh ourselves. Dey thinks wese all ignorant as it is, and dey thinks wese all alike, and dat dey knows us inside and out, but you know better. Dey wouldn't make no great 'miration if you had uh tole 'em Hattie had all dem mens. Dey spectin' dat. Dey wouldn't zarn 'tween uh woman lak Hattie and one lak Lucy, uh yo' wife befo' she died. Dey thinks all colored folks is de same dat way. De only difference dey makes is 'tween uh nigger dat works hard and don't sass 'em, and one dat don't. De hard worker is uh good nigger. De loafer is bad. Otherwise wese all de same. Dass how come Ah got up and said, 'Yeah, Ah done it,' 'cause dey b'lieved it anyhow, but dey b'lieved de same thing 'bout all de rest."

It was late afternoon when John stumbled out of the courthouse with his freedom that had been granted to Hattie.

"You tellin' de truth, John," Hambo agreed at last, "but don't you come puttin' me in wid dem other crabs. Don't you come talkin' tuh *me* lak dat! Ah knock yuh so dead dat yuh can't eben fall. Dey'll have tuh push yuh over. Pick up dem damn big foots uh your'n and come on up tuh mah house. Ah got barbecued spare-ribs and death puddin' ready cooked."

On the way over there was a great deal of surface chatter out of Hambo. John kept silent except when he had to answer. At Hambo's gate he paused. "Ain't it funny, Hambo, you know all uhbout me. Us been friends fuh twenty years. Don't it look funny, dat all mah ole pleasures done got tuh be new sins? Maybe iss 'cause Ahm gittin' ole. Havin' women didn't useter be no sin. Jus' got sinful since Ah got ole."

" 'Tain't de sin so much, John. You know our people is jus' lak uh passle uh crabs in uh basket. De minute dey see one climbin' up too high, de rest of 'em reach up and grab 'em and pull 'im back. Dey ain't gonna let nobody git nowhere if dey kin he'p it."

CHAPTER 24

✦

Second Sunday in the month came rolling around. Pastoral day. Covenant meeting. Communion service. But before all this must come Conference meeting on the Saturday night before, and John knew and everybody knew what the important business of the meeting would be. Zion Hope, after seventeen years, was going to vote on a pastor. Was John Pearson to be given a vote of confidence? Not if Hattie's faction prevailed. Would Felton Cozy receive the call? Not if Hambo and the John Pearson faction was still alive.

Everybody was there. John opened the meeting as usual, then stepped down and turned the chair over to Deacon Hoffman. "I know we all come here tuhnight tuh discuss some things. Ah'd ruther not tuh preside. Deacon Hoffman."

Hoffman took the chair. "Y'all know whut we come here for. Less get thru wid de most urgent business and den we kin take up new business."

He fumbled with the pile of hymnals on the table and waited. There was an uneasy shuffling of feet all over the room, but nobody arose to put a motion. Finally Hattie got up about the middle of the center aisle.

"Brother Cherman."

"Sister Pearson."

171

"Ah wants tuh lay charges 'ginst mah husband."

Hambo was on his feet.

"Brother Cherman! Brother Cherman!"

"Sister Pearson got de flo', Brer Hambo."

"She ain't got no business wid it. She's entirely out uh order."

"She ain't. She says she got charges tuh make uhginst her husband. Dat's whut uh Conference meetin' is for in uh Baptis' Church—tuh hear charges and tuh rectify, ain't it?"

"Yeah," Hambo answered, "but dis woman ain't got no husband in dis church, Brother Cherman. We ain't got no right listenin' tuh nothin' she got tuh say. G'wan back where you come from, Hattie, and try to improve up from uh turpentine still."

"Dat's right, too," shouted Sister Watson, "been divorced two weeks tuh mah knowin'."

"Better set down, Sister Pearson, 'til we kin git dis straight," Hoffman said, reluctantly.

"Iss straight already," Andrew Berry shouted, "when uh woman done gone tuh de cotehouse and divorcted uh man she done got her satisfaction. She ain't got no mo' tuh say. Let de mess drop. Ah ain't goin' tuh hear it."

"And another thing," Hambo put in. "Elder Pearson, you oughta git up and tell whut you found in yo' bed. Course he beat uh, and 'tain't uh man under de sound uh mah voice but whut wouldn't uh done de same. G'wan tell it, Rev'und."

"Naw, no use tuh sturry up de stink. Let it rest. Y'all g'wan do whut yuh want tuh."

There was a long, uncomfortable silence.

"G'wan talk, Harris, you and de rest dat's so anxious tuh ground-mole de pastor, but be sho and tell where *you* wuz yo'self when you seen him do all of dis y'all talkin' 'bout. Be sho and tell dat too. Humph! Youse jes' ez deep in de mud ez he is in de mire."

Another long silence. Finally Hoffman said, "De hour is growin' late. Less table dis discussion and open up de house fuh new business."

Soon the meeting was over. John, Hambo and Berry walked home together.

"If Harris and dem had uh called dat meetin' de nex' day after cote, it would a been uh smuttie rub, nelly eve'ybody would have been uhginst yuh, but two weeks is too long fuh colored tuh hold onto dey feeling. Most of 'em don't keer one way uh 'nother by now."

"Still plenty of 'em is 'ginst me," John spoke at last. "It made mah flesh crawl—Ah felt it so when Ah wuz in dere."

"But dey ain't got no guts. Dey wants tuh do dey work under cover. Dey got tuh fight war if dey wants tuh win dis battle, and dey needs cannon-guns. You can't fight war wid uh brick."

John said nothing. His words had been very few since his divorce. He was going about learning old truths for himself as all men must, and the knowledge he got burnt his insides like acid. All his years as pastor at Zion Hope he had felt borne up on a silken coverlet of friendship, but the trial had shown him that he reclined upon a board, thinly disguised. Hambo had tried vainly to bring him around. A few others had done their share. A few he recognized among the congregation as foes, avowedly; a few friends in the same degree. The rest he saw would fall in line and toady if he triumphed, and execrate him if he failed. He felt inside as if he had been taking calomel. The world had suddenly turned cold. It was not new and shiny and full of laughter. Mouldy, maggoty, full of suck-holes—one had to watch out for one's feet. Lucy must have had good eyes. She had seen so much and told him so much it had wearied him, but she hadn't seen all this. Maybe she had, and spared him. She would. Always spreading carpets for his feet and breaking off the points of thorns. But and oh, her likes were no more on this earth! People whom he had never injured snatched at his shoddy bits of carpet and sharpened the thorns for his flesh.

Nobody pushed him uphill, but everybody was willing to lend a hand to the downward shove. Oh for the wings, for the wings of a dove! That he might see no more what men's faces held!

Sunday afternoon, the sunlight filtered thru the colored glass on the packed and hushed church. Women all in white. Three huge bouquets of red hibiscus below him and behind the covered Communion table. As he stood looking down into the open Bible and upon the snow-white table, his feelings ran riot over his body. "He that soppeth in the dish with me." He knew he could not preach that Last Supper. Not today. Not for many days to come. He turned the pages while he swallowed the lump in his throat and raised:

> Beloved, Beloved, now are we the sons of God
> And it doth not yet appear what we shall be
> But we know, but we know
> When He shall appear, when He shall appear
> We shall be like Him
> We shall see Him as He is.

The audience sang with him. They always sang with him well because group singers follow the leader.

Then he began in a clear, calm voice.

"Brothers and Sisters: De song we jus' sung, and seein' so many uh y'all out here tuh day, it reaches me in uh most particular manner. It wakes up uh whole family uh thoughts, and Ahm gointer speak tuh yuh outa de fullness uh mah heart. Ah want yuh tuh pray wid me whilst Ah break de bread uh life fuh de nourishment uh yo' souls.

"Our theme this morning is the wounds of Jesus. When the father shall ast, 'What are these wounds in thine hand?' He shall answer, 'Those are they with which I was wounded in the house of my friends.' Zach. 13:6.

"We read in the 53rd Chapter of Isaiah where He was wounded for our transgressions and bruised for our iniquities, and the apostle Peter affirms that His blood was spilt from before the foundation of the world.

"I have seen gamblers wounded. I have seen desperadoes

174

wounded; thieves and robbers and every other kind of characters, law-breakers and each one had a reason for his wounds. Some of them was unthoughtful, and some for being overbearing, and some by the doctor's knife, but all wounds disfigure a person.

"Jesus was not unthoughtful. He was not overbearing. He was never a bully. He was never sick. He was never a criminal before the law and yet He was wounded. Now, a man usually gets wounded in the midst of his enemies, but this man was wounded, says the text, in the house of His friends. It is not your enemies that harm you all the time. Watch that close friend. Every believer in Christ is considered His friend, and every sin we commit is a wound to Jesus. The blues we play in our homes is a club to beat up Jesus, and these social card parties.

Jesus have always loved us from the foundation of the world
When God
Stood out on the apex of His power
Before the hammers of creation
Fell upon the anvils of Time and hammered out the ribs of the
      earth
Before He made any ropes
By the breath of fire
And set the boundaries of the ocean by the gravity of His
      power
When God said, ha!
Let us make man
And the elders upon the altar cried, ha!
If you make man, ha!
He will sin
God my master, ha!
Father!! Ha-aa!
I am the teeth of time
That comprehended de dust of de earth
And weighed de hills in scales
That painted de rainbow dat marks de end of de parting storm
Measured de seas in de holler of my hand

That held de elements in a unbroken chain of controllment.
Make man, ha!
If he sin I will redeem him
I'll break de chasm of hell
Where de fire's never quenched
I'll go into de grave
Where de worm never dies, Ah!
So God A'mighty, Ha!
Got His stuff together
He dipped some water out of de mighty deep
He got Him a handful of dirt
From de foundation sills of de earth
He seized a thimble full of breath
From de drums of de wind, ha!
God, my master!
Now I'm ready to make man
Aa-aah!
Who shall I make him after? Ha!
Worlds within worlds begin to wheel and roll
De Sun, Ah!
Gethered up de fiery skirts of her garments
And wheeled around de throne, Ah!
Saying, Ah, make man after me, ha!
God gazed upon the sun
And sent her back to her blood-red socket
And shook His head, ha!
De Moon, ha!
Grabbed up de reins of de tides.
And dragged a thousand seas behind her
As she walked around de throne
Ah-h, please make man after me
But God said "NO!"
De stars bust out from their diamond sockets
And circled de glitterin' throne cryin'
A-aah! Make man after me
God said, "NO!"
I'll make man in my own image, ha!

I'll put him in de garden
And Jesus said, ha!
And if he sin,
I'll go his bond before yo' mighty throne
Ah, He was yo' friend
He made us all, ha!
Delegates to de judgment convention
Ah!
Faith hasn't got no eyes, but she' long-legged
But take de spy-glass of Faith
And look into dat upper room
When you are alone to yourself
When yo' heart is burnt with fire, ha!
When de blood is lopin' thru yo' veins
Like de iron monasters (monsters) on de rail
Look into dat upper chamber, ha!
We notice at de supper table
As He gazed upon His friends, ha!
His eyes flowin' wid tears, ha! He said
"My soul is exceedingly sorrowful unto death, ha!
For this night, ha!
One of you shall betray me, ha!
It were not a Roman officer, ha!
It were not a centurion
But one of you
Who I have chosen my bosom friend
That sops in the dish with me shall betray me."
I want to draw a parable.
I see Jesus
Leaving heben with all of His grandeur
Dis-robin' Hisself of His matchless honor
Yielding up de scepter of revolvin' worlds
Clothing Hisself in de garment of humanity
Coming into de world to rescue His friends.
Two thousand years have went by on their rusty ankles
But with the eye of faith, I can see Him
Look down from His high towers of elevation

177

I can hear Him when He walks about the golden streets
I can hear 'em ring under His footsteps
Sol me-e-e, Sol do
Sol me-e-e, Sol do
I can see Him step out upon the rim bones of nothing
Crying I am de way
De truth and de light
Ah!
God A'mighty!
I see Him grab de throttle
Of de well ordered train of mercy
I see kingdoms crush and crumble
Whilst de archangels held de winds in de corner chambers
I see Him arrive on dis earth
And walk de streets thirty and three years
Oh-h-hhh!
I see Him walking beside de sea of Galilee wid His disciples
This declaration gendered on His lips
"Let us go on to the other side"
God A'mighty!
Dey entered de boat
Wid their oarus (oars) stuck in de back
Sails unfurled to de evenin' breeze
And de ship was now sailin'
As she reached de center of de lake
Jesus was sleep on a pillow in de rear of de boat
And de dynamic powers of nature became disturbed
And de mad winds broke de heads of de Western drums
And fell down on de lake of Galilee
And buried themselves behind de gallopin' waves
And de white-caps marbilized themselves like an army
And walked out like soldiers goin' to battle
And de zig-zag lightning
Licked out her fiery tongue
And de flying clouds
Threw their wings in the channels of the deep
And bedded de waters like a road-plow

And faced de current of de chargin' billows
And de terrific bolts of thunder—they bust in de clouds
And de ship begin to reel and rock
God A'mighty!
And one of de disciples called Jesus
"Master!! Carest Thou not that we perish?"
And He arose
And de storm was in its pitch
And de lightnin' played on His raiments as He stood on the
    prow of the boat
And placed His foot upon the neck of the storm
And spoke to the howlin' winds
And de sea fell at His feet like a marble floor
And de thunders went back in their vault
Then He set down on de rim of de ship
And took de hooks of His power
And lifted de billows in His lap
And rocked de winds to sleep on His arm
And said, "Peace, be still."
And de Bible says there was a calm.
I can see Him wid de eye of faith.
When He went from Pilate's house
Wid the crown of seventy-two wounds upon His head
I can see Him as He mounted Calvary and hung upon de cross
    for our sins.
I can see-eee-ee
De mountains fall to their rocky knees when He cried
"My God, my God! Why hast Thou forsaken me?"
The mountains fell to their rocky knees and trembled like a
    beast
From the stroke of the master's axe
One angel took the flinches of God's eternal power
And bled the veins of the earth
One angel that stood at the gate with a flaming sword
Was so well pleased with his power
Until he pierced the moon with his sword
And she ran down in blood

And de sun
Batted her fiery eyes and put on her judgment robe
And laid down in de cradle of eternity
And rocked herself into sleep and slumber
He died until the great belt in the wheel of time
And de geological strata fell aloose
And a thousand angels rushed to de canopy of heben
With flamin' swords in their hands
And placed their feet upon blue ether's bosom, and looked
     back at de dazzlin' throne
And de arc angels had veiled their faces
And de throne was draped in mournin'
And de orchestra had struck silence for the space of half an
     hour
Angels had lifted their harps to de weepin' willows
And God had looked off to-wards immensity
And blazin' worlds fell off His teeth
And about that time Jesus groaned on de cross, and
Dropped His head in the locks of His shoulder and said, "It
     is finished, it is finished."
And then de chambers of hell exploded
And de damnable spirits
Come up from de Sodomistic world and rushed into de smoky
     camps of eternal night,
And cried, "Woe! Woe! Woe!"
And then de Centurion cried out,
"Surely this is the Son of God."
And about dat time
De angel of Justice unsheathed his flamin' sword and ripped
     de veil of de temple
And de High Priest vacated his office
And then de sacrificial energy penetrated de mighty strata
And quickened de bones of de prophets
And they arose from their graves and walked about in de
     streets of Jerusalem
I heard de whistle of de damnation train

Dat pulled out from Garden of Eden loaded wid cargo goin'
    to hell
Ran at break-neck speed all de way thru de law
All de way thru de prophetic age
All de way thru de reign of kings and judges—
Plowed her way thru de Jurdan
And on her way to Calvary, when she blew for de switch
Jesus stood out on her track like a rough-backed mountain
And she threw her cow-catcher in His side and His blood
    ditched de train
He died for our sins.
Wounded in the house of His friends.
That's where I got off de damnation train
And dat's where you must get off, ha!
For in dat mor-ornin', ha!
When we shall all be delegates, ha!
To dat Judgment Convention
When de two trains of Time shall meet on de trestle
And wreck de burning axles of de unformed ether
And de mountains shall skip like lambs
When Jesus shall place one foot on de neck of de sea, ha!
One foot on dry land, ah
When His chariot wheels shall be running hub-deep in fire
He shall take His friends thru the open bosom of an un-
    clouded sky
And place in their hands de "hosanna" fan
And they shall stand 'round and 'round his beatific throne
And praise His name forever, Amen.

    There had been a mighty response to the sermon all thru its
length. The "bearing up" had been almost continuous, but as
Pearson's voice sank dramatically to the final Amen, Anderson
lifted a chant that kept the church on fire for several seconds
more. During this frenzy John Pearson descended from the
pulpit. Two deacons sprang to assist him at the Communion
table, but he never stopped there. With bowed head he
walked down the center aisle and out of the door—leaving
stupefaction in his wake. Hoffman and Nelse Watson posted

after him and stopped him as he left the grounds, but he brushed off their hands.

"No, chillun, Ah—Ah can't break—can't break de bread wid y'all no mo'," and he passed on.

"Man, ain't you goin' on back tuh yo' pulpit lak you got some sense?" Hambo asked that night. "If you don't some of 'em is sho tuh strow it uhround dat you wuz put out."

"Naw, Hambo. Ah don't want y'all fightin' and scratchin' over me. Let 'em talk all dey wanta."

"Ain't yuh never tuh preach and pastor no mo'?"

"Ah won't say never 'cause— Never is uh long time. Ah don't b'lieve Ahm fitted tuh preach de gospel—unless de world is wrong. Yuh see dey's ready fuh uh preacher tuh be uh man uhmongst men, but dey ain't ready yet fuh 'im tuh be uh man uhmongst women. Reckon Ah better stay out de pulpit and carpenter fuh mah livin'. Reckon Ah kin do dat 'thout uh whole heap uh rigmarole."

But after a while John was not so certain. Several people who formerly had felt that they would rather wait for him several weeks to do a job now discovered that they didn't even have time to get him word. Some who already had work done shot angry, resentful looks after him and resolved not to pay him. It would be lacking in virtue to pay carpenter-preachers who got into trouble with congregations. Two men who had been glad of a chance to work under him on large jobs kept some of his tools that he had loaned them and muttered that it was no more than their due. He had worked them nearly to death in the damp and cold and hadn't paid them. One man grew so indignant that he pawned a spirit-level and two fine saws.

John was accused of killing one man by exposure and over-work. It was well known that he died of tuberculosis several months after he had worked a day or two for John, but nobody was going to be behind hand in accusations. Every bawdy in town wept over her gin and laid her downfall at John's door. He was the father of dozens of children by women he had never seen. Felton Cozy had stepped into his shoes at Zion

Hope and made it a point to adjust his glasses carefully each time he saw John lest too much sin hit him in his virtuous eye. John came to recognize all this eventually and quit telling people his troubles or his plans. He found that they rejoiced at the former and hurried away to do what they could to balk the latter.

As one man said, "Well, since he's down, less keep 'im down."

He saw himself growing shabby. It was hard to find food in variety.

One evening he came home most dejected.

"Whuss de matter, big foots?" Hambo asked. "You look all down in de mouf."

"Look lak lightnin' done struck de po' house. Dey got me in de go-long Ah reckon. All de lies dese folks strowing 'round 'bout me done got some folks in de notion Ah can't drive uh clean nail in they lumber. Look lak dey spectin' uh house Ah build tuh git tuh fornication befo' dey could get de paint on it. Lawd Jesus!"

"Come in and eat some dese snap peas and okra Ah got cooked. It'll give you mo' guts than uh goat."

"Naw thankee, Hambo. Ahm goin' lie down."

He went into his room and shut the door. "Oh Lucy! Lucy! Come git me. You knowed all dis—whut yuh leave me back heah tuh drink dis cup? Please, Lucy, take dis curse offa me. Ah done paid and paid. Ah done wept and Ah done prayed. If you see God where you is over dere ast Him tuh have mercy! Oh Jesus, Oh Jesus, Oh-wonder-workin' God. Take dis burden offa mah sobbin' heart or else take me 'way from dis sin-sick world!"

He sought Lucy thru all struggles of sleep, mewing and crying like a lost child, but she was not there. He was really searching for a lost self and crying like the old witch with her shed skin shrunken by red pepper and salt, "Ole skin, doncher know me?" But the skin was never to fit her again. Sometimes in the dark watches of the night he reproached Lucy bitterly for leaving him. "You meant to do it," he would sob. "Ah saw yo' eyes."

By day he gave no sign of his night-thoughts. His search and his tears were hidden under bed quilts.

When Hambo woke him for breakfast next morning he didn't get up.

"Don't b'lieve Ahm goin' out tuhday, 'cause if Ah meet Cozy wid dat sham-polish smile uh his'n de way Ah feel tuhday, dey'll be tryin' me fuh murder nex' time."

His courage was broken. He lay there in bed and looked back over days that had had their trial and failure. They had all been glorious tomorrows once gilded with promise, but when they had arrived, they turned out to be just days with no more fulfillment—no more glad realities than those that had preceded—more betrayal, so why look forward? Why get up?

His divorce trial stayed with him. He saw that though it was over at the courthouse the judge and jury had moved to the street corners, the church, the houses. He was on trial everywhere, and unlike the courthouse he didn't have a chance to speak in his own behalf.

Sisters White and Carey came over around sundown with a gingerbread and melon-rind preserves.

"Always remembered you had uh sweet tooth," Sister Carey said.

They wanted to know if he was thinking of pastoring again. Certain people had crowded Cozy in, but the real folks had "chunked him out again. His shirttail may be long but we kin still spy his hips."

"He never could preach, nohow," Sister White complained, "and he been strainin' hisself tryin' tuh be stronger wid de women folks than you wuz. Settin' 'round de houses drinkin' and sayin' toastes 'bout, 'Luck tuh de duck dat swims de pond—' Bet if some dese men folks ketch 'im dey'll luck his duck fuh 'im. Since you won't consider, us callin' uh man from Savannah."

184

"Oh, he's more'n welcome to all de women folks," John rejoined.

"Where you keepin' yo'self dese days, anyhow, and whut you doin'?"

"Oh well, Sister White, since yuh ast me, Ah do any kind of uh job Ah kin git tuh make uh dollar, and Ah keeps mahself at home. Sometimes Ah reads de Bible and sometimes Ah don't feel tuh. Den Ah jus' knock uhround from pillar tuh post and sort of dream. Seem lak de dreams is true sho 'nuff sometime—iss so plain befo' me, but after while dey fades. But even while they be fadin', Ah have others. So it goes from day tuh day."

One night John had a dream. Lucy sat beside a stream and cried because she was afraid of a snake. He killed the snake and carried Lucy across in his arms to where Alf Pearson stood at the cross roads and pointed down a white shell road with his walking cane and said, "Distance is the only cure for certain diseases," and he and Lucy went racing down the dusty white road together. Somehow Lucy got lost from him, but there he was on the road—happy because the dead snake was behind him, but crying in his loneliness for Lucy. His sobbing awoke him and he said, "Maybe it's meant for me tuh leave Sanford. Whut Ahm hangin' 'round heah for, anyhow?"

At breakfast he said to Hambo, "Well, Hambo, Ah been thinkin' and thinkin' and Ah done decided dat Ahm goin' tuh give you dis town. You kin have it."

"You better say Joe, 'cause you don't know. Us been here batchin' tuhgether and gittin 'long fine. Ahm liable not tuh let yuh go. Me, Ahm in de 'B' class, be here when you leave and be here when you git back."

"Oh yeah, Ahm goin'. Gointer spread mah jenk in unother town."

"Where you figgerin' on goin'?"

"Don't know yet. When Ah colleck dem few pennies Ah got owing tuh me, iss good bye Katy, bar de door. Some uh dese mawnin's, and it won't be long, you goin' tuh wake up callin' me and Ah'll be gone."

And that is the way he went. It was equally haphazard that he landed in Plant City and went about looking for work.

Several times he passed the big white building that Baptist pride had erected and that he had been invited as Moderator to dedicate, but he passed it now with shuttered eyes. He avoided the people who might remember him.

A week and no work. Walking the streets with his tool kit. Hopeful, smiling ingratiatingly into faces like a dog in a meat house. Desperation nettling his rest.

"How yuh do, suh? Ain't you Rev'und Pearson?"

He looked sidewise quickly into the face of a tall black woman who smiled at him over a gate. Yard chock full of roses in no set pattern.

"Yes ma'am. Well, Ah thank yuh."

"Thought Ah knowed yuh. Heard yuh preach one time at our church."

"Pilgrim Rest Baptis' Church?"

"Dat's right. Dat wuz uh sermon! Come in."

John was tired. He sat heavily upon the step.

"Don't set on de do' step. Elder, heah's uh chear."

"Iss all right, Sister, jus' so Ahm settin' down."

"Naw, it 'tain't. If you set on de steps you'll git all de pains in de house. Ha, ha! Ah reckon you say niggers got all de signs and white folks got all de money."

He sat in the comfortable chair she placed for him and surrendered his hat.

"You got tuh eat supper wid me, lessen you got somewhere puhticklar tuh go. Mah dead husband said you wuz de best preacher ever borned since befo' dey built de Rocky Mountains."

Rev. Pearson laughed a space-filling laugh and waited on her lead.

"You goin' tuh be in our midst uh while?"

"Don't know, Sister—er—"

"Sister Lovelace. Knowed you wouldn't know me. Maybe you would eben disremember mah husband, but Ah sho is glad tuh have yuh in our midst. 'Scuse me uh minute whilst

Ah go skeer yuh up suppin' tuh eat."

She bustled inside but popped out a moment later with a palm-leaf fan.

"Cool yo'self off, Rev'und."

She was back in a few minutes with a pitcher clinking with ice.

"Have uh cool drink uh water, Elder—mighty hot. Ain't aimin' tuh fill yuh up on water, ha! ha! jes' keepin' yuh cool 'til it git done."

From the deep porch, smothered in bucket flowers the street looked so different. The world and all seemed so different—it seemed changed in a dream way. "Maybe nothin' ain't real sho 'nuff. Maybe 'tain't no world. No elements, no nothin'. Maybe wese jus' somewhere in God's mind," but when he wiggled his tired toes the world thudded and throbbed before him.

"Walk right intuh de dinin'-room and take uh chear, Rev'und. Right in dis big chear at de head uh de table. Maybe you kin make uh meal outa dis po' dinner Ah set befo' yuh, but yuh know Ahm uh widder woman and doin' de bes' ah kin."

"Dis po' dinner," consisted of fried chicken, hot biscuits, rice, mashed sweet potatoes, warmed over greens, rice pudding and iced tea.

"You goin' tuh set down and eat wid me, ain't yuh Sister Lovelace?"

"Naw, you go right uhead and eat. Ahm goin' tuh fan de flies. Dey right bad dese days. Ah been laying off tuh have de place screened, but jes' ain't got 'round tuh it. De wire is easy tuh git but dese carpenters 'round heah does sich shabby work 'til Ah ruther not be bothered."

"Ahm uh carpenter."

"You ain't got time tuh fool wid nothin' lak dat. Youse too big uh man."

"Oh, Ah got plenty time."

John felt warm heart-beats that night in his room. He decided to drop a line or two to Sanford. He sent a cheerful line to Hambo first of all.

He wrote to Mamie Lester for news and comfort. She never answered. She felt injured that he should ask such a thing of her. Her indignation burst out of her. She asked many people, "Who do John Pearson think Ah am to be totin' news for him? He ain't nothin'." She said "nothin' " as if she had spat a stinking morsel out of her mouth.

After a long time, when he didn't get an answer, John Pearson understood, and laughed in his bed. The virtuous indignation of Mamie Lester! He could see her again as he had first seen her twenty years ago, as she had tramped into Sanford as barefooted as a yard dog with her skimpy, dirty calico dress and uncombed head; and her guitar hanging around her neck by a dirty red ribbon. How she had tried to pick him up and instead had gotten an invitation to his church. Respectability and marriage to a deacon. She, who had had no consciousness of degradation on the chain-gang and in the brothel, had now discovered she had no time for talk with fallen preachers.

Now that he had work to do, he wrote to George Gibson, asking him to return his tools that George had borrowed. George ignored the letter. He was really angry, "The son of a bum! Won't pay nobody and then come astin' me 'bout dem tools. Ah wish he would come to my face and ast me for 'em."

"Do Pearson owe you too?" another impostor asked.

"Do he? Humph!" he left the feeling that if he only had the money that John Pearson owed him, he need never worry any more.

George was indignant at being asked favors by the weak. His blood boiled.

It became the fashion that whoever was in hard luck, whoever was in debt—John Pearson had betrayed him. Gibson habitually wore a sorrowful look of infinite betrayal. In the meanwhile he used John's tools and came finally to feel that he deserved them.

The next day after the chance meeting John began his task of screening the house of Sally Lovelace, and when he was thru he hesitated over taking the money agreed upon.

"You done fed me more'n de worth uh de job," he said.

"Aw shucks, man, uh woman dat's useter havin' uh man tuh do fuh got tuh wait on somebody. Take de money. You goin' tuh be tuh church dis Sunday?"

"Er—er—Ah don't jus' exactly know, tuh tell yuh truth, Sister Lovelace."

"You jokin', Ah know. Whut you goin' tuh do, if you don't go?"

"Not tuh turn yuh no short answer, Ah don't know."

"Oh come uhlong wid me. Deacon Turner and dem wuz overglad tuh know youse in town. Dey wants yuh tuh run our revival meetin' and dey did say suppin' 'bout yuh preachin' Communion Service."

John flinched, and Mrs. Lovelace saw it. He had to stay to supper then, and at eleven o'clock that night she knew everything. He had not spared himself, and lay with his head in her lap sobbing like a boy of four.

"Well, youse gointer pastor right here at Pilgrim Rest and none of 'em bet' not come 'round here tryin' tuh destroy yo' influence!" Sally blazed. "Ain't doodley squat dey self and goin' 'round tromplin' on folks dat's 'way uhbove 'em." She ran her fingers soothingly thru John's curly hair, and he fell asleep at her knee.

John escorted Sally to church on Sunday and preached.

"Man, you preached!" Sally said warmly during dinner—"only thing Ah heahed so many folks wuz shoutin' Ah couldn't half hear whut you wuz sayin'. You got tuh preach dat at home some time. Special fuh me."

"Preach it anytime you say, but sho 'nuff Ah felt lak ole times tuhday. Felt lak Samson when his hair begin tuh grow out agin."

"Dat's de way fuh yuh tuh feel, John. Oh yeah, 'fo' Ah fuhgit it, dere's uh lady got twenty-seben houses. She wants you tuh look over and patch up wherever dey needs fixin'. Ain't been nothin' done on 'em in two years. 'Bout two weeks steady work and den de Meth'dis' parsonage got tuh have new shingles all over and me and de pastor's wife stands in. Oh you goin' tuh git 'long good in this town.''

John had finished the work on the houses before he found out that they belonged to Sally. The Methodist preacher had paid him. He found himself displeased when he heard of Sally's ownership. What would she with all that property, want with him?

"John, dey's fixin' tuh loose de pastor uh Pilgrim Rest and Ahm quite sho dey's 'bout tuh call you. So go git yo' things tuhgether and less git married tuhday so nobody can't start no talk.''

"Thank yuh, Sally.''

"You wuz aimin' tuh ast me anyhow, wuzn't yuh?''

"Sho wuz, jus' ez soon ez Ah could git tuh de place where Ah could make support fuh yuh.''

"Well, den eve'ything is all right between us. We ain't no chillun no mo', and we don't need tuh go thru uh whole lot uh form and fashion—uh kee-kee-in' and eatin' up pocket handkerchers. You done got de church and dat calls fuh over uh hund'ed dollars uh month and besides whut you got comin' in from carpenterin', and Ah got three hund'ed dollars eve'y month from de rent uh dem houses. Ahm gointer marry you, 'cause Ah love yuh and Ah b'lieve you love me, and 'cause you needs marryin'.''

"Ah sho do, Sally. Less go git married and den got set on de fish pond and ketch us uh mess uh speckled perches fuh supper. Iss uh heap mo' fun than buyin' 'em.''

"Less do. Ah always wanted tuh go sich places, but Oscar never would take me. He wuz uh good puhvider tho'.''

Sally went to bed as a matter of course that night, but John was as shy as a girl—as Lucy had been. His bride wondered at that. He stayed a long time on his knees and Sally never knew how fervently he prayed that Sally might never look at him out of the eyes of Lucy. How abjectly he begged his God to keep his path out of the way of snares and to bear him up lest he bruise his feet against a stumbling-stone, and he vowed vows, if God would only keep his way clean. "Let Lucy see it too, Lawd, so she kin rest. And be so pleased as to cast certain memories in de sea of fuhgitfulness where dey will never rise tuh condemn me in de judgment. Amen and thang God."

CHAPTER 25

❖

S ally, you never ought tuh bought me no car. Dat's too much money tuh take out de bank."

"Who else Ahm goin' tuh spend it on? Ah ain't got uh chick nor uh chile 'ceptin' you. If us ever goin' tuh enjoy ourselves, dis is de world tuh do it in."

"But uh Chevrolet would uh done me. You didn't hafta go buy no Cadillac."

"Wanted yuh tuh set up in uh Cadillac. Dat's yo' weddin' present and our first anniversary present all two together."

"Don't look lak us been married no year, Sally."

"But us is. Dat's 'cause we happy. Tuh think Ah lived tuh git forty-eight 'fo' Ah ever knowed whut love is."

"Ah love you de same way, Sally."

"Look here, John, you ain't been back tuh Sanford since yuh lef' dere."

"Don't keer if Ah never see it no mo' 'twill be too soon."

"Yeah, but honey, yo' buddy Hambo done been down here and paid you uh visit. You oughter go up and spend uh few days wid him, and let dem niggers see how well you gittin' uhlong."

"Awright; when you wanta go?"

"Me? Ah ain't goin'. Ah got mah guava jelly tuh put up. Ah don't trust ridin' so fur in dese cars, nohow. You go and tell me all uhbout it. You been right up under me ever since us been married. Do yuh good tuh git off uh spell."

"Naw, Sally, Ah don't want tuh go 'thout you."

"Fool, how you goin' tuh git uh rest from me and take me wid yuh? You jes' lak uh li'l' boy and dass whut make Ah love yuh so, but you g'wan."

"Naw, Ah promised mahself never tuh sleep uh night 'way from you. Ah don't wanta break mah vow."

Sally exulted in her power and sipped honey from his lips, but she made him go, seeing the pain in John's face at the separation. It was worth her own suffering ten times over to see him that way for her.

The next morning he turned the long nose of his car north-wards and pulled up at Hambo's gate. He was affectionately called every vile name in the language and fed on cow peas, but it seemed good to be there.

Three girls in their late teens stood about his gleaming chariot when he emerged towards sundown to visit the new pastor of Zion Hope church. They admired it loudly and crudely hinted for rides, but John coolly drove off without taking any hints. He was used to admiration of his car now and he had his vows.

Sanford was warm. From what he heard now as he sat under the wheel of his car, Sanford had had not a moment of happiness since he left. Zion Hope was desolate. The choir in heaven had struck silence for the space of half an hour. Wouldn't he consider a recall?

"Naw, it would be de same ole soup-bone—jus' warmed over—dat's all. Ah got uh church bigger'n dis one."

"You could give dem two Sundays and us two, couldn't yuh?" Trustee John Hall pled.

"Ah couldn't see de way tuh be 'way from home dat much. We got too much proppity down dere fuh me tuh look after."

"You got proppity?"

"Yep. Thirty houses tuh rent. Three of 'em brand new. Ah jus' finished 'em off las' week and dey was rented 'fo' de roof got on." He pulled out the huge roll of bills in his pocket,

194

"And Ah jus' got th'ew collectin' de month's rent 'fo' Ah come off."

"God uhmighty man, youse rich! You got bucks above suspicion! Oh shucks, Ah lak tuh fuhgit. Here's dat fo' dollars Ah owe you fuh buildin' dat shed-room 'fo' you went way from here. Ah could uh been done paid yuh, but Ah let talk keep me from it."

John pocketed the money without thanking him. He was grinning sardonically inside, thinking of the heat of the pavements and empty belly, the cold cruelty of want, how much men hit and beat at need when it pleads its gauntness.

But Hall was looking upon plenty and heard no miserable inside gnawings. He heard not John's cold lack of courtesy.

"But you got tuh preach for us dis comin' Sunday. Dat's Communion service. Nobody in de world kin preach dat lak you. Lemme go put it out right now, so's de whole church will know."

"You reckon Ah'd fine uh welcome, Hall?"

"Lawd yes, Rev. Pearson. You left a welcome at Zion Hope when you left here, and you kerried a welcome wid yuh where you went and you brought a welcome back wid you. Come preach for us one mo' time. God a'mighty man, Zion Hope couldn't hold all de folks dat would be dere. We'd lift a collection lak on big rally day."

But John was fingering the four dollars in his mind. He would buy a chicken for supper. Hambo would like that. He would still have enough left over to service the car and take him home.

"Nope, Brother Hall. Thankee for de invitation, but Ah feels to get on back home tuh mah wife. Can't be off too long."

He went on thinking how to show Sally how he could guard their money. Sure three dollars and a quarter would take him home. Maybe less. He wrote Sally about it, wrote her some kind of a letter every day.

While he and Hambo ate supper he heard voices on the porch—gay giggling. He motioned to see who it was.

"Aw, don't go," Hambo continued, " 'Tain't nobody but

dem three li'l' chippies from up de street. Dey gone crazy 'bout dat car. Dat kinda plump one is Ora Patton—jes' ez fresh ez dishwater. Always grinnin' up in some man's face. She's after yo' money right now. I seen her pass here eve'y few minutes—switchin' it and lookin' back at it. Set down and finish yo' supper man. Ah wouldn't pay her no rabbit-foot. She ain't wuth it.''

"Oh, Ah ain't studyin' 'bout dem gals. Jus' don't want no-body tuh mess wid dat car. Dat radiator cap cost twenty-six dollars. Soon ez Ah git th'ew supper Ahm goin' tuh put de car up.''

"You better, dey steal gas 'round here too, but dat Ora is hot after yuh. Her egg-bag ain't gonna rest easy 'til she git nex' tuh yuh. Money crazy. Don't give 'er uh damn cent. Be lak me. Ah wouldn't give uh bitch uh bone if she treed uh terra-pin.''

"She won't git nothin' outa me. Ahm lak de cemetery. Ahm takin' in, but never no put out. 'Ceptin' tuh Sally. She come tuh me in hell and Ah love her for it.''

When John stepped to the door of his car he found Ora on the running-board.

"Hello, daddy.''

"Oh, er, hello, daughter.''

"Don't call me no daughter. Take me fuh uh short ride.''

"Ahm jus' goin' tuh de garage. Two—three blocks, you kin ride dat fur if you wanta.''

"Okay, stingy papa. You eben wear uh stingy-rim hat.'' As the car moved off silently, "Lawd! Ah wonder how it feels tuh be drivin' uh great big ole 'Kitty.' ''

"Kin you drive?''

"Yeah. Lemme take de wheel jes' uh minute. Every body in town is talkin' 'bout dis blue and silver 'Kitty.' You mus' got money's mammy, and grandpa change.''

"Nope, broke ez uh he-ha'nt in torment. All dis b'longs tuh mah wife. Here's de garage. Youse goin' on past it.''

"Aw, gimme uh li'l' bit uh ride, daddy. Don't be so mean and hateful.''

"Nope, Ahm goin' home tuhmorrer and Ah got tuh be in bed so Ah wont go tuh sleep drivin'. Move over."

He reached for the wheel and Ora shot down on the gas. They had nosed out on the road to Osteen before John dared to struggle for possession of the wheel. He hated to think of even a scratch on his paint. Then Ora pulled to the side of the road and parked and threw her arms about his neck and began to cry.

"Ora so bad and now, big, good-looking daddy is mad wid her! Po' Ora can't he'p who she like. Please don't be mad, you pretty, curly headed man."

John unwrapped her arms from 'round his neck gently.

"Well, Ah'll give you uh li'l' short ride, if thass all yuh want. Can't burn up too much gas."

Ora kissed him fleshily, "Dat's right sweet daddy. Let de wheels roll, Ah loves cars. Ride me 'til Ah sweat."

In twenty minutes John was back at the garage and Ora got out pouting. "You mus' figger Ah sweats mighty easy, papa. Ah ast yuh fuh uh ride, but you ain't gimme none hardly."

Friday came and John was glad. He was going home and Ora had failed of her purpose. He was convincing himself that God and Sally could trust him.

Friday night Ora waited for him outside the garage. Standing in the dark of a clump of hibiscus.

"Thought you wuz goin' home Tuesday?" she accused. "Here 'tis Friday night and you ain't gone yet. Ah know you jes' wants tuh git rid uh me."

"Naw, 'tain't dat. First place Ah got uh wife and second place Ahm goin' home sho 'nuff tuhmorrer and therefo' Ah ain't got no time tuh talk. Needs mah sleep. Ahm gittin' ole."

"Aw, naw, you ain't. Come on less take uh good bye ride. Less don't make it stingy lak de las' time. Less ride out tuh Oviedo and back."

She climbed in beside him and put her hands on top of his wheel and eye-balled him sweetly.

"Don't go in dis ole garage. Drive on."

CHAPTER 26

✦

Two hours later when John found himself dressing in a dingy back room in Oviedo he was mad—mad at his weakness—mad at Ora, though she did not know it as yet. She was putting on her shoes on the other side of the bed.

"Daddy, you got twenty dollars you kin gimme? Ah needs so many things and you got plenty."

"Naw, Ah tole you befo' Ah didn't have nothin'. Anything you see on me b'longs tuh Sally." He laced his shoes and put on his vest, then he remembered the remainder of the four dollars he had collected. He pulled it out of his pocket and threw it at her, "Here! Take dat. Iss all Ah got, and Ah hope you rot in hell! Ah hope you never rise in judgment!" He seized his coat and put it on as he hurried out to the car. Ora grabbed up her dress and dashed after him, but he was under the wheel before she left the room, and the motor was humming when she reached the running-board. John viciously thrust her away from the car door without uttering a word. He shoved her so hard that she stumbled into the irrigation ditch, as the car picked up speed and in a moment was a red eye in the distance.

"Well, de ole gray-head bastard! Wonder whut got intuh him? Dis li'l' ole three dollars and some odd change is gonna do me uh lot uh good. Ah been strainin' up tuh git tuh Oviedo

199

fuh de last longest and here Ah is, but Ah wisht Ah knowed whut he flew hot over. Sho do. He done lef' me right where Ah wants tuh be, wid pay-day at de packin' house tuhmorrer. Jes' lak de rabbit in de briar patch.

"Bright and soon tuhmorrer Ah means tuh git me uh bottle uh perfume and some new garters—one red one tuh draw love and one yeller one tuh draw money. Hey, hey, Ah can't lose—not wid de help Ah got."

When Hambo awoke John was gone. Ten dollars was on the dresser beside the clock, and a couple of brand new night-shirts were on a chair.

"Well de hen-fired son-of-a-gun done slipped off and never tole me good bye again! Bet de wop-sided, holler-headed—— thought Ah wuz gointer cry, but he's uh slew-footed liar!" Whereupon Hambo cried over the stove as he fried his sow-bosom and made a flour hoe-cake. Then he found he couldn't eat. Frog in his throat or something so that even his coffee choked him.

The ground-mist lifted on a Florida sunrise as John fled homeward. The car droned, "ho-o-ome" and tortured the man. False pretender! Outside show to the world! Soon he would be in the shelter of Sally's presence. Faith and no questions asked. He had prayed for Lucy's return and God had answered with Sally. He drove on but half-seeing the railroad from looking inward.

The engine struck the car squarely and hurled it about like a toy. John was thrown out and lay perfectly still. Only his foot twitched a little.

"Damned, if I kin see how it happened," the engineer declared. "He musta been sleep or drunk. God knows I blowed for him when I saw him entering on the track. He wasn't drunk. Couldn't smell no likker on him, so he musta been asleep. Hell, now I'm on the carpet for carelessness, but I got witnesses I blowed."

Sally wept hard. "Naw, Ah don't want de seben thousand

dollars from de railroad. Ahm goin' tuh give it tuh his chillun. Naw, Ah don't want none of it. Ah loved 'im too much tuh rob his chillun. Jes' lemme be buried right side uh him when Ah die. Us two off by ourselves. Dass how come Ah bought uh new burial lot. Ah can't git over it, people. Jes' ez he wuz gittin ready tuh live, he got tuh git taken uhway, but Ah got one consolation, he sho wuz true tuh me. Jes' tuh think Ah had tuh live fifty years tuh git one sweet one and it throwed de light over all de other ones. Ah'll never regret uh thing. He wuz true tuh me." She said it over and over. It was a song for her heart and she kept singing it.

She sat shining darkly among the multitudes from all over the State who had come to do John Pearson homage. She sat among his children and made them love her, and when he was laid to rest she was invited to attend memorial services in twenty or more cities.

Sanford was draped in mourning on the second Sunday when Zion Hope held her memorial for John Pearson. The high-backed, throne-like chair was decorated. Tight little sweaty bouquets from the woods and yards were crowded beside ornate floral pieces. Hattie in deep mourning came back to town for the service.

She would have seated herself on the front seat before the flower-banked chair that represented the body of Rev. Pearson, but someone stopped her. "His wife is in de seat," they whispered and showed her to a place among the crowd.

Hambo rolled his eyes at the black-veiled Hattie and gritted his teeth, and whispered to Watson:

"Uhhunh, Ad done heered she wuz comin' back tuh ast us all tuh he'p her git his lodge insurances. Wisht Ah wuz God. Ah'd take and turn her intuh uh damn hawg and den Ah'd concrete de whole world over, so she couldn't find uh durned place tuh root."

And the preacher preached a barbaric requiem poem. On the pale white horse of Death. On the cold icy hands of Death. On the golden streets of glory. Of Amen Avenue. Of Halleluyah Street. On the delight of God when such as John

201

appeared among the singers about His throne. On the weeping sun and moon. On Death who gives a cloak to the man who walked naked in the world. And the hearers wailed with a feeling of terrible loss. They beat upon the O-go-doe, the ancient drum. O-go-doe, O-go-doe, O-go-doe! Their hearts turned to fire and their shinbones leaped unknowing to the drum. Not Kata-Kumba, the drum of triumph, that speaks of great ancestors and glorious wars. Not the little drum of kidskin, for that is to dance with joy and to call to mind birth and creation, but O-go-doe, the voice of Death—that promises nothing, that speaks with tears only, and of the past.

So at last the preacher wiped his mouth in the final way and said, "He wuz uh man, and nobody knowed 'im but God," and it was ended in rhythm. With the drumming of the feet, and the mournful dance of the heads, in rhythm, it was ended.

GLOSSARY

❖

Lidard knot, fat pine wood, generally used for kindling.   p. 2

Chaps, children. Old English use.   p. 13

Buckra, white people.   p. 7

Patter roller, "Patrollers," an organization of the late slavery days that continued through the Reconstruction period. Its main objective was the intimidation of Negroes. Similar to the KKK.   p. 7

Hagar's chillun, Negroes, as against Sarah's children, the whites.
   p. 10

Apin' down de road, running away.   p. 10

Talkin' at de big gate, boasting. Making pretence of bravery behind the back of a powerful person. The allusion comes from the old slavery-time story of the Negro who boasted to another that he had given Ole Massa a good cussin' out. The other one believed him and actually cussed Ole Massa out the next time that he was provoked, and was consequently given a terrible beating. When he was able to be at work again he asked the first Negro how it was that he was not whipped for cussing Ole Massa. The first Negro asked the other if he had cussed Ole Massa to his face. "Sho Ah did. Ain't dat whut you tole me you done?" "Aw naw, fool. Ah ain't tole yuh nothin' uh de kind. As said Ah give Ole Massa uh good cussin' out and Ah did. But when Ah did dat, he wuz settin' up on de verandah and Ah

203

wuz down at de big gate. You sho is uh big fool. It's uh wonder Ole Massa didn't kill you dead." p. 14

Shickalacked, a sound-word to express noise of a locomotive.

p. 15

Nable string, umbilical cord. p. 19

Boogers, head lice. p. 24

Make 'miration, pay flattering compliments. p. 28

Parched peanuts, roasted peanuts. p. 29

Cuffy, West African word meaning Negro. p. 29

Branch, colloquial for small stream. p. 34

Smell hisself, reaching puberty (girl or boy becoming conscious of). p. 45

Lies, stories, tales. p. 61

Tush hawg, wild boar, very vicious, hence a tough character. The tusks of the wild boar curve out and are dangerous weapons.

p. 63

Seben years ain't too long fuh uh coudar tuh wear uh ruffled bosom shirt, it's never too late for me to get even with you.

p. 64

Coudar, a striped, hard-shell fresh-water turtle. p. 64

Bucket flower, potted plant. Old buckets and tubs being used for flower pots. A delicate, well-cared-for person. p. 68

Lay-over, hen with a full drooping comb. Domestic animals and fowls often named for some striking characteristic. p. 77

Jook, the pleasure houses near industrial work. A combination of bawdy, gaming, and dance hall. Incidentally the cradle of the "blues." p. 90

Strowin', spreading abroad. p. 90

Sheep shadney, tea made from sheep droppings. It is sweetened and fed to very young babies. p. 92

Old Hannah, the sun. p. 93

Piney wood rooters, razor-back hogs. Wild hogs. They never get really fat. Inclined to toughness. p. 94

Justice been beggin' righteous tuh do, this is your duty so clearly that it is not debatable. p. 95

He ain't goin' tuh let his shirt-tail touch 'im, he won't sit down. p. 95

Ah'll give mah case tuh Miss Bush and let Mother Green stand mah bond, I'll hide in the woods. I won't need a lawyer because I'll be hidden and no one will have to stand my bond for I have put my person in care of the bushes. p. 95

Squat dat rabbit, let the matter drop, cease. p. 95

De caboose uh dat, the end; i.e., the caboose is the tail end of a freight train. p. 96

Loud talk me, making your side appear right by making more noise than the others. p. 96

Big Moose done come down from de mountain, "When the half-gods go, the gods arrive." He will make all that has gone before seem trivial beside his works. p. 113

Porpoise, pauper. p. 113

Gopher, land tortoise, native of Florida which is locally known as a gopher. p. 113

Better say Joe, that is doubtful. p. 113

Big britches goin' tuh fit li'l' Willie, he who was small is now grown. The underdog is now in position to fight for topdog place. p. 113

Bitter bone, the all-power black-cat bone. Some hoodoo doctors select it by boiling the cat alive with appropriate ceremonies (see "Hoodoo in America," *Journal of American Folk-Lore,* Vol. 44, No. 174, p. 387) and passing the bones thru the mouth until one arrives at the bitter bone. p. 126

Catbone, same as above, though some doctors do not seek a bone by taste (see "Hoodoo in America," *Journal of American Folk-Lore,* Vol. 44, No. 174, p. 396). p. 126

God don't eat okra, okra when cooked is slick and slimy, i.e., God does not like slickness, crooked ways. p. 128

When Ahm dying don't you let 'em take de pillow from under mah head. The pillow is removed from beneath the head of the dying because it is said to prolong the death struggle if left in place. All mirrors, and often all glass surfaces, are covered because it is believed the departing spirit will pause to look in them and if it does they will be forever clouded afterwards. p. 130

Doodly-squat, nothing more valuable than dung. Hence the person is in extreme poverty. p. 138

Cold preach, cold used as a superlative to mean unsurpassed. Very common usage. p. 153

Black Herald, Black Dispatch, Negro gossip. p. 157

In his cooler passages the colored preacher attempts to achieve what to him is grammatical correctness, but as he warms up he goes natural. The "ha" in the sermon marks a breath. The congregation likes to hear the preacher breathing or "straining." p. 157

Sow-bosom, salt pork, a very important item in the diet of both Negroes and poor whites in the South. p. 200

AFTERWORD

❖

ZORA NEALE HURSTON:
"A NEGRO WAY OF SAYING"

I.

The Reverend Harry Middleton Hyatt, an Episcopal priest whose five-volume classic collection, *Hoodoo, Conjuration, Witchcraft, and Rootwork*, more than amply returned an investment of forty years' research, once asked me during an interview in 1977 what had become of another eccentric collector whom he admired. "I met her in the field in the thirties. I think," he reflected for a few seconds, "that her first name was Zora." It was an innocent question, made reasonable by the body of confused and often contradictory rumors that make Zora Neale Hurston's own legend as richly curious and as dense as are the black myths she did so much to preserve in her classic anthropological works. *Mules and Men* and *Tell My Horse,* and in her fiction.

A graduate of Barnard, where she studied under Franz Boas, Zora Neale Hurston published seven books—four novels, two books of folklore, and an autobiography—and more than fifty shorter works between the middle of the Harlem Renaissance and the end of the Korean War, when she was the dominant black woman writer in the United States. The dark obscurity into which her career then lapsed reflects her staunchly independent political stances rather than any deficiency of craft or vision. Virtually ignored after the early fifties, even by the Black Arts movement in the sixties, an otherwise noisy and intense spell of black image- and myth-making that rescued so many black writers from remaindered oblivion, Hurston embodied a more or less harmonious but nevertheless problematic unity of opposites. It is this complexity that refuses to lend itself to the glib categories of "radical" or "conservative," "black" or "Negro," "revolutionary" or "Uncle Tom"—categories of little use in literary criticism. It is this same complexity, embodied in her fiction, that, until Alice Walker published her important essay ("In Search of Zora Neale Hurston") in *Ms.* magazine in 1975, had made Hurston's place in black literary history an ambiguous one at best.

The rediscovery of Afro-American writers has usually turned on larger political criteria, of which the writer's work is supposedly a mere reflection. The deeply satisfying aspect of the rediscovery of Zora Neale Hurston is that black women generated it primarily to establish a maternal literary ancestry. Alice Walker's moving essay recounts her attempts to find Hurston's unmarked grave in the Garden of the Heavenly Rest, a segregated cemetery in Fort Pierce, Florida. Hurston became a metaphor for the black woman writer's search for tradition. The craft of Alice Walker, Gayl Jones, Gloria Naylor, and Toni Cade Bambara bears, in markedly different ways, strong affinities with Hurston's. Their attention to Hurston signifies a novel sophistication in black literature: they read Hurston not only for the spiritual kinship inherent in such relations but because she used black vernacular speech and rituals, in ways subtle and various, to chart the coming to consciousness of black women, so glaringly absent in other black fiction. This use of the vernacular became the fundamental framework for all but one of her novels and is particularly effective in her classic work *Their Eyes Were Watching God,* published in 1937, which is more closely related to Henry James's *The Portrait of a Lady* and Jean Toomer's *Cane* than to Langston Hughes's and Richard Wright's proletarian literature, so popular in the Depression.

The charting of Janie Crawford's fulfillment as an autonomous imagination, *Their Eyes* is a lyrical novel that correlates the need of her first two husbands for ownership of progressively larger physical space (and the gaudy accoutrements of upward mobility) with the suppression of self-awareness in their wife. Only with her third and last lover, a roustabout called Tea Cake whose unstructured frolics center around and about the Florida swamps, does Janie at last bloom, as does the large pear tree that stands beside her grandmother's tiny log cabin.

> She saw a dust bearing bee sink into the sanctum of a
> bloom; the thousand sister calyxes arch to meet the love
> embrace and the ecstatic shiver of the tree from root to
> tiniest branch creaming in every blossom and frothing with
> delight. So this was a marriage!

To plot Janie's journey from object to subject, the narrative of the novel shifts from third to a blend of first and third person (known as "free indirect discourse"), signifying this awareness of self in Janie. *Their Eyes* is a bold feminist novel, the first to be explicitly so in the Afro-American tradition. Yet in its concern with the project of finding a voice, with language as an instrument of injury and salvation, of selfhood and empowerment, it suggests many of the themes that inspirit Hurston's oeuvre as a whole.

II.

One of the most moving passages in American literature is Zora Neale Hurston's account of her last encounter with her dying mother, found in a chapter entitled "Wandering" in her autobiography, *Dust Tracks on a Road* (1942):

> As I crowded in, they lifted up the bed and turned it around so that Mama's eyes would face east. I thought that she looked to me as the head of the bed reversed. Her mouth was slightly open, but her breathing took up so much of her strength that she could not talk. But she looked at me, or so I felt, to speak for her. She depended on me for a voice.

We can begin to understand the rhetorical distance that separated Hurston from her contemporaries if we compare this passage with a similar scene published just three years later in *Black Boy* by Richard Wright, Hurston's dominant black male contemporary and rival: "Once, in the night, my mother called me to her bed and told me that she could not endure the pain, and she wanted to die. I held her hand and begged her to be quiet. That night I ceased to react to my mother; my feelings were frozen." If Hurston represents her final moments with her mother in terms of the search for voice, then Wright attributes to a similar experience a certain "somberness of spirit that I was never to lose," which "grew into a symbol in my mind, gathering to itself . . . the poverty, the ignorance, the helplessness. . . ." Few authors in the black tradition have less in common than Zora Neale Hurston and Richard Wright. And whereas Wright would reign through the forties as our predominant author, Hurston's fame reached its zenith in 1943 with a *Saturday Review* cover story honoring the success of *Dust Tracks.* Seven years later, she would be serving as a maid in Rivo Alto, Florida; ten years after that she would die in the County Welfare Home in Fort Pierce, Florida.

How could the recipient of two Guggenheims and the author of four novels, a dozen short stories, two musicals, two books on black mythology, dozens of essays, and a prizewinning autobiography virtually "disappear" from her readership for three full decades? There are no easy answers to this quandary, despite the concerted attempts of scholars to resolve it. It is clear, however, that the loving, diverse, and enthusiastic responses that Hurston's work engenders today were not shared by several of her influential black male contemporaries. The reasons for this are complex and stem largely from what we might think of as their "racial ideologies."

Part of Hurston's received heritage—and perhaps the paramount received notion that links the novel of manners in the Harlem Renaissance, the social realism of the thirties, and the cultural nationalism of the Black Arts movement—was the idea that racism had reduced black people to mere ciphers, to beings who only react to an omnipresent racial oppression, whose culture is "deprived" where different, and whose psyches are in the main "pathological." Albert Murray, the writer and social critic, calls this "the Social Science Fiction Monster." Socialists, separatists, and civil rights advocates alike have been devoured by this beast.

Hurston thought this idea degrading, its propagation a trap, and railed against it. It was, she said, upheld by "the sobbing school of Negrohood who hold that nature somehow has given them a dirty deal." Unlike Hughes and Wright, Hurston chose deliberately to ignore this "false picture that distorted. . . ." Freedom, she wrote in *Moses, Man of the Mountain,* "was something internal. . . . The man himself must make his own emancipation." And she declared her first novel a manifesto against the "arrogance" of whites assuming that "black lives are only defensive reactions to white actions." Her strategy was not calculated to please.

What we might think of as Hurston's mythic realism, lush and dense within a lyrical black idiom, seemed politically retrograde to the proponents of a social or critical realism. If Wright, Ellison, Brown, and Hurston were engaged in a battle over ideal fictional modes with which to represent the Negro, clearly Hurston lost the battle.

But not the war.

After Hurston and her choice of style for the black novel

211

were silenced for nearly three decades, what we have witnessed since is clearly a marvelous instance of the return of the repressed. For Zora Neale Hurston has been "rediscovered" in a manner unprecedented in the black tradition: several black women writers, among whom are some of the most accomplished writers in America today, have openly turned to her works as sources of narrative strategies, to be repeated, imitated, and revised, in acts of textual bonding. Responding to Wright's critique, Hurston claimed that she had wanted at long last to write a black novel, and "not a treatise on sociology." It is this urge that resonates in Toni Morrison's *Song of Solomon* and *Beloved,* and in Walker's depiction of Hurston as our prime symbol of "racial health—a sense of black people as complete, complex, *undiminished* human beings, a sense that is lacking in so much black writing and literature." In a tradition in which male authors have ardently denied black literary paternity, this is a major development, one that heralds the refinement of our notion of tradition: Zora and her daughters are a tradition-within-the-tradition, a black woman's voice.

The resurgence of popular and academic readerships of Hurston's works signifies her multiple canonization in the black, the American, and the feminist traditions. Within the critical establishment, scholars of every stripe have found in Hurston texts for all seasons. More people have read Hurston's works since 1975 than did between that date and the publication of her first novel, in 1934.

III.

Rereading Hurston, I am always struck by the density of intimate experiences she cloaked in richly elaborated imagery. It is this concern for the figurative capacity of black language, for what a character in *Mules and Men* calls "a hidden meaning, jus' like de Bible . . . de inside meanin' of words," that unites Hurston's anthropological studies with her fiction. For the folklore Hurston collected so meticulously as Franz Boas's student at Barnard became metaphors, allegories, and performances in her novels, the traditional recurring canonical metaphors of black culture. Always more of a novelist than a social scientist, even Hurston's academic collections center on the quality of imagination that makes these lives whole and splendid. But it is in the novel that Hurston's use of the black idiom realizes its fullest effect. In *Jonah's Gourd Vine,* her first novel, for instance, the errant preacher, John, as described by Robert Hemenway "is a poet who graces his world with language but cannot find the words to secure his own personal grace." This concern for language and for the "natural" poets who "bring barbaric splendor of word and song into the very camp of the mockers" not only connects her two disciplines but also makes of "the suspended linguistic moment" a thing to behold indeed. Invariably, Hurston's writing depends for its strength on the text, not the context, as does John's climactic sermon, a *tour de force* of black image and metaphor. Image and metaphor define John's world; his failure to interpret himself leads finally to his self-destruction. As Robert Hemenway, Hurston's biographer, concludes, "Such passages eventually add up to a theory of language and behavior."

Using "the spy-glass of Anthropology," her work celebrates rather than moralizes; it shows rather than tells, such that "both behavior and art become self-evident as the tale texts and hoodoo rituals accrete during the reading." As author, she functions as "a midwife participating in the birth of a body of folklore, . . . the first wondering contacts with natural law." The myths she describes so accurately are in fact "alternative modes for perceiving reality," and never just condescending depictions of the quaint. Hurston sees "the Dozens," for example, that age-old black ritual of graceful insult, as, among other things, a verbal defense of the sanctity of the family, conjured through ingenious plays on words. Though attacked by Wright and virtually ignored by his literary heirs, Hurston's ideas about language and craft undergird many of the most successful contributions to Afro-American literature that followed.

213

IV.

We can understand Hurston's complex and contradictory legacy more fully if we examine *Dust Tracks on a Road,* her own controversial account of her life. Hurston did make significant parts of herself up, like a masquerader putting on a disguise for the ball, like a character in her fictions. In this way, Hurston *wrote* herself, and sought in her works to rewrite the "self" of "the race," in its several private and public guises, largely for ideological reasons. That which she chooses to reveal is the life of her imagination, as it sought to mold and interpret her environment. That which she silences or deletes, similarly, is all that her readership would draw upon to delimit or pigeonhole her life as a synecdoche of "the race problem," an exceptional part standing for the debased whole.

Hurston's achievement in *Dust Tracks* is twofold. First, she gives us a *writer's* life, rather than an account, as she says, of "the Negro problem." So many events in this text are figured in terms of Hurston's growing awareness and mastery of books and language, language and linguistic rituals as spoken and written both by masters of the Western tradition and by ordinary members of the black community. These two "speech communities," as it were, are Hurston's great sources of inspiration not only in her novels but also in her autobiography.

The representation of her sources of language seems to be her principal concern, as she constantly shifts back and forth between her "literate" narrator's voice and a highly idiomatic black voice found in wonderful passages of free indirect discourse. Hurston moves in and out of these distinct voices effortlessly, seamlessly, just as she does in *Their Eyes* to chart Janie's coming to consciousness. It is this usage of a *divided* voice, a double voice unreconciled, that strikes me as her great achievement, a verbal analogue of her double experiences as a woman in a male-dominated world and as a black person in a nonblack world, a woman writer's revision of W. E. B. Du Bois's metaphor of "double consciousness" for the hyphenated African-American.

Her language, variegated by the twin voices that intertwine throughout the text, retains the power to unsettle:

There is something about poverty that smells like death.
Dead dreams dropping off the heart like leaves in a dry
season and rotting around the feet; impulses smothered too
long in the fetid air of underground caves. The soul lives
in a sickly air. People can be slave-ships in shoes.

Elsewhere she analyzes black "idioms" used by a culture "raised on simile and invective. They know how to call names," she concludes, then lists some, such as 'gator-mouthed, box-ankled, puzzle-gutted, shovel-footed: "Eyes looking like skint-ginny nuts, and mouth looking like a dishpan full of broke-up crockery!"

Immediately following the passage about her mother's death, she writes:

The Master-Maker in His making had made Old Death.
Made him with big, soft feet and square toes. Made him
with a face that reflects the face of all things, but neither
changes itself, nor is mirrored anywhere. Made the body of
death out of infinite hunger. Made a weapon of his hand to
satisfy his needs. This was the morning of the day of the
beginning of things.

Language, in these passages, is not merely "adornment," as Hurston described a key black linguistic practice; rather, manner and meaning are perfectly in tune: she says the thing in the most meaningful manner. Nor is she being "cute," or pandering to a condescending white readership. She is "naming" emotions, as she says, in a language both deeply personal and culturally specific.

The second reason that *Dust Tracks* succeeds as literature

arises from the first: Hurston's unresolved tension between her double voices signifies her full understanding of modernism. Hurston uses the two voices in her text to celebrate the psychological fragmentation both of modernity and of the black American. As Barbara Johnson has written, hers is a rhetoric of division, rather than a fiction of psychological or cultural unity. Zora Neale Hurston, the "real" Zora Neale Hurston that we long to locate in this text, dwells in the silence that separates these two voices: she is both, and neither; bilingual, and mute. This strategy helps to explain her attraction to so many contemporary critics and writers, who can turn to her works again and again only to be startled at her remarkable artistry.

But the life that Hurston could write was not the life she could live. In fact, Hurston's life, so much more readily than does the standard sociological rendering, reveals how economic limits determine our choices even more than does violence or love. Put simply, Hurston wrote well when she was comfortable, wrote poorly when she was not. Financial problems—book sales, grants and fellowships too few and too paltry, ignorant editors and a smothering patron—produced the sort of dependence that affects, if not determines, her style, a relation she explored somewhat ironically in "What White Publishers Won't Print." We cannot oversimplify the relation between Hurston's art and her life; nor can we reduce the complexity of her postwar politics, which, rooted in her distaste for the pathological image of blacks, were markedly conservative and Republican.

Nor can we sentimentalize her disastrous final decade, when she found herself working as a maid on the very day the *Saturday Evening Post* published her short story "Conscience of the Court" and often found herself without money, surviving after 1957 on unemployment benefits, substitute teaching, and welfare checks. "In her last days," Hemenway concludes dispassionately, "Zora lived a difficult life—alone, proud, ill, obsessed with a book she could not finish."

The excavation of her buried life helped a new generation

read Hurston again. But ultimately we must find Hurston's legacy in her art, where she "ploughed up some literacy and laid by some alphabets." Her importance rests with the legacy of fiction and lore she constructed so cannily. As Hurston herself noted, "Roll your eyes in ecstasy and ape his every move, but until we have placed something upon his street corner that is our own, we are right back where we were when they filed our iron collar off." If, as a friend eulogized, "She didn't come to you empty," then she does not leave black literature empty. If her earlier obscurity and neglect today seem inconceivable, perhaps now, as she wrote of Moses, she has "crossed over."

HENRY LOUIS GATES, JR.

SELECTED BIBLIOGRAPHY

WORKS BY ZORA NEALE HURSTON

Jonah's Gourd Vine. Philadelphia: J. B. Lippincott, 1934.

Mules and Men. Philadelphia: J. B. Lippincott, 1935.

Their Eyes Were Watching God. Philadelphia: J. B. Lippincott, 1937.

Tell My Horse. Philadelphia: J. B. Lippincott, 1938.

Moses, Man of the Mountain. Philadelphia: J. B. Lippincott, 1939.

Dust Tracks on a Road. Philadelphia: J. B. Lippincott, 1942.

Seraph on the Suwanee. New York: Charles Scribner's Sons, 1948.

I Love Myself When I Am Laughing . . . & Then Again When I Am Looking Mean and Impressive: A Zora Neale Hurston Reader. Edited by Alice Walker. Old Westbury, N.Y.: The Feminist Press, 1979.

The Sanctified Church. Edited by Toni Cade Bambara. Berkeley: Turtle Island, 1981.

Spunk: The Selected Short Stories of Zora Neale Hurston. Berkeley: Turtle Island, 1985.

WORKS ABOUT ZORA NEALE HURSTON

Baker, Houston A., Jr. *Blues, Ideology, and Afro-American Literature: A Vernacular Theory,* pp. 15–63. Chicago: University of Chicago Press, 1984.

Bloom, Harold, ed. *Zora Neale Hurston.* New York: Chelsea House, 1986.

———, ed. *Zora Neale Hurston's "Their Eyes Were Watching God."* New York: Chelsea House, 1987.

Byrd, James W. "Zora Neale Hurston: A Novel Folklorist." *Tennessee Folklore Society Bulletin* 21 (1955): 37–41.

Cooke, Michael G. "Solitude: The Beginnings of Self-Realization in Zora Neale Hurston, Richard Wright, and Ralph Ellison." In Michael G. Cooke, *Afro-American Literature in the Twentieth Century,* pp. 71–110. New Haven: Yale University Press, 1984.

Dance, Daryl C. "Zora Neale Hurston." In *American Women Writers: Bibliographical Essays,* edited by Maurice Duke, et al. Westport, Conn.: Greenwood Press, 1983.

Gates, Henry Louis, Jr. "The Speakerly Text." In Henry Louis Gates, Jr., *The Signifying Monkey,* pp. 170–217. New York: Oxford University Press, 1988.

Giles, James R. "The Significance of Time in Zora Neale Hurston's *Their Eyes Were Watching God."* *Negro American Literature Forum* 6 (Summer 1972): 52–53, 60.

Hemenway, Robert E. *Zora Neale Hurston: A Literary Biography.* Chicago: University of Illinois Press, 1977.

Holloway, Karla. *The Character of the Word: The Texts of Zora Neale Hurston.* Westport, Conn.: Greenwood Press, 1987.

Holt, Elvin. "Zora Neale Hurston." In *Fifty Southern Writers After 1900,* edited by Joseph M. Flura and Robert Bain, pp. 259–69. Westport, Conn.: Greenwood Press, 1987.

Howard, Lillie Pearl. *Zora Neale Hurston.* Boston: Twayne, 1980.

———. "Zora Neale Hurston." In *Dictionary of Literary Biography,* vol. 51, edited by Trudier Harris, pp. 133–45. Detroit: Gale, 1987.

Jackson, Blyden. "Some Negroes in the Land of Goshen." *Tennessee Folklore Society Bulletin* 19 (4) (December 1953): 103–7.

Johnson, Barbara. "Metaphor, Metonymy, and Voice in *Their Eyes.*" In *Black Literature and Literary Theory,* edited by Henry Louis Gates, Jr., pp. 205–21. New York: Methuen, 1984.

———. "Thresholds of Difference: Structures of Address in Zora Neale Hurston." In *"Race," Writing and Difference,* edited by Henry Lewis Gates, Jr. Chicago: University of Chicago Press, 1986.

Jordan, June. "On Richard Wright and Zora Neale Hurston." *Black World* 23 (10) (August 1974): 4–8.

Kubitschek, Missy Dehn. " 'Tuh de Horizon and Back': The Female Quest in *Their Eyes.*" *Black American Literature Forum* 17 (3) (Fall 1983): 109–15.

Lionnet, Françoise. "Autoethnography: The Anarchic Style of *Dust Tracks on a Road.*" In Françoise Lionnet, *Autobiographical Voices: Race, Gender, Self-Portraiture,* pp. 97–130. Ithaca: Cornell University Press, 1989.

Lupton, Mary Jane. "Zora Neale Hurston and the Survival of the Female." *Southern Literary Journal* 15 (Fall 1982): 45–54.

Meese, Elizabeth. "Orality and Textuality in Zora Neale Hurston's *Their Eyes.*" In Elizabeth Meese, *Crossing the Double Cross: The Practice of Feminist Criticism,* pp. 39–55. Chapel Hill: University of North Carolina Press, 1986.

Newson, Adele S. *Zora Neale Hurston: A Reference Guide.* Boston: G. K. Hall, 1987.

Rayson, Ann. *"Dust Tracks on a Road:* Zora Neale Hurston and the Form of Black Autobiography." *Negro American Literature Forum* 7 (Summer 1973): 42–44.

Sheffey, Ruthe T., ed. *A Rainbow Round Her Shoulder: The Zora Neale Hurston Symposium Papers.* Baltimore: Morgan State University Press, 1982.

Smith, Barbara. "Sexual Politics and the Fiction of Zora Neale Hurston." *Radical Teacher* 8 (May 1978): 26–30.

Stepto, Robert B. *From Behind the Veil.* Urbana: University of Illinois Press, 1979.

Walker, Alice. "In Search of Zora Neale Hurston." *Ms.*, March 1975, pp. 74–79, 85–89.

Wall, Cheryl A. "Zora Neale Hurston: Changing Her Own Words." In *American Novelists Revisited: Essays in Feminist Criticism,* edited by Fritz Fleischmann, pp. 370–93. Boston: G. K. Hall, 1982.

Washington, Mary Helen. "Zora Neale Hurston: A Woman Half in Shadow." Introduction to *I Love Myself When I Am Laughing,* edited by Alice Walker. Old Westbury, N.Y.: Feminist Press, 1979.

———. " 'I Love the Way Janie Crawford Left Her Husbands': Zora Neale Hurston's Emergent Female Hero." In Mary Helen Washington, *Invented Lives: Narratives of Black Women, 1860–1960.* New York: Anchor Press, 1987.

Willis, Miriam. "Folklore and the Creative Artist: Lydia Cabrera and Zora Neale Hurston." *CLA Journal* 27 (September 1983): 81–90.

Wolff, Maria Tai. "Listening and Living: Reading and Experience in *Their Eyes.*" *BALF* 16 (1) (Spring 1982): 29–33.

CHRONOLOGY

❖

January 7, 1891	Born in Eatonville, Florida, the fifth of eight children, to John Hurston, a carpenter and Baptist preacher, and Lucy Potts Hurston, a former schoolteacher.
September 1917– June 1918	Attends Morgan Academy in Baltimore, completing the high school requirements.
Summer 1918	Works as a waitress in a nightclub and a manicurist in a black-owned barbershop that serves only whites.
1918–19	Attends Howard Prep School, Washington, D.C.
1919–24	Attends Howard University; receives an associate degree in 1920.
1921	Publishes her first story, "John Redding Goes to Sea," in the *Stylus,* the campus literary society's magazine.
December 1924	Publishes "Drenched in Light," a short story, in *Opportunity.*
1925	Submits a story, "Spunk," and a play, *Color Struck,* to *Opportunity*'s literary contest. Both

win second-place awards; publishes "Spunk" in the June number.

1925–27   Attends Barnard College, studying anthropology with Franz Boas.

1926   Begins field work for Boas in Harlem.

January 1926   Publishes "John Redding Goes to Sea" in *Opportunity*.

Summer 1926   Organizes *Fire!* with Langston Hughes and Wallace Thurman; they publish only one issue, in November 1926. The issue includes Hurston's "Sweat."

August 1926   Publishes "Muttsy" in *Opportunity*.

September 1926   Publishes "Possum or Pig" in the *Forum*.

September–November 1926   Publishes "The Eatonville Anthology" in the *Messenger*.

1927   Publishes *The First One,* a play, in Charles S. Johnson's *Ebony and Topaz*.

February 1927   Goes to Florida to collect folklore.

May 19, 1927   Marries Herbert Sheen.

September 1927   First visits Mrs. Rufus Osgood Mason, seeking patronage.

October 1927   Publishes an account of the black settlement at St. Augustine, Florida, in the *Journal of Negro History;* also in this issue: "Cudjo's Own Story of the Last African Slaver."

December 1927   Signs a contract with Mason, enabling her to return to the South to collect folklore.

1928   Satirized as "Sweetie Mae Carr" in Wallace Thurman's novel about the Harlem Renaissance *Infants of the Spring;* receives a bachelor of arts degree from Barnard.

January 1928   Relations with Sheen break off.

May 1928	Publishes "How It Feels to Be Colored Me" in the *World Tomorrow*.
1930–32	Organizes the field notes that become *Mules and Men*.
May–June 1930	Works on the play *Mule Bone* with Langston Hughes.
1931	Publishes "Hoodoo in America" in the *Journal of American Folklore*.
February 1931	Breaks with Langston Hughes over the authorship of *Mule Bone*.
July 7, 1931	Divorces Sheen.
September 1931	Writes for a theatrical revue called *Fast and Furious*.
January 1932	Writes and stages a theatrical revue called *The Great Day*, first performed on January 10 on Broadway at the John Golden Theatre; works with the creative literature department of Rollins College, Winter Park, Florida, to produce a concert program of Negro music.
1933	Writes "The Fiery Chariot."
January 1933	Stages *From Sun to Sun* (a version of *Great Day*) at Rollins College.
August 1933	Publishes "The Gilded Six-Bits" in *Story*.
1934	Publishes six essays in Nancy Cunard's anthology, *Negro*.
January 1934	Goes to Bethune-Cookman College to establish a school of dramatic arts "based on pure Negro expression."
May 1934	Publishes *Jonah's Gourd Vine*, originally titled *Big Nigger;* it is a Book-of-the-Month Club selection.

September 1934	Publishes "The Fire and the Cloud" in the *Challenge.*
November 1934	*Singing Steel* (a version of *Great Day*) performed in Chicago.
January 1935	Makes an abortive attempt to study for a Ph.D in anthropology at Columbia University on a fellowship from the Rosenwald Foundation. In fact, she seldom attends classes.
August 1935	Joins the WPA Federal Theatre Project as a "dramatic coach."
October 1935	*Mules and Men* published.
March 1936	Awarded a Guggenheim Fellowship to study West Indian Obeah practices.
April–September 1936	In Jamaica.
September–March 1937	In Haiti; writes *Their Eyes Were Watching God* in seven weeks.
May 1937	Returns to Haiti on a renewed Guggenheim.
September 1937	Returns to the United States; *Their Eyes Were Watching God* published, September 18.
February–March 1938	Writes *Tell My Horse;* it is published the same year.
April 1938	Joins the Federal Writers Project in Florida to work on *The Florida Negro.*
1939	Publishes "Now Take Noses" in *Cordially Yours.*
June 1939	Receives an honorary Doctor of Letters degree from Morgan State College.
June 27, 1939	Marries Albert Price III in Florida.

Summer 1939	Hired as a drama instructor by North Carolina College for Negroes at Durham; meets Paul Green, professor of drama, at the University of North Carolina.
November 1939	*Moses, Man of the Mountain* published.
February 1940	Files for divorce from Price, though the two are reconciled briefly.
Summer 1940	Makes a folklore-collecting trip to South Carolina.
Spring–July 1941	Writes *Dust Tracks on a Road*.
July 1941	Publishes "Cock Robin, Beale Street" in the *Southern Literary Messenger*.
October 1941–January 1942	Works as a story consultant at Paramount Pictures.
July 1942	Publishes "Story in Harlem Slang" in the *American Mercury*.
September 5, 1942	Publishes a profile of Lawrence Silas in the *Saturday Evening Post*.
November 1942	*Dust Tracks on a Road* published.
February 1943	Awarded the Anisfield-Wolf Book Award in Race Relations for *Dust Tracks;* on the cover of the *Saturday Review*.
March 1943	Receives Howard University's Distinguished Alumni Award.
May 1943	Publishes "The 'Pet Negro' Syndrome" in the *American Mercury*.
November 1943	Divorce from Price granted.
June 1944	Publishes "My Most Humiliating Jim Crow Experience" in the *Negro Digest*.
1945	Writes *Mrs. Doctor;* it is rejected by Lippincott.

March 1945	Publishes "The Rise of the Begging Joints" in the *American Mercury.*
December 1945	Publishes "Crazy for This Democracy" in the *Negro Digest.*
1947	Publishes a review of Robert Tallant's *Voodoo in New Orleans* in the *Journal of American Folklore.*
May 1947	Goes to British Honduras to research black communities in Central America; writes *Seraph on the Suwanee;* stays in Honduras until March 1948.
September 1948	Falsely accused of molesting a ten-year-old boy and arrested; case finally dismissed in March 1949.
October 1948	*Seraph on the Suwanee* published.
March 1950	Publishes "Conscience of the Court" in the *Saturday Evening Post,* while working as a maid in Rivo Island, Florida.
April 1950	Publishes "What White Publishers Won't Print" in the *Saturday Evening Post.*
November 1950	Publishes "I Saw Negro Votes Peddled" in the *American Legion* magazine.
Winter 1950–51	Moves to Belle Glade, Florida.
June 1951	Publishes "Why the Negro Won't Buy Communism" in the *American Legion* magazine.
December 8, 1951	Publishes "A Negro Voter Sizes Up Taft" in the *Saturday Evening Post.*
1952	Hired by the *Pittsburgh Courier* to cover the Ruby McCollum case.
May 1956	Receives an award for "education and human relations" at Bethune-Cookman College.

June 1956	Works as a librarian at Patrick Air Force Base in Florida; fired in 1957.
1957–59	Writes a column on "Hoodoo and Black Magic" for the *Fort Pierce Chronicle.*
1958	Works as a substitute teacher at Lincoln Park Academy, Fort Pierce.
Early 1959	Suffers a stroke.
October 1959	Forced to enter the St. Lucie County Welfare Home.
January 28, 1960	Dies in the St. Lucie County Welfare Home of "hypertensive heart disease"; buried in an unmarked grave in the Garden of Heavenly Rest, Fort Pierce.
August 1973	Alice Walker discovers and marks Hurston's grave.
March 1975	Walker publishes "In Search of Zora Neale Hurston," in *Ms.,* launching a Hurston revival.

About the author

About the book

Insights,
Interviews
& More ...

Read on

"In Search of Zora Neale Hurston"

by Alice Walker

The work of Zora Neale Hurston was relatively unknown in 1975, when Alice Walker, beloved author of The Color Purple, *wrote her groundbreaking essay "In Search of Zora Neale Hurston" (Ms. magazine, March 1975). In this seminal piece, reprinted here in its entirety, Walker illuminates her idol's life and work.*

"ON JANUARY 16, 1959, Zora Neale Hurston, suffering from the effects of a stroke and writing painfully in longhand, composed a letter to the 'editorial department' of Harper & Brothers inquiring if they would be interested in seeing 'the book I am laboring upon at the present—a life of Herod the Great.' One year and twelve days later, Zora Neale Hurston died without funds to provide for her burial, a resident of the St. Lucie County, Florida, Welfare Home. She lies today in an unmarked grave in a segregated cemetery in Fort Pierce, Florida, a resting place generally symbolic of the black writer's fate in America.

"Zora Neale Hurston is one of the most significant unread authors in America, the author of two minor classics and four other major books."

—*Robert Hemenway, "Zora Hurston and the Eatonville Anthropology," from* The Harlem Renaissance Remembered, *edited by Arna Bontemps (Dodd, 1972)*

Courtesy of the Estate of Carl Van Vechten, Joseph Solomon, Executor

ON AUGUST 15, 1973, I wake up just as the plane is lowering over Sanford, Florida, which means I am also looking down on Eatonville, Zora Neale Hurston's birthplace. I recognize it from Zora's description in *Mules and Men*: "the city of five lakes, three croquet courts, three hundred brown skins, three hundred good swimmers, plenty guavas, two schools, and no jailhouse." Of course I cannot see the guavas, but the five lakes are still there, and it is the lakes I count as the plane prepares to land in Orlando.

From the air, Florida looks completely flat, and as we near the ground this impression does not change. This is the first time I have seen the interior of the state, which Zora wrote about so well, but there are the acres of orange groves, the sand, mangrove trees, and scrub pine that I know from her books. Getting off the plane I walk through the hot moist air of midday into the tacky but air-conditioned airport. I search for Charlotte Hunt, my companion on the Zora Hurston expedition. She lives in Winter Park, Florida, very near Eatonville, and is writing her graduate dissertation on Zora. I see her waving—a large pleasant-faced white woman in dark glasses. We have written to each other for several weeks, swapping our latest finds (mostly hers) on Zora, and trying to make sense out of the mass of information obtained (often erroneous or simply confusing) from Zora herself—through her stories and autobiography—and from people who wrote about her.

Eatonville has lived for such a long time in my imagination that I can hardly believe it will be found existing in its own right. ▶

"In Search of Zora Neale Hurston" *(continued)*

But after twenty minutes on the expressway, Charlotte turns off and I see a small settlement of houses and stores set with no particular pattern in the sandy soil off the road. We stop in front of a neat gray building that has two fascinating signs: EATONVILLE POST OFFICE and EATONVILLE CITY HALL.

Inside the Eatonville City Hall half of the building, a slender, dark, brown-skin woman sits looking through letters on a desk. When she hears we are searching for anyone who might have known Zora Neale Hurston, she leans back in thought. Because I don't wish to inspire foot-dragging in people who might know something about Zora they're not sure they should tell, I have decided on a simple, but I feel profoundly *useful*, lie.

"I am Miss Hurston's niece," I prompt the young woman, who brings her head down with a smile.

"I think Mrs. Moseley is about the only one still living who might remember her," she says.

"Do you mean *Mathilda* Moseley, the woman who tells those 'woman-is-smarter-than-man' lies in Zora's book?"

"Yes," says the young woman. "Mrs. Moseley is real old now, of course. But this time of day, she should be at home."

I stand at the counter looking down on her, the first Eatonville resident I have spoken to. Because of Zora's books, I feel I know something about her; at least I know what the town she grew up in was like years before she was born.

"Tell me something," I say, "do the schools teach Zora's books here?"

"No," she says, "they don't. I don't think most people know anything about Zora Neale Hurston, or knew about any of the great things she did. She was a fine lady. I've read all of her books myself, but I don't think many other folks in Eatonville have."

"Many of the church people around here, as I understand it," says Charlotte in a murmured aside, "thought Zora was pretty loose. I don't think they appreciated her writing about them."

"Well," I say to the young woman, "thank you for your help." She clarifies her directions to Mrs. Moseley's house and smiles as Charlotte and I turn to go.

"The letter to Harper's does not expose a publisher's rejection of an unknown masterpiece, but it does reveal how the bright promise of the

Harlem Renaissance deteriorated for many of the writers who shared in its exuberance. It also indicates the personal tragedy of Zora Neale Hurston: Barnard graduate, author of four novels, two books of folklore, one volume of autobiography, the most important collector of Afro-American folklore in America, reduced by poverty and circumstance to seek a publisher by unsolicited mail."

—*Robert Hemenway*

"Zora Neale Hurston was born in 1901, 1902, or 1903—depending on how old she felt herself to be at the time someone asked."

—*Librarian, Beinecke Library, Yale University*

THE MOSELEY HOUSE is small and white and snug, its tiny yard nearly swallowed up by oleanders and hibiscus bushes. Charlotte and I knock on the door. I call out. But there is no answer. This strikes us as peculiar. We have had time to figure out an age for Mrs. Moseley—not dates or a number, just old. I am thinking of a quivery, bedridden invalid when we hear the car. We look behind us to see an old black-and-white Buick—paint peeling and grillwork rusty—pulling into the drive. A neat old lady in a purple dress and white hair is straining at the wheel. She is frowning because Charlotte's car is in the way.

Mrs. Moseley looks at us suspiciously. "Yes, I knew Zora Neale," she says, unsmilingly and with a rather cold stare at Charlotte (who I imagine feels very *white* at that moment), "but that was a long time ago, and I don't want to talk about it."

"Yes ma'am," I murmur, bringing all my sympathy to bear on the situation.

"Not only that," Mrs. Moseley continues, "I've been sick. Been in the hospital for an operation. Ruptured artery. The doctors didn't believe I was going to live, but you see me alive, don't you?"

"Looking well, too," I comment.

Mrs. Moseley is out of her car. A thin, sprightly woman with nice gold-studded false teeth, uppers and lowers. I like her because she stands there *straight* beside her car, with a hand on her hip and her straw pocketbook on her arm. She wears white T-strap shoes with heels that show off her well-shaped legs.

"I'm eighty-two years old, you know," she says. "And I just can't remember things the way I used to. Anyhow, Zora Neale left here to go ▶

5

to school and she never really came back to live. She'd come here for material for her books, but that was all. She spent most of her time down in South Florida."

"You know, Mrs. Moseley, I saw your name in one of Zora's books."

"You did?" She looks at me with only slightly more interest. "I read some of her books a long time ago, but then people got to borrowing and borrowing and they borrowed them all away."

"I could send you a copy of everything that's been reprinted." I offer. "Would you like me to do that?"

"No," says Mrs. Moseley promptly. "I don't read much any more. Besides, all of that was *so* long ago. . . ."

Charlotte and I settle back against the car in the sun. Mrs. Moseley tells us at length and with exact recall every step in her recent operation, ending with: "What those doctors didn't know—when they were expecting me to die (and they didn't even think I'd live long enough for them to have to take out my stitches!)—is that Jesus is the best doctor, and if *He* says for you to get well, that's all that counts."

With this philosophy, Charlotte and I murmur quick assent: being Southerners and church bred, we have heard that belief before. But what we learn from Mrs. Moseley is that she does not remember much beyond the year 1938. She shows us a picture of her father and mother and says that her father was Joe Clarke's brother. Joe Clarke, as every Zora Hurston reader knows, was the first mayor of Eatonville; his fictional counterpart is Jody Starks of *Their Eyes Were Watching God*. We also get directions to where Joe Clarke's store *was*—where Club Eaton is now. Club Eaton, a long orange-beige nightspot we had seen on the main road, is apparently famous for the good times in it regularly had by all. It is, perhaps, the modern equivalent of the store porch, where all the men of Zora's childhood came to tell "lies," that is, black folktales, that were "made and used on the spot," to take a line from Zora. As for Zora's exact birthplace, Mrs. Moseley has no idea.

After I have commented on the healthy growth of her hibiscus bushes, she becomes more talkative. She mentions how much she *loved* to dance, when she was a young woman, and talks about how good her husband was. When he was alive, she says, she was completely happy because he allowed her to be completely free. "I was so free I had to pinch myself sometimes to tell if I was a married woman."

Relaxed now, she tells us about going to school with Zora. "Zora and I went to the same school. It's called Hungerford High now. It *was* only to the eighth-grade. But our teachers were so good that by the time you left you knew college subjects. When I went to Morris Brown in Atlanta, the teachers there were just teaching me the same things I had already learned right in Eatonville. I wrote Mama and told her I was going to come home and help her with her babies. I wasn't learning anything new."

"Tell me something, Mrs. Moseley," I ask, "why do you suppose Zora was against integration? I read somewhere that she was against school desegregation because she felt it was an insult to black teachers." ▶

"In Search of Zora Neale Hurston" *(continued)*

"Oh, one of them [white people] came around asking me about integration. One day I was doing my shopping. I heard 'em over there talking about it in the store, about the schools. And I got on out of the way because I knew if they asked me, they wouldn't like what I was going to tell 'em. But they came up and asked me anyhow. 'What do you think about this integration?' one of them said. I acted like I thought I had heard wrong. 'You're asking *me* what *I* think about integration?' I said. 'Well, as you can see I'm just an old colored woman'—I was seventy-five or seventy-six then—'and this is the first time anybody ever asked me about integration. And nobody asked my grandmother what she thought, either, but her daddy was one of you all.'" Mrs. Moseley seems satisfied with this memory of her rejoinder. She looks at Charlotte. "I have the blood of three races in my veins," she says belligerently, "white, black, and Indian, and nobody asked me *anything* before."

"Do you think living in Eatonville made integration less appealing to you?"

"Well, I can tell you this: I have lived in Eatonville all my life and I've been in the governing of this town. I've been everything but Mayor and I've been *assistant* Mayor. Eatonville was and is an all-black town. We have our own police department, post office, and town hall. Our own school and good teachers. Do I need integration?

"They took over Goldsboro, because the black people who lived there never incorporated like we did. And now I don't even know if any black folks live there. They built big houses up there around the lakes. But we didn't let that happen in Eatonville, and we don't sell land to just anybody. And you see, we're still here."

When we leave, Mrs. Moseley is standing by her car, waving. I think of the letter Roy Wilkins wrote to a black newspaper blasting Zora Neale for her lack of enthusiasm about the integration of schools. I wonder if he knew the experience of Eatonville she was coming from. Not many black people in America have come from a self-contained, all-black community where loyalty and unity are taken for granted. A place where black pride is nothing new.

There is, however, one thing Mrs. Moseley said that bothered me.

"Tell me, Mrs. Moseley," I had asked, "Why is it that thirteen years after Zora's death, no marker has been put on her grave?"

And Mrs. Moseley answered: "The reason she doesn't have a stone is because she wasn't buried here. She was buried down in South Florida somewhere. I don't think anybody really knew where she was."

"Only to reach a wider audience, need she ever write books—because she is a perfect book of entertainment in herself. In her youth she was always getting scholarships and things from wealthy white people, some of whom simply paid her just to sit around and represent the Negro race for them, she did it in such a racy fashion. She was full of sidesplitting anecdotes, humorous tales, and tragicomic stories, remembered out of her life in the South as a daughter of a traveling minister of God. She could make you laugh one minute and cry the next. To many of her white friends, no doubt, she was a perfect 'darkie,' in the nice meaning they give the term—that is, a naïve, childlike, sweet, humorous, and highly colored Negro.

"But Miss Hurston was clever, too—a student who didn't let college give her a broad 'a' and who had great scorn for all pretentions, academic or otherwise. That is why she was such a fine folklore collector, able to go among the people and never act as if she had been to school at all. Almost nobody else could stop the average Harlemite on Lenox Avenue and measure his head with a strange-looking, anthropological device and not get bawled out for the attempt, except Zora, who used to stop anyone whose head looked interesting, and measure it."

—*Langston Hughes,* The Big Sea *(Knopf)*

"What does it matter what white folks must have thought about her?"
—*Student, Black Women Writers Class, Wellesley College*

MRS. SARAH PEEK PATTERSON is a handsome, red-haired woman in her late forties, wearing orange slacks and gold earrings. She is the director of Lee-Peek Mortuary in Fort Pierce, the establishment that handled Zora's burial. Unlike most black funeral homes in Southern towns that sit like palaces among the general poverty, Lee-Peek has a run-down, *small* look. Perhaps this is because it is painted purple and white, as are its Cadillac chariots. These colors do not age well. The rooms are cluttered and grimy, and the bathroom is a tiny, stale-smelling prison, with a bottle of black hair dye (apparently used to touch up the hair of the corpses) dripping into the face bowl. Two pine burial boxes are resting in the bathtub. ▶

"In Search of Zora Neale Hurston" *(continued)*

Mrs. Patterson herself is pleasant and helpful.

"As I told you over the phone, Mrs. Patterson," I begin, shaking her hand and looking into her penny-brown eyes, "I am Zora Neale Hurston's niece, and I would like to have a marker put on her grave. You said, when I called you last week, that you could tell me where the grave is."

By this time I am, of course, completely into being Zora's niece, and the lie comes with perfect naturalness to my lips. Besides, as far as I'm concerned, she *is* my aunt—and that of all black people as well.

"She was buried in 1960," exclaims Mrs. Patterson. "That was when my father was running this funeral home. He's sick now or I'd let you talk to him. But I know where she's buried. She's in the old cemetery, the Garden of the Heavenly Rest, on Seventeenth Street. Just when you go in the gate there's a circle, and she's buried right in the middle of it. Hers is the only grave in that circle—because people don't bury in that cemetery any more."

She turns to a stocky, black-skinned woman in her thirties, wearing a green polo shirt and white jeans cut off at the knee. "This lady will show you where it is," she says.

"I can't tell you how much I appreciate this," I say to Mrs. Patterson, as I rise to go. "And could you tell me something else? You see, I never met my aunt. When she died I was still a junior in high school. But could you tell me what she died of, and what kind of funeral she had?"

"I don't know exactly what she died of," Mrs. Patterson says, "I know she didn't have any money. Folks took up a collection to bury her. . . . I believe she died of malnutrition."

"Malnutrition?"

Outside, in the blistering sun, I lean my head against Charlotte's even more blistering cartop. The sting of the hot metal only intensifies my anger. *"Malnutrition?"* I manage to mutter. "Hell, our condition hasn't changed *any* since Phillis Wheatley's time. *She* died of malnutrition!"

"Really?" says Charlotte, "I didn't know that."

"One cannot overemphasize the extent of her commitment. It was so great that her marriage in the spring of 1927 to Herbert Sheen was short-lived. Although divorce did not come officially until 1931, the two separated amicably after only a few months, Hurston to continue her collecting, Sheen to attend Medical School. Hurston never married again."

—*Robert Hemenway*

"WHAT IS YOUR NAME?" I ask the woman who has climbed into the back seat.

"Rosalee," she says. She has a rough, pleasant voice, as if she is a singer who also smokes a lot. She is homely, and has an air of ready indifference.

"Another woman came by here wanting to see the grave," she says, lighting up a cigarette. "She was a little short, dumpty white lady from one of these Florida schools. Orlando or Daytona. But let me tell you something before we get started. All I know is where the cemetery is. I don't know one thing about that grave. You better go back in and ask her to draw you a map." ▶

"In Search of Zora Neale Hurston" *(continued)*

A few moments later, with Mrs. Patterson's diagram of where the grave is, we head for the cemetery.

We drive past blocks of small, pastel-colored houses and turn right onto Seventeenth Street. At the very end, we reach a tall curving gate, with the words "Garden of Heavenly Rest" fading into the stone. I expected, from Mrs. Patterson's small drawing, to find a small circle—which would have placed Zora's grave five or ten paces from the road. But the "circle" is over an acre large and looks more like an abandoned field. Tall weeds choke the dirt road and scrape against the sides of the car. It doesn't help either that I step out into an active anthill.

"I don't know about y'all," I say, "but I don't even believe this." I am used to the haphazard cemetery-keeping that is traditional in most Southern black communities, but this neglect is staggering. As far as I can see there is nothing but bushes and weeds, some as tall as my waist. One grave is near the road, and Charlotte elects to investigate it. It is fairly clean, and belongs to someone who died in 1963.

Rosalee and I plunge into the weeds; I pull my long dress up to my hips. The weeds scratch my knees, and the insects have a feast. Looking back, I see Charlotte standing resolutely near the road.

"Aren't you coming?" I call.

"No," she calls back. "I'm from these parts and I know what's out there." She means snakes.

"Shit," I say, my whole life and the people I love flashing melodramatically before my eyes. Rosalee is a few yards to my right.

"How're you going to find anything out here?" she asks. And I stand still a few seconds, looking at the weeds. Some of them are quite pretty, with tiny yellow flowers. They are thick and healthy, but dead weeds under them have formed a thick gray carpet on the ground. A snake could be lying six inches from my big toe and I wouldn't see it. We move slowly, very slowly, our eyes alert, our legs trembly. It is hard to tell where the center of the circle is since the circle is not really round, but more like half of something round. There are things crackling and hissing in the grass. Sandspurs are sticking to the inside of my skirt. Sand and ants cover my feet. I look toward the road and notice that there are, indeed, *two* large curving stones, making an entrance and exit to the cemetery. I take my bearings from them and try to navigate to exact center. But the center of anything can be very large, and a grave is not a pinpoint. Finding the grave seems positively hopeless. There is only one thing to do:

"Zora!" I yell as loud as I can (causing Rosalee to jump), "are you out here?"

"If she is, I sho hope she don't answer you. If she do, I'm gone."

"Zora!" I call again, "I'm here. Are you?"

"If she is," grumbles Rosalee, "I hope she'll keep it to herself."

"Zora!" Then I start fussing with her. "I hope you don't think I'm going to stand out here all day, with these snakes watching me and these ants having a field day. In fact, I'm going to call you just one or two more times." On a clump of dried grass, near a small busy tree, my eye falls on one of the largest bugs I have ever seen. It is on its back, and is as large as three of my fingers. I walk toward it, and yell "Zo-ra!" and my foot sinks into a hole. I look down. I am standing in a sunken rectangle that is about six feet long and about three or four feet wide. I look up to see where the two gates are.

"Well," I say, "this is the center, or approximately anyhow. It's also the only sunken spot we've found. Doesn't this look like a grave to you?"

"For the sake of not going no farther through these bushes," Rosalee growls, "yes, it do."

"Wait a minute," I say, "I have to look around some more to be sure this is the only spot that resembles a grave. But you don't have to come."

Rosalee smiles—a grin, really—beautiful and tough.

"Naw," she says, "I feels sorry for you. If one of these snakes got a hold of you out here by yourself I'd feel *real* bad." She laughs. "I done come this far, I'll go on with you."

"Thank you, Rosalee," I say. "Zora thanks you too."

"Just as long as she don't try to tell me in person," she says, and together we walk down the field.

"The gusto and flavor of Zora Neal[e] Hurston's storytelling, for example, long before the yarns were published in *Mules and Men* and other books, became a local legend which might . . . have spread further under different conditions. A tiny shift in the center of gravity could have made them bestsellers."
　　　　　　—*Arna Bontemps*, Personals *(Paul Bremen, Ltd., London; 1963)*

"Bitter over the rejection of her folklore's value, especially in the black community, frustrated by what she felt was her failure to convert the ▶

"In Search of Zora Neale Hurston" *(continued)*

Afro-American world view into the forms of prose fiction, Hurston finally gave up."
—*Robert Hemenway*

WHEN CHARLOTTE AND I drive up to the Merritt Monument Company, I immediately see the headstone I want.

"How much is this one?" I ask the young woman in charge, pointing to a tall black stone. It looks as majestic as Zora herself must have been when she was learning voodoo from those root doctors down in New Orleans.

"Oh, *that* one," she says, "that's our finest. That's Ebony Mist."

"Well, how much is it?"

"I don't know. But wait," she says, looking around in relief, "here comes somebody who'll know."

A small, sunburned man with squinty green eyes come sup. He must be the engraver, I think, because his eyes are contracted into slits as if he has been keeping stone dust out of them for years.

"That's Ebony Mist," he says. "That's our best."

"How much is it?" I ask, beginning to realize I probably *can't* afford it.

He gives me a price that would feed a dozen Sahelian drought victims for three years. I realize I must honor the dead, but between the dead great and the living starving, there is no choice.

"I have a lot of letters to be engraved," I say, standing by the plain gray marker I have chosen. It is pale and ordinary, not at all like Zora, and makes me momentarily angry that I am not rich.

We got into his office and I hand him a
sheet of paper that has:

ZORA NEALE HURSTON
"A GENIUS OF THE SOUTH"
NOVELIST   FOLKLORIST
ANTHROPOLOGIST
1960

"A genius of the South" is from one of Jean
Toomer's poems.

"Where is this grave?" the monument man
asks. "If it's in a new cemetery, the stone has to
be flat."

"Well, it's not a new cemetery and Zora—
my aunt—doesn't need anything flat because
with the weeds out there, you'd never be able
to see it. You'll have to go out there with me."

He grunts.

"And take a long pole and 'sound' the
spot," I add. "Because there's no way of telling
it's a grave, except that it's sunken."

"Well," he says, after taking my money and
writing up a receipt, in the full awareness that
he's the only monument dealer for miles, "you
take this flag" (he hands me a four-foot-long
pole with a red-metal marker on top) "and
take it out to the cemetery and put it where
you think the grave is. It'll take us about three
weeks to get the stone out there."

I wonder if he knows he is sending me to
another confrontation with the snakes. He
probably does. Charlotte has told me she
will cut my leg and suck out the blood, if I
am bit.

"At least send me a photograph when it's
done, won't you?"

He says he will. ▶

"In Search of Zora Neale Hurston" *(continued)*

"Hurston's return to her folklore-collecting in December of 1927 was made possible by Mrs. R. Osgood Mason, an elderly white patron of the arts, who at various times also helped Langston Hughes, Alain Locke, Richmond Barthe, and Miguel Covarrubias. Hurston apparently came to her attention through the intercession of Locke, who frequently served as a kind of liaison between the young black talent and Mrs. Mason. The entire relationship between this woman and the Harlem Renaissance deserves extended study, for it represents much of the ambiguity involved in white patronage of black artists. All her artists were instructed to call her 'Godmother'; there was a decided emphasis on the 'primitive' aspects of black culture, apparently a holdover from Mrs. Mason's interest in the Plains Indians. In Hurston's case there were special restrictions imposed by her patron: although she was to be paid a handsome salary for her folklore collecting, she was to limit her correspondence and publish nothing of her research without prior approval."

—*Robert Hemenway*

"You have to read the chapters Zora *left out* of her autobiography."
—*Student, Special Collections Room*
Beinecke Library, Yale University

DR. BENTON, a friend of Zora's and a practicing M.D. in Fort Pierce, is one of those old, good-looking men whom I always have trouble not liking. (It no longer bothers me that I may be constantly searching for father figures; by this time, I have found several and dearly enjoyed knowing them all.) He is shrewd, with steady brown eyes under hair that is almost white. He is probably in his seventies, but doesn't look it. He carries himself with dignity, and has cause to be proud of the new clinic where he now practices medicine. His nurse looks at us with suspicion, but Dr. Benton's eyes have the penetration of a scalpel cutting through skin. I guess right away that if he knows anything at all about Zora Hurston, he will not believe I am her niece. "Eatonville?" Dr. Benton says, leaning forward in his chair, looking first at me, then at Charlotte. "Yes, I know Eatonville, I grew up not far from there. I knew the whole bunch of Zora's family." (He looks at the shape of my cheekbones, the size of my eyes, and the nappiness of my hair.) "I knew her daddy. The old man. He was a hardworking, Christian man. Did the best he could for his family. He was the mayor of Eatonville for a while, you know.

"My father was the mayor of Goldsboro. You probably never heard of it. It never incorporated like Eatonville did, and has just about disappeared. But Eatonville is still all-black."

He pauses and looks at me. "And you're Zora's niece," he says wonderingly.

"Well," I say with shy dignity, yet with some tinge, I hope, of a nineteenth-century blush, "I'm illegitimate. That's why I never knew Aunt Zora."

I love him for the way he comes to my rescue. "You're *not* illegitimate!" he cries, his eyes resting on me fondly. "All of us are God's children! Don't you even *think* such a thing!"

And I hate myself for lying to him. Still I ask myself, would I have gotten this far toward getting the headstone and finding out about Zora Hurston's last days without telling my lie? Actually I probably would have. But I don't like taking chances that could get me stranded in Central Florida.

"Zora didn't get along with her family. I don't know why. Did you read her autobiography, *Dust Tracks on a Road*?"

"Yes, I did," I say. "It pained me to see Zora pretending to be naïve and grateful about the old white 'Godmother' who helped finance her research, but I loved the part where she ran off from home after falling out with her brother's wife.

Dr. Benton nodded. "When she got sick, I tried to get her to go back to her family, but she refused. There wasn't any real hatred; they just never had gotten along and Zora wouldn't go to them. She didn't want to go to the country home, either, but she had to, because she couldn't do a thing for herself."

"I was surprised to learn she died of malnutrition."

Dr. Benton seems startled. "Zora *didn't* die of malnutrition," he says indignantly. "Where did you get that story from? She had a stroke and she died in the welfare home." He seems particularly upset, distressed, but sits back reflectively in his chair: "She was an incredible woman," he muses. "Sometimes when I closed my office, I'd go by her house and just talk to her for an hour or two. She was a well-read, well-traveled woman and always had her own ideas about what was going on . . ."

"I never knew her, you know. Only some of Carl Van Vechten's photographs and some newspaper photographs. . . . What did she look like?"

"When I knew her, in the fifties, she was a big woman, *erect*. Not quite ▶

as light as I am [Dr. Benton is dark beige], and about five foot, seven inches, and she weighed about two hundred pounds. Probably more. She . . ."

"What! Zora was *fat!* She wasn't in Van Vechten's pictures!"

"Zora loved to eat," Dr. Benton says complacently. "She could sit down with a mound of ice cream and just eat and talk till it was all gone."

While Dr. Benton is talking, I recall that the Van Vechten pictures were taken when Zora was still a young woman. In them she appears tall, tan, and healthy. In later newspaper photographs—when she was in her forties—I remembered that she seemed heavier and several shades lighter. I reasoned that the earlier photographs were taken while she was busy collecting folklore materials in the hot Florida sun.

"She had high blood pressure. Her health wasn't good. . . . She used to live in one of my houses—on School Court Street. It's a block house . . . I don't recall the number. But my wife and I used to invite her over to the house for dinner. *She always ate well,*" he says emphatically.

"That's comforting to know," I say, wondering where Zora ate when she wasn't with the Bentons.

"Sometimes she would run out of groceries—after she got sick—and she'd call me. 'Come over here and see 'bout me,' she'd say. And I'd take her shopping and buy her groceries.

"She was always studying. Her mind—before the stroke—just worked all the time. She was always going somewhere, too. She once went to Honduras to study something. And when she died, she was working on that book about Herod the Great. She was so intelligent! And really had perfect expressions. Her English was beautiful." (I suspect that is a clever way to let me know Zora herself didn't speak in the "black English" her characters used.)

"I used to read all of her books," Dr. Benton continues, "but it was a long time ago. I remember one about . . . it was called, I think, 'The Children of God' [*Their Eyes Were Watching God*], and I remember Janie and Teapot [Teacake] and the mad dog riding on the cow in that hurricane and bit old Teapot on the cheek. . . ."

I am delighted that he remembers even this much of the story, even if the names are wrong, but seeing his affection for Zora I feel I must ask him about her burial. "Did she *really* have a pauper's funeral?"

"She *didn't* have a pauper's funeral!" he says with great heat. "Everybody around here *loved* Zora."

"We just came back from ordering a headstone," I say quietly, because he *is* an old man and the color is coming and going on his face, "but to tell the truth, I can't be positive what I found is the grave. All I know is the spot I found was the only grave-size hole in the area."

"I remember it wasn't near the road," says Dr. Benton, more calmly. "Some other lady came by here and we went out looking for the grave and I took a long iron stick and poked all over that part of the cemetery but we didn't find anything. She took some pictures of the general area. Do the weeds still come up to your knees?" ▶

"And beyond," I murmur. This time there isn't any doubt. Dr. Benton feels ashamed.

As he walks us to our car, he continues to talk about Zora. "She couldn't really write much near the end. She had the stroke and it left her weak; her mind was affected. She couldn't think about anything for long.

"She came here from Daytona, I think. She owned a houseboat over there. When she came here, she sold it. She lived on that money, then she worked as a maid—for an article on maids she was writing—and she worked for the *Chronicle* writing the horoscope column.

"I think black people here in Florida got mad at her because she was for some politician they were against. She said this politician *built* schools for blacks while the one they wanted just talked about it. And although Zora wasn't egotistical, what she thought, she thought; and generally what she thought, she said."

When we leave Dr. Benton's office, I realize I have missed my plane back home to Jackson, Mississippi. That being so, Charlotte and I decide to find the house Zora lived in before she was taken to the country welfare home to die. From among her many notes, Charlotte locates a letter of Zora's she has copied that carries the address: 1734 School Court Street. We ask several people for directions. Finally, two old gentlemen in a dusty gray Plymouth offer to lead us there. School Court Street is not paved, and the road is full of mud puddles. It is dismal and squalid, redeemed only by the brightness of the late afternoon sun. Now I can understand what a "block" house is. It is a house shaped like a block, for one thing, surrounded by others just like it. Some houses are blue and some are green or yellow. Zora's is light green. They are tiny—about fifty by fifty feet, squatty with flat roofs. The house Zora lived in looks worse than the others, but that is its only distinction. It also has three ragged and dirty children sitting on the steps.

"Is this where y'all live?" I ask, aiming my camera.

"No, ma'am" they say in unison, looking at me earnestly. "We live over yonder. This Miss So-and-So's house; but she in the hospital."

We chatter inconsequentially while I take more pictures. A car drives up with a young black couple in it. They scowl fiercely at Charlotte and don't look at me with friendliness, either. They get out and stand in their doorway across the street. I go up to them to explain. "Did you know Zora Hurston used to live right across from you?" I ask.

"Who?" They stare at me blankly, then become curiously attentive, as if they think I made the name up. They are both Afro-ed and he is somberly dashiki-ed.

I suddenly feel frail and exhausted. "It's too long a story," I say, "but tell me something, is there anybody on this street who's lived here for more than thirteen years?"

"That old man down there," the young man says, pointing. Sure enough, there is a man sitting on his steps three houses down. He has graying hair and is very neat, but there is a weakness about him. He reminds me of Mrs. Turner's husband in *Their Eyes Were Watching God*. He's rather "vanishing"-looking, as if his features have been sanded down. In the old days, before black was beautiful, he was probably considered attractive, because he has wavy hair and light-brown skin; but now, well, light skin has ceased to be its own reward.

After the preliminaries, there is only one thing I want to know: "Tell me something," I begin, looking down at Zora's house, "did Zora like flowers?"

He looks at me queerly. "As a matter of fact," he says, looking regretfully at the bare, rough yard that surrounds her former house, "she was crazy about them. And she was a great gardener. She loved azaleas, and that running and blooming vine [morning glories], and she really loved that night-smelling flower [gardenia]. She kept a vegetable garden year-round, too. She raised collards and tomatoes and things like that.

"Everyone in this community thought well of Miss Hurston. When she died, people all up and down this street took up a collection for her burial. We put her away nice."

"Why didn't somebody put up a headstone?"

"Well, you know, one was never requested. Her and her family didn't get along. They didn't even come to the funeral."

"And did she live there by herself?"

"Yes, until they took her away. She lived with—just her and her companion, Sport."

My ears perk up. "Who?"

"Sport, you know, her dog. He was her only companion. He was a big brown-and-white dog."

When I walk back to the car, Charlotte is talking to the young couple on their porch. They are relaxed and smiling. ▶

"I told them about the famous lady who used to live across the street from them," says Charlotte as we drive off. "Of course they had no idea Zora ever lived, let alone that she lived across the street. I think I'll send some of her books to them."

"That's real kind of you," I say.

"I am not tragically colored. There is no great sorrow dammed up in my soul, nor lurking behind my eyes. I do not mind at all. I do not belong to the sobbing school of Negrohood who hold that nature somehow has given them a lowdown dirty deal and whose feelings are all hurt about it.... No, I do not weep at the world—I am too busy sharpening my oyster knife."

—*Zora Neale Hurston, "How It Feels to Be Colored Me,"* World Tomorrow, *1928*

THERE ARE TIMES—and finding Zora Hurston's grave was one of them—when normal responses of grief, horror, and so on, do not make sense because they bear no real relation to the depth of the emotion one feels. It was impossible for me to cry when I saw the field full of weeds where Zora is. Partly this is because I have come to know Zora through her books and she was not a teary sort of person herself; but partly, too, it is because there is a point at which even grief feels absurd. And at this point laughter gushes up to retrieve sanity.

It is only later, when the pain is not so direct a threat to one's own existence that what was learned in that moment of comical lunacy is understood. Such moments rob us of both youth and vanity. But perhaps they are also times when greater disciplines are born. ∾

Alice Walker is the author of Revolutionary Petunias and Other Poems *(Harcourt), which was nominated for a National Book Award, and* In Love & Trouble: Stories of Black Women *(Harcourt), which received the Rosenthal Foundation Award from the National Institute of Arts and Letters.*

"A Series of Linguistic Moments"
Robert E. Hemenway on *Jonah's Gourd Vine*

The following is excerpted from Robert E. Hemenway's Zora Neale Hurston: A Literary Biography *(The University of Illinois Press, 1977) and is reprinted by permission of The University of Illinois Press.*

THE WRITING OF *Jonah's Gourd Vine* is a good example of Hurston's dedication to her craft. She had no means of support while writing. She lived in a one-room house in Saford renting for $1.50 per week. She composed on a flimsy card table and survived on the fifty cents for groceries her cousin lent her each Friday. By the time the manuscript was completed, she owed eighteen dollars in rent, and on the morning of October 16 the landlord evicted her, despite the fact that she was about to earn her first money in three months by booking some folksingers for a city festival. She opened the publisher's telegram in the afternoon while purchasing shoes to replace her worn scraps of leather, and when she saw the figure $200 she "tore out of that place with one old shoe and one new one on and ran to the Western Union office." The book was published in the first week of May, 1934.

Jonah's Gourd Vine is an autobiographical novel, not a document for understanding Hurston's private life. It is usually dealt with as a fictionalization of her parents' marriage—complete with her father's philandering, her mother's steady strength, and Zora's reaction to them both. The novel's main characters are named John and Lucy; their history is the Hurston family history. The plot takes John from life on an Alabama plantation to a ministerial position in Eatonville. Zora even uses the deathbed scene that she remembered as a major trauma of her youth, when her dying mother asked her to stop the neighbors from removing her pillow at the moment of passing. Having observed such parallels between art and life, the reader should be wary of accepting Hurston's fictional characters as autobiographical admissions. Often the novel portrays John and Lucy in ways in which she apparently never thought of her parents, and the novel's plot does not follow exactly the family story. For example, there is more than a hint that Lucy's death is caused by the workings of a hoodoo doctor, an idea with dramatic potential but apparently no basis in fact.

The novel is basically John's story. He rises from a life as an illiterate laborer to become moderator of a Baptist convention in central Florida. The seeds of his tragedy are sown early: he cannot resist women, and although he is a powerful man of God when in the pulpit, he is a man among women when his inspiration ends. Lucy, who is in many ways the strongest character in the novel, serving as both a mainstay for John and a cohesive force for her family, all but wills him the backbone necessary to rise in the world. But after she dies, his lusts predominate. Eventually his congregation rejects him, and he dies just as he has begun to understand both his success and his failure.

John is the bastard child of Amy ▶

Crittenden, a slave on the Pearson plantation before Emancipation. His father was probably the master, Alf Pearson, but John never knows it, and Amy never admits it. After the Civil War, Amy struggles to make a life with her cruel husband, Ned, and it is his rejection of John that causes the teenager to leave home for work at Pearson's. John is such a strong, handsome, striking figure that he is soon sent to school and put in a position of responsibility. He also falls in love with his schoolmate, Lucy Potts, the smartest girl in the class. Even though she is barely past puberty, they become engaged. Her parents object because John is from "over the creek," without money or status; but the lovers persevere, Lucy showing great courage in the face of the familial opposition. After their marriage, John is unfaithful, although he continues to express his love. He always returns to Lucy, and he violently defends wife and family when they are endangered. The Alabama portion of the novel ends when John savagely beats Lucy's brother for collecting a debt at the time she is having her third child. John is arrested and arraigned, but Pearson secures his release, advising him that "distance is the only cure for certain diseases." He runs away, ending up in Eatonville where "uh man kin be sumpin' . . . 'thout folks tramplin' all over yuh. Ah wants mah wife and chillum heah." After they arrive, Lucy encourages John in his preaching, and he becomes a major figure in the community. The family prospers despite John's indiscretions. Eventually Lucy grows sick, and all John can think of, despite the intensity of their love, is the release her death will bring from the guilt she instills in him.

After Lucy's death John marries his mistress, to the distress of his children and parishioners. The church begins to plot his downfall, and his enemies are eventually joined by his new wife, Hattie, who has become a woman scorned. John realizes that her attraction is only physical, and he is bewildered to even find himself married. After he beats Hattie for attempting to conjure him, she asks for a divorce. John refuses to contest because he recognizes the racism of the white court. He tells his friend: "Dey thinks wese all ignorant as it is, and dey thinks wese all alike, and dat dey knows us inside and out. . . . De only difference dey makes is 'tween uh nigger that work hard and don't sass 'em, and one dat don't." Although the church tries again to remove him, John deflects their efforts with powerful preaching. Finally, he voluntarily removes himself from the pulpit and discovers how quickly people relish the hardship of the dispossessed. One man says, "Well, since he's down, less keep 'im down." After moving to a nearby town he meets a good woman, who becomes his third wife and helps him understand some of the forces within him. He returns to preaching, but is killed accidentally just as he approaches his great self-awareness.

The title of the novel is addressed not so much to this total story as to a specific act of cruelty caused by the "brute-beast" in John. In a crucial scene Lucy is lying sick, on a bed that will shortly be turned to the East so that she can die peaceably. John resents this illness because it makes him feel guilty about his mistress, and he tries to take out his frustrations on Lucy. He accuses her of always complaining, "always doggin' me bout 'sumptin." When she replies with references to his love affairs, he tells her to "shut up! Ahm sick an' tired uh yp' yawin and jawin'. 'Taint nothing ah hate lak gittin sin throwed in mah face dat done got cold. Ah do ez Ah please. You jus' uh hold back tuh me nohow … uh man can't utilize hisself." When she replies, "Big talk ain't chagin' what you doin.' You can't clean yo self wd yo tongue lak uh cat," he hits her for the first and only time of their marriage. From this moment John's descent begins. He dreams of Lucy, begs her forgiveness and tries to forget his act. He cannot do so, and it seems likely that this scene was what Hurston had in mind when she explained the novel's title to Carl Van Vechten: "Oh yes, the title you didn't understand. (Jonah 4:6–10). You see the prophet of God sat up under a gourd vine that had grown up in one night. But a cut worm came along and cut it down. Great and sudden growth. One act of malice and it is withered and gone."

This sort of conventional analysis for *Jonah's Gourd Vine* does not address what seems most important in reading the novel. There is little preparation for the horror of the scene; for all his faults, John has not been portrayed as a man likely to slap his wife on her deathbed. Although the episode is intended to haunt John, the haunting gets lost in the hypocrisy he encounters; he becomes as much the victim of others as of himself. This is a good example of why *Jonah's Gourd Vine* cannot be properly represented by a plot outline or a discussion of character development. The novel is less a narrative than a series of linguistic moments representing the folklife of the black South. A statement of one's independence is "Ahm three times seben and uh button." At parting people say, "Seeyuh later, and tell yuh straighter." At birth a child's "nable string" is buried under a chinaberry tree. A game of "Hide and Seek" is accompanied by a standard rhyme, probably adapted from jump-rope chants: ▶

"A Series of Linguistic Moments" *(continued)*

Ah got up 'bout half-past fo'
Fourty fo' robbers wuz round mah do'
Ah got up and let 'em in
Hit 'em ovah de head wid uh rollin' pin
All hid? All hid?

In the critical speeches of the novel, characters express themselves in the traditional metaphors of the culture. An enemy of Lucy's announces, "Ah means tuh beat her 'til she rope lak okra, and den again Ah'll stomp her 'til she slack lak lime." When John proposes, he asks Lucy if she pays attention to birds. She deliberately misunderstands him, referring to a folk belief about the blue jay, who goes "to hell ev'ry Friday and totes uh grain uh sand in his mouf tuh put out de fire." But what John wants to know is, "Which would you ruther be, if you had yo' ruthers—uh lark uh flyin', uh dove uh settin?" He proposes in a ritual (discussed earlier) handed down from slavery; somewhere he was taught the words and ways of courtship, the poetic ceremonies that adorned life under an oppressive system.

Hurston's purpose in the novel, as she stated in a letter to James Weldon Johnson, was to emphasize this quality in her characters' lives. John was to be "a Negro preacher who is neither funny nor an imitation Puritan ram rod in pants. Just the human being and poet that he must be to succeed in a Negro pulpit. I do not speak of those among us who have been tampered with and consequently have gone Presbyterian or Episcopal. I mean the common run of us who love magnificence, beauty, poetry and color so much that there can never be too much of it." The preacher as a poet is the dominant theme in the novel, and it is the quality of imagination—his image-making faculty—that always redeems John's human failings. When in pulpit, John is an inspired artist who consecrates language. He can speak as God creating the world:

> I am the teeth of time
> That comprehended de dust of the de earth
> And weighed de hills in scales
> That painted de rainbow dat marks de end of de
>   parting storm
> Measured de seas in de holler of my hand
> That held de elements in an unbroken chain of
>   controllment

Yet this inspiration is only an elevated form of the verbal skill common to the group; he can also say, "Ahm jus' lak uh old shoe— soft when yuh rain on me and cool me off, and hard when yuh shine on me and git me hot."

As the two passages indicate, John's poetic powers operate in both spiritual and physical worlds; he is a poet who attempts to reconcile the secular and the religious, the spirit and the flesh. Hurston told James Weldon Johnson shortly after the book was published:

> I suppose that you have seen the criticism of my book in the *New York Times*. He means well, I guess, but I never saw such a lack of information about us. It just seems that he is unwilling to believe that a Negro preacher could have so much poetry in him. When you and I (who seem to be the only ones even among the Negroes who recognize the barbaric poetry in their sermons) know that there are hundreds of preachers who ▶

are equaling that sermon weekly. He does not know that merely being a good man is not enough to hold a Negro preacher in an important charge. He must also be an artist. He must be both a poet and an actor of a very high order, and then he must have the voice and figure. He does not realize or is unwilling to admit that the light that shone from GOD'S TROMBONES was handed to you, as was the sermon to me in *Jonah's Gourd Vine*.

The review was typical of the book's reception by the white press. Everyone liked it, primarily for its rich language. Most reviewers also demonstrated their cultural bias, so much so that even their praise becomes suspect. Margaret Wallace, in the *New York Times Book Review*, assumed that all her readers were white, and wrote that John and Lucy were "part and parcel of the tradition of their race, which is as different from ours as night and day." The *Times Literary Supplement* read the English edition and found that the marriage "is described with delicacy not often encountered in negro fiction." The *New Republic*'s review was entitled "Darktown Strutter." The *Boston Chronicle* said that the novel "presents openly the greatest problem of the Negro in all its universality: the utterly inescapable interrelation of sex, success, and society." What Hurston objected to in the *Times* review was criticism of John's climactic sermon "is too good, too brilliantly splashed with poetic imagery to be the product of any one Negro preacher." Presumably no single uneducated black man could be so poetic, so powerful in his language-shaping art. Only *Opportunity* and the *Crisis* reviewed the book without a racist bias, and the *Crisis* objected to her imposition of folklore on the story.

These reviews had to be disappointing, not because they were negative—in fact, all reporters praised the book—but for their ignorance of Hurston's purpose. Although she had no control over the racist misreadings, she had been very clear about what she was trying to portray in John, and somehow the message had gotten lost. She identified his ability to pronounce the Word as a culturally derived characteristic. Belligerently, she had originally titled the novel *Big Nigger*, hardly a casual decision. She was well aware of the controversy aroused by Van Vechten's *Nigger Heaven*, and her title could only have been meant to challenge readers acknowledging the ethnic heritage John Pearson brought to Christianity. Hurston was definitely stating that a "nigger," supposedly a downtrodden, inarticulate, ignorant, semi-human being, was a Christian poet of extraordinary talent. That talent exposed the incredible irony that whites should ever call John such a name; his poetic gift also gave the label special significance when used by blacks among themselves. Her original dedication in *Jonah's Gourd Vine* stressed the courage of John, persons of Afro-American history, creators of beauty in the face of such epithets: "To the first and only real Negro poet in America—the preachers, who bring barbaric splendor of word and song into the very camp of the mockers."

John's poetic faculties are part of the esthetic matrix of black fold culture. Hurston surrounds her character with a world of metaphor and image that makes John's ability only heightened example of a native esthetic. If it is the language-making faculty that best defines him, that is what also defines his world. John is a man who seeks beauty, lives intensely each moment, and loves language as an end in itself. Moreover, he lives in this way because his culture honors an improvisational oral art. He tells his wife, "Lucy, don't you worry 'bout yo' folks, hear? Ahm goitner be uh father and uh mother tuh you. You jes' look tuh me, girl chile. Jes' you put yo' pendence in me. Ah means tuh prop you up on ev'y leanin' side." His human inability to fulfill this promise does not detract from the poetry in its expression. Similarly, John's vulnerability to the "brute-beast" in him coexists with his ability to thank his God for living through another night:

> We thank thee that our sleeping couch
> Was not our cooling board
> Our cover was not our winding sheet

Such passages eventually add up to a theory of language and behavior: an ability to adorn with words the day-to-day ceremonies of living may indicate a life of profound wisdom despite observable human failings. Although a devout prayer coming from a lustful man might be thought hypocritical, John is never a hypocrite. He lives each moment sincerely, and his life deserves to be judged on its own terms. He is both spirit and flesh, a coexistence manifest in the image-making faculty that is John's special gift.

There is a contradiction at the center of *Jonah's Gourd Vine* that arises directly from Hurston's emphasis on the transcendent moment of language growing from this first. John creates poetry perceiving the world in striking images, but he can never really understand himself. ▶

31

"A Series of Linguistic Moments" *(continued)*

He is a poet who graces his world with language but cannot find the words to secure his own personal grace. A captive of the community's need for a public giver of words, after he has served his neighbors he is washed out, voided, left only with instincts which he does not understand and for which he is condemned. No passage demonstrates the book's contradiction more sharply that the long sermon that John preaches on the same communion Sunday when he will renounce his pulpit. It is a linguistic tour de force; traditional metaphors and similes well known in the black community are skillfully improvised. In fact, the language is so powerful that the reader forgets that the sermon is intended as a climax to the novel. As we become captured by John's language, his personal crisis—whether to remain as a man of God—fades into the background. John's crisis is not important to the sermon; only his language compels, and it is this separation of confused self from inspired utterance that frustrates him.

The climactic sermon begins with the test of Zechariah 13:6, taken to be about the wounds of Jesus received in the house of his friends. This text then becomes part of a traditional sermon topic: the story of God's creation of the world and his gift of Jesus as an agent of salvation. Jesus loved man since the "foundations of the world," well before "the hammers of creation / Fell upon the anvils of Time and hammered out the / ribs of the earth." Christ's long-standing love makes his betrayal by his friends all the more tragic and it causes John Pearson, at this moment the inspired agent of God, to call upon his allegorical faculties:

> I want to draw a parable.
> I see Jesus
> Leaving heben will all of His grandeur
> Dis-robin' Hisself of His matchless honor
> Yielding up de scepter of revolvin' worlds
> Clothing Hisself in de garment of humanity
> Coming into de world to rescue His friends

It is "with the eye of faith" that John can see his saviour: "I can see Him step out upon the rim bones of nothing / Crying I am de way / De truth and de light." He can see him "grab de throttle of de well ordered train of mercy." John's sermon becomes a vision; the visionary cries out, "I can see-eee-ee," and his congregation shares in the sight. The vision is not an ethereal abstraction, but a living metaphor, created from blood, metal, and bones. John cannot only see, he can even hear:

> I heard de whistle of se damnation train
> Dat pulled out from Garden of Eden loaded wid
>   cargo goin' to hell
> Ran at break-neck speed all de way thru de law
> All de way thru de prophetic age
> All de way thru de reign of kings and judges—
> Plowed her way thru de Jurdan
> And on her way to Calvary, when she blew for
>   de switch
> Jesus stood out on her track like a rough-backed
>   mountain
> And she threw her cow-catcher in His side and
>   His blood ditched de train
> He died for our sins
> Wounded in the house of His friends

These images and themes were familiar to most black congregations in the South, and ▶

"A Series of Linguistic Moments" *(continued)*

many of them can still be heard in black churches. The train motif is well known; Bernard Bell has identified it, for example, as the source for the epic sermon from the Reverend Homer Barbee in Ralph Ellison's *Invisible Man*. But the sermon itself is the important literary event at this point in the novel—not the fact that it is John's final sermon before his congregation. One could remove the sermon, place it in another context, and the language would command virtually the same response: the power of the passage is in the text, not the context. It is instructive to note that the sermon was taken almost verbatim from Hurston's field notes; this is the reason she told Johnson that it was "handed" to her. It does not grow from the novelist's trying to create an appropriate sermon for John's crisis. It was collected from the Reverend C. C. Lovelace of Eau Gallie, Florida, on May 3, 1929, and Hurston had published it before, in her *Negro* essay. Lovelace was apparently not giving his last sermon, and presumably he had a good relationship with his congregation. The sermon's power, then, is inherent. Its effect comes primarily from the self-contained text. Although it supports the theme of the black preacher as poet and represents John's inspired powers, it gives us few insights into John's interior struggle. His language does serve to articulate his personal problems because it is directed away from the self toward the communal celebration. John, the man of words, becomes the victim of his bardic function. He is the epic poet of the community who sacrifices himself for the group vision.

This sermon scene reveals why the novel finally becomes as frustrating for the reader as for John. The book works at cross-purposes; it is a story of individual character in which language directs one away from the individual and toward the documentation of communal esthetic. While John should be in harmony with his community—and is, at the moment of inspiration—usually he is at odds, although his poetic gift expresses the communal experience in its highest form. If the separation between John and his group were meant to be his tragedy, then John's individual story would affect us deeply. But John is not finally a tragic character, because this potentially tragic theme becomes subordinated to the cultural argument that is used to explain his struggle.

Hurston suggests that this lack of control over one's destiny is the obvious product of Afro-American history. Uprooted from his homeland, thrown into alien culture, the African adapted as best he could to barbaric institutions offered him by the white man. But the

African heritage was never lost. It joined with white ideas, so that when white men's music wearied, Africa inspired, just as it did during John's sermons:

"Hey you, dere, us ain't no whote folks! Put down dat fiddle! Us don't want no fiddles, neither no guitars, neither no banjoes. Less clap!"

So they danced. They called for the instrument that they had brought to America in their skins—the drum—and they played upon it. With their hands they played upon the little dance drums of Africa. The drums of kid-skin. With their feet they stomped it, and the voice of Kata-Kumba, the great drum, lifted itself within them and they heard it. The great drum that is made by priests and sits in majesty in the juju house. The drum with the man skin that is dressed with human blood, that is beaten with a human shinbone and speaks to gods as a man and to men as a God. Then they beat upon the drum and danced. It was said, "He will serve us better if we bring him from Africa naked and thingless." So the burka reasoned. They tore away his clothes that Cuffy might bring nothing away, but Cuffy seized his drum and hid it in his skin under the skull bones. The shin-bones he bore openly, for he thought, "Who shall rob me of shim bones when they see no drum?" So he laughed with cunning and said, "I, who am borne away to become an orphan, carry my parents with me. For *Rhythm* is she not my mother and Drama is her man?" So he groaned aloud in the ships and hid his drum and laughed.

The only problem with this passage is that it serves poorly its novelistic context. There is no preparation for the intensity of feeling; yet the rhythmic ceremony is intended to symbolize John's dilemma. His concept of spirituality springs, as Larry Neal has argued, "from a formerly enslaved communal society, non-Christian in background, where there is really no clean cut dichotomy between the world of spirit and the world of flesh." The significance of the passage for John's personal troubles is unclear, however, and its implications remain unfulfilled until the penultimate paragraph of the book. There, when John's funeral sermon is preached, the Kata-Kumba comes to have a special meaning:

And the preacher preached a barbaric requiem poem. On the pale white horse of Death. On the cold icy hands of Death. On the golden streets of glory. Of Amen Avenue. Of Halleluyah Street. On the delight of God when such as John appeared among the singers about His throne. On the weeping sun and moon. On Death who gives a cloak to the man who walked naked in the world. And the hearers wailed with a feeling of terrible loss. They beat upon the O-go-doe, the ancient drum. O-go-doe, O-go-doe, O-go-doe! Their hearts turned to fire ▶

and their shin-ones leaped unknowing to the drum. Not Kata-Kumba, the drum of triumph, that speaks of great ancestors and glorious wars. Not the little drum of kid-skin, for that is to dance with joy and to call to mind birth and creation, but O-go-doe, the voice of Death—that promises nothing, that speaks with tears only, and of the past.

So at last the preacher wiped his mouth in the final way and said, "He wuz uh man, and nobody knowed 'him but God," and it was ended in rhythm. With the drumming of the feet, and mournful dance of the heads, in rhythm, it was ended.

Hurston demonstrates here John's conflicting impulses; she implies that his struggle is more than a person conflict. Neal has argued that in adopting Christianity blacks still were "able to shape out of it unique forms of expression that reflected the most retrievable, thence the most important, aspects of the pre-Christian cultural memory." By evoking this African past, the Kata-Kumba and the O-go-doe are meant to explain John's struggle. He is capable of great inspiration because he has access to a pre-Christian cultural memory. He is also capable of so-called Christian immorality, an immorality arising less from personal inadequacy, Hurston implies, than the limitations of American culture, a civilization that denies the beat of the drum, as it denies John's manhood. Yet within the action of the novel it is primarily John's function as a giver of words that denies him the self-awareness that could lead to a resolution of his problem. Hurston was writing a traditional novel of character about internalized conflict, while denying her hero the possibility of discovering the cultural dilemma that created his frustration. It is not by chance that John is killed in a deus ex machina ending, driving into the side of a train, which is throughout the novel a symbol of the white man's mechanized world. He is doomed to cultural collision rather than to self-understanding.

It is John's lack of self-awareness that has troubled so many readers, as Nick Aaron Ford realized long ago. In his *Contemporary Negro Novel* (1936), Ford objected to *Jonah's Gourd Vine* because John's "rise to religious prominence and financial ease is but a millstone around his neck. He is held back by some unseen cord which seems to be tethered to his racial heritage. Life crushes him almost to death, but he comes out of the mills with no graded insight into the deep mysteries which surround him."

Hurston had not yet worked out a way to fictionally resolve either the bicultural trade-offs inherent in being black in America or the relationship between the individual artist and the community that artist serves. Nor had she discovered a way to structure a novel around the image-making faculty, the suspended linguistic moment, and to sustain that structure through plot, character, setting—all the ingredients of successful fiction. *Jonah's Gourd Vine* is a fascinating first novel, written in the three months, filled with the folklore Zora had been collecting, told out of the experience of her own family. Its beauty derives from its moments of traditional, poetic language. Although the sum may be less than the parts, the parts are remarkable indeed. ᥲ

Have You Read?
More by
Zora Neale Hurston

THEIR EYES WERE WATCHING GOD

The epic tale of Janie Crawford, whose quest for identity takes her on a journey during which she learns what love is, experiences life's joys and sorrows, and comes home to herself in peace. Her passionate story prompted Alice Walker to say, "There is no book more important to me than this one."

MULES AND MEN

The fruit of Hurston's labors as a folklorist and anthropologist, this celebrated treasury of black American folklore includes stories, "big old lies," songs, Vodou customs, superstitions—all the humor and wisdom that is the matchless heritage of American blacks.

THE COMPLETE STORIES

This landmark gathering of Zora Neale Hurston's short fiction—most of which appeared only in literary magazines during her lifetime and some of which has never before been published—reveals the evolution of one of the most important African American writers. Spanning her career from 1921 to 1955, these stories attest to Hurston's tremendous range and establish themes that recur in her longer fiction. The stories in this collection map, in rich language and imagery, Hurston's development and concerns as a writer and provide an invaluable reflection of the mind and imagination of the author of the acclaimed novel *Their Eyes Were Watching God*.

TELL MY HORSE

This firsthand account of the mysteries of Vodou is based on Hurston's personal experiences in Haiti and Jamaica, where she participated as an initiate and not just an observer of Vodou practices in the 1930s. Of great cultural interest, her travelogue paints a vividly authentic picture of ceremonies, customs, and superstitions.

MOSES, MAN OF THE MOUNTAIN

Based on the familiar story of the Exodus, Hurston blends the Moses of the Old Testament with the Moses of black folklore and song to create a compelling allegory of power, redemption, and faith.

DUST TRACKS ON A ROAD

First published in 1942 at the crest of her popularity as a writer, this is Hurston's imaginative and exuberant account of her rise from childhood poverty in the rural South to a prominent place among the leading artists and intellectuals of the Harlem Renaissance. It is a book full of the wit and wisdom of a proud and spirited woman who started off low and climbed high.

SERAPH ON THE SUWANEE

Hurston's novel of turn-of-the-century white Florida "crackers" marks a daring departure for the author famous for her complex accounts of black culture and heritage. Hurston explores the evolution of a marriage full of love but very little communication and the desires of a young woman in search of herself and her place in the world.

EVERY TONGUE GOT TO CONFESS

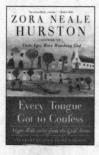

African American folklore was Zora Neale Hurston's first love. Collected in the late 1920s, these hilarious, bittersweet, often saucy folktales—some of which date back to the Civil War—provide a fascinating, verdant slice of African American life in the rural South at the turn of the twentieth century. Arranged according to subject—from God Tales, Preacher Tales, and Devil Tales to Heaven Tales, White-Folk Tales, and Mistaken Identity Tales—they reveal attitudes about slavery, faith, race relations, family, and romance that have been passed on for generations. They capture the heart and soul of the vital, independent, and creative community that so inspired Zora Neale Hurston.